"With a uniquely h[...]
laugh-out-loud mo[...]
delight!"

—Melissa Ferguson, bestselling author of *How to Plot a Payback*

"*An Overdue Match* is the perfect book for anyone who has ever felt unseen or unloved. Monzon has a way of taking the reader on a heart journey, and Evangeline Kelly is a fantastic heroine to effect change. She empowers the reader to become the heroine of their story."

—Toni Shiloh, Christy Award–winning author

"I can always count on Sarah Monzon for romance that makes me swoon and inspiring stories that keep me fully engaged . . . heart, mind, and soul. I will continue to read anything she writes, forever."

—Bethany Turner, author of *Cole and Laila Are Just Friends: A Love Story*

AN
OVERDUE
Match

AN OVERDUE

Match

Sarah Monzon

BETHANYHOUSE

a division of Baker Publishing Group
Minneapolis, Minnesota

Published by Bethany House Publishers
Minneapolis, Minnesota
BethanyHouse.com

Bethany House Publishers is a division of
Baker Publishing Group, Grand Rapids, Michigan

Printed in the United States of America

Library of Congress Cataloging-in-Publication Data
Names: Monzon, Sarah, author.
Title: An overdue match / Sarah Monzon.
Description: Minneapolis, Minnesota : Bethany House Publishers, a division of
   Baker Publishing Group, 2025. | Series: Checking Out Love ; 1
Identifiers: LCCN 2024032329 | ISBN 9780764243745 (paper) | ISBN
   9780764244582 (casebound) | ISBN 9781493448968 (ebook)
Subjects: LCGFT: Christian fiction. | Romance fiction. | Novels.
Classification: LCC PS3613.O5496 O94 2025 | DDC 813/.6--dc23/eng/20230320
LC record available at https://lccn.loc.gov/2024032329

This book is a work of fiction. Names, characters, places, and incidents are the product
of the author's imagination or are used fictitiously. Any resemblance to actual events,
locales, or persons, living or dead, is coincidental.

Cover design and illustration by Camila Gray

The author is represented by Rachel McMillan.

Baker Publishing Group publications use paper produced from sustainable forestry
practices and postconsumer waste whenever possible.

25 26 27 28 29 30 31   7 6 5 4 3 2 1

For my mom and all the bold, beautiful,
and bald ladies in the world.
This one is dedicated to you.

1

Libraries aren't famous for their penal codes, but some literary offenses deserve due punishments. I haven't decided yet where I stand on late fees—for or against—as I truly can see both sides of the argument on that one. As someone who has impatiently waited in the digital queue for my turn for a book to become available, a little incentive to the lackadaisical reader to get a move on is useful. However, I also understand the desire to linger between the pages of certain books and how hard it is to move on after a literary hangover.

On the issue of mishandling of books, however, I am firmly in the camp of some sort of consequence, for to mistreat a book is most certainly a punishable crime.

I unfold the dog-eared corner and smooth out the cream-colored paper of the hardcover in my hands, making soothing, cooing noises under my breath. A book doesn't have feelings, but it does have a soul. Life exhaled into every word by the author and then breathed into each person who reads those same words. So, in a sense, books are both alive themselves and give life to others simultaneously. Which is why they should be treated with care and not irresponsibly—something the patron who folded these pages clearly disagrees with. I turn the page and unfold another corner.

"Uh-oh. I know that look. Did someone write in a book again, Evangeline?" Hayley teases as she retrieves a paper from the printer, one bearing the list of titles to be pulled from the shelves and set aside for patrons who put in holds on the library's website.

I turn to her, frowning. "I'm not against writing in books. The margins are great for that and so are a rainbow of highlighters. If someone wants to commit marginalia by engaging with the text in their own copies, who am I to judge? What I'm against is people writing in *library* books. There's a big difference." I turn a few more pages and hold up the offending evidence. "But some Neanderthal dog-eared at least seventy percent of this title. Seventy percent! He should be dragged from his cave and beaten with his own club." I mutter that last part under my breath.

Hayley gasps in mock horror. "A duel for the author's honor must be in order. It's pistols at dawn."

I shake my head while swallowing back a grin. "You know I prefer swords for a duel."

"Swords? Really?" Her button nose scrunches. "I'd imagine they'd be really heavy to hold out in front of you. Wouldn't your muscles tremble and your palms get so sweaty they'd lose their grip on the hilt? Then you'd be run through and I'd be left alone to do the reshelving by myself. Oooh!" Her eyes alight with mischief the second a new thought enters her head. "Unless you're dueling some regency rogue and he decides that instead of running you through, he'll teach you the proper way to wield that deadly weapon." She shimmies her shoulders. "The perfect excuse to get close and use his charms to seduce and disarm you."

My cheeks twitch at her theatrics, a smile threatening to unleash. With sheer willpower, I force a deadpan look onto my face. "I changed my mind. I choose pistols. Pull the trigger. Bam. Done."

She tries to push out her bottom lip to pout, but her laughing makes it impossible. "You're no fun, you know that? Besides, the hero coming up with an excuse to teach the heroine a skill, eliciting the need to put his arms around her, is a well-established device of romance novels for a reason. Plus, bullet wounds bleed a lot. You don't want that. Think of the mess you'd have to clean up."

I'd rather not think about it, thank you very much. Somehow our conversation has gotten off topic, although that's not exactly unusual when it comes to Hayley.

She extends the paper with the list of holds out to me. "Want to keep an eye on the dastardly dog-eared deviant under the guise of getting actual work done?"

"Nice alliteration, and yes, I do." I take the paper.

I'd only gotten a quick look at the retreating form of the patron who'd turned in this mistreated book. He'd headed toward the nonfiction aisles, specifically the biography shelves near the back corner, opposite the children's section.

I quickly scan the library's barcode on the cover and return the book in the system, noting the borrower's name. Tai Davis. I'd only moved to Little Creek (pronounced *crick*, like the ache you'd get in your neck) six months ago, and though the town is small, the name Tai Davis doesn't ring any bells.

But if he's willing to mutilate almost every page of a book, I really don't trust him to roam the aisles of the library unsupervised. I take my job as protector of free thought, untold universes, awaiting adventures, and expanding personal perspectives seriously. Because books are more than just paper and ink. They're a portal leading to anywhere you ever wanted to go—heart, mind, or soul.

Hayley and Martha, the children's librarian, like to tease me about my strict standards when it comes to the treatment of books. Martha points out that at least my patrons don't chew on the pages of paperbacks, the books coming back soggy, slobbery, and smelling of spit-up. She has a point, and I also concede that I may go beyond the bounds of what's deemed the appropriate amount of caring when it comes to library property, but I can't help it. Books are my friends, and I can't stand to see them bullied. Call it my quirk.

I straighten my leopard-print pencil skirt, then run my thumb along the waistband to make sure my vintage library due date card graphic tee is tucked in before I step around the beveled corner of the desk and head toward the back of the library.

Between the *J* and *K* shelves, I spot him. The same black leather jacket pulled taut between impressively wide shoulders and ending in large silver buckles at a trim waist. His head is bent, and although I can't see what's in his hands, it doesn't take Sherlock Holmes on the case to figure out it must be an open book. Location is a dead giveaway.

I walk softly in my red canvas high-tops to the aisle of shelves just on the other side of him. I can watch him through the small space between the top of Walter Isaacson's published works and the bottom of the metal shelf holding our copy of Antonia Fraser's writings on Mary, Queen of Scots, and Oliver Cromwell.

The man isn't that tall. Maybe a smidge over an inch of my own five-foot-three frame. With my restricted view between the shelves, I can only really see from the top of his shoulders to the middle of the back of his head. His hair is thick, black as an inkwell, and swirls softly over the large collar of his biker-style jacket like an artistic script font. He turns, putting himself in profile, and I suck in a sharp breath.

I blame my reaction on surprise and the ingrained teachings of my granny, Carol Sykes. I've never seen anyone with a neck tattoo in person before. According to her, the only people who would permanently mark themselves in such a visible location on their bodies are "dangerous" and I should "stay away for my safety" because they probably "got their tattoos either in jail or as a gang sign." Which, to be fair, maybe was the case fifty years ago? I don't know. I wasn't alive fifty years ago, and things do tend to change over the course of a couple generations.

Even though I read profusely and open my mind to many different viewpoints, the voice of my childhood—of my granny—is still loudest overall. Which is probably the reason I subconsciously take a step back. It's definitely not because I correlate a human canvas with anything deviant or think that he "put graffiti on God's temple," or that he will "regret his decisions when he's old and wrinkled."

But even from this distance, the beautiful artwork draws my eye—so much so that granny's voice in my mind fades as my focus pools to one location. It's a simple red rose with unfolding petals so soft looking that I want to run my finger over the bloom to feel the velvety texture. It's delicate. Intricate. Beautiful. Made even more so because of the contrast of the hard lines framing the picture. The strong angle of the man's stern jaw ends in a powerful set chin. Even his neck is corded muscle and thrumming veins, a juxtaposition against the soft blossom.

Guilt sits heavy in my stomach, though I can't pinpoint its exact cause. There are too many options to choose from, starting with the fact that I haven't turned on my heel and distanced myself from a man I've been conditioned since childhood to see as dangerous. Or maybe it's because I'm openly staring at a man, ogling the lines of his neck—both natural and inked—instead of acting like a proper lady and averting my eyes. Or maybe it's as simple as being at work and not actually getting any work done at the moment.

Whatever the reason, the guilt isn't enough to propel me into any sort of action. I stand there and I stare, tracing the different weighted lines with my gaze.

In reading fiction, I've learned that there are, in essence, three types of people. There are main characters, who are your heroes and heroines. The stars of the story. They may see conflict within their journey, but ultimately they receive their happily-ever-after in the end. Then there are the secondary characters. The supporting cast, if you will. Their job is to be a sort of shining light for the main characters, adding just enough spice to the story to bring out the flavor but never steal the show. And finally, the third category is the villain. The antagonist to the protagonist. Whether slightly sinister or downright diabolical, this is the fictional persona readers love to hate.

Personally, I'm a secondary character. For reasons that shall not be named at this time, I will likely never fit into the heroine role. Not in my own story. Not in any story. Contrarily, the level of my ability to be nefarious is set at exactly zero, therefore I don't fit into the mold of a villain either. Which is fine by me. Everyone loves a good sidekick.

But where does Mr. Tai Davis fit? I can tell that under no circumstance would he ever be mistaken for a secondary character. Maybe it's the way his presence commands the space even though he's currently the only patron in the J–K aisle, no underling for him to direct. That, along with the width of his stance and set of shoulders, is just the first entry of proof that he would steal the attention on every page he stepped onto.

Which only leaves villain or hero as options. The fact that he's in a library does give him a tally mark under the Hero heading, in my opinion. All good heroes should be well-read. However, his handling of books—or mishandling, rather—is definitely a slash against him. (No, I'm not harping on the dog-ear thing too much. If people want to treat library books as their own personal collection, then they can keep the book they ruined and buy the library a new copy.) Then there's his neck tattoo. Of a rose. Does that make him bad? Or good?

It makes him neither because tattoos have no moral standing on a person's character.

The cover of a book closing with a puff of air on the other side of the shelves snaps me out of . . . whatever *that* was. Mr. Davis pivots to face the opposite direction and strides toward the exit. I wait a couple of seconds so he can get ahead of me before tailing him again since I don't know if he will bank left toward the fiction section or right toward the audiobooks and DVDs. I'm not exactly sure what he would do to mar those media platforms, but as long as I'm around, the answer will be nothing. Unless, of course, he checks them out. There's not much I can do once inventory leaves the library.

"Excuse me." A woman's voice behind me stops my feet from moving after Mr. Davis.

I turn around and smile pleasantly at the woman with her arm slung across a young boy's shoulders. "How can I help you?"

The mother looks down at her son. "Go ahead and ask," she encourages him with a small push between his shoulder blades.

"Um." The boy raises his bright blue eyes from underneath a shock of wheat-colored hair, then lowers them back down to the patterned carpet again. "I'm looking for a book."

I sneak a quick peek over my shoulder, but my mark is gone. Next time I'll just tag his return as damaged and charge him for a new copy. I glance back down at the boy in front of me and feel the muscles in my face relax. There's no question here. *This* boy is hero material, on par with Henry Huggins or Max Crumbly.

I squat down to eye level. "Then you've come to the right place. What book are you looking for?"

He shrugs. "A good one?"

I sneak one more peek toward the exit as I lead the mother and son toward the children's section. This time I get a glimpse of black leather as the automatic doors close, a single book tucked between the muscular curve of a hip and arm.

Pistols at dawn, I think facetiously at his retreating form before turning to introduce my new little friend to the wonderful world of Perodia, where Tag and his squirrel companion, Skyla, meet the last firehawk. Boy, is he in for an adventure.

2

The reasons I'm not heroine material, based on genre:

- Sci-fi—I'm afraid of heights. I have trouble even crossing bridges and would pass out if forced to, say, go to the top of the Space Needle (ask me how I know). There's no way that I could explore intergalactic regions and interact with extraterrestrial intelligence from a spaceship in actual space.
- Western—I'm allergic to horses. I found this out the hard way one year in sleepaway camp. I was so excited to flex my inner Annie Oakley only to find out that if I got within ten feet of a horse, my eyes would swell shut and I'd break out in a rash that would give me the nickname Blind Ketchup Girl for a week. A little on the nose, as far as demeaning names go, but nine-year-old bullies aren't particularly bright. The point is, you really can't have a compelling western without horses.
- Mystery/Thriller/Suspense—A search-and-rescue team had to get me out of a corn maze once. Also, I've never been able to win even a single game of Clue. Being able to puzzle out scenarios seems like a pretty basic prerequisite for the genre.

- Fantasy—Sadly, I have no magical powers with which to save humanity.
- Historical—Automatically disqualified by being born in the current century. Also, I'm kind of partial to breathing deeply and thus would refuse to wear a corset. There's also my love of indoor plumbing.

And that leaves romance. This genre took me a little longer than the others to realize I also didn't qualify for a leading role. My ex-fiancé, Brett, was the first to let me in on the secret, although I missed the clues to begin with because, as I've established, I'd never make it as a mystery-solving sleuth. But looking back, I can see the hints along the way even before he sat me down for the big reveal.

The ebbing interest in his eyes when he looked at me. The loss of touch that coincided with the loss of my hair. The tie of attraction that had at one time bound him to me unraveling, until one day it just wasn't there anymore. At least for him.

At first, I convinced myself Brett's actions and words had nothing to do with my heroine status and everything to do with demoting him from leading man to villain. I mean, it was classic villainous behavior for him to have such a shallow depth of feeling that he was no longer attracted to me and stopped loving me when I developed alopecia, an autoimmune disease in which my T cells sound the bugle cry to attack my hair follicles like the swarm of bees that kept Winnie the Pooh from the honey in the tree (that's probably a strange analogy, but I subbed for Martha at story time yesterday and the toddlers and preschoolers made buzzing sounds when we came to that page, so it's still fresh in my mind).

That reflects on Brett and his character, not me. If it were true love, then when my hair fell out—first in patches, then at an increased rate that I ended up shaving the remaining valiant strands that had resisted the attack—he would've still run his fingers over the soft buzz of fuzz around my crown, kissed the widening spots that were as smooth as a baby's bottom, and tried to convince me that I was still beautiful, hair or no hair.

But Brett's rejection wasn't a quiet confession in an empty room. It was more like a kid at the top of a mountain shouting into the wind so his words bounce off the range in an endless echo. The same words reverberating over and over and over again.

There's a study someone conducted somewhere about how a person can disbelieve something told to them once as a lie, but when that same thing is repeated x amount of times, they accept it as truth. I can probably look up the study in the reference section, but I really don't want to.

The point is, Brett might have been the first voice to tell me I'm not heroine material, but it wasn't until I kept hearing the echo from sources all around me that I began to believe he might be right.

Echoes like the ones from romance books themselves, in fact.

I pick up a stack of books from a basket at the end of the A–E aisle of fiction. Books that people have taken off the shelves to look at but ultimately decided not to check out. Instead of reshelving the titles themselves, we encourage patrons to place the books in the baskets so we librarians can reshelve them properly. You'd be surprised how many people will just put a book willy-nilly on a shelf instead of paying attention to alphabetical and numerical order. Melvil Dewey would roll over in his grave.

I shuffle the trio of books, looking at their covers. Romances, all of them. And all proving my point. The first is a bodice-ripper from the early 2000s, with a Fabio-esque cover model. His luscious locks flow in the breeze, and the woman in his arms, décolletage on full display, has a head of hair that Pantene would be privileged to put in one of their commercials. The next is a book with a contemporary setting. The military man with a black past has a high and tight crew cut, but the woman he's staring at broodily has a mane of curls running the full length of her back. The third is much the same.

I don't have to read the stories within to know that (A) every hero dreams of running his fingers through the woman's hair, and (B) every hero equates anything false—I'm talking even a little bit of lipstick or rouge, in the case of the bodice-ripper—as some sort of moral deficiency in the heroine, stripping her of heroine status.

Yep. I no longer have any hair for a man to be tempted by (A). The disease that started as alopecia areata, or spot balding, has progressed past even alopecia totalis, where I didn't have any hair on my head but still had hair on other places on my body. Now, it's alopecia universalis, which, as I'm sure you've guessed, is a complete and universal loss of hair. Everywhere. I no longer have to shave my legs (yay!), but I also have lost characteristics that are essentially associated with being human. The face radically changes when it no longer sports eyebrows or eyelashes.

Which, of course, leads to (B) and the fact that not only do I apply makeup, as do probably ninety-five percent of modern women, but a lot of what I wear is fake. Fake eyelashes. Fake temporary eyebrow tattoos. Fake hair in the form of a wig.

I quickly reshelve the trio of books and make my way back to the front desk. I don't often think of my character status anymore. Not since I moved to Little Creek and began my fresh start, anyway. But for some reason, my stalking of Tai Davis earlier brought it all back. Maybe because I wasn't able to clearly classify him, although, again, I'm not sure why I even tried. I don't often make a habit of judging people without talking to them first. Even then, I try to give them the benefit of the doubt if the first impression isn't the best. Life isn't a Jane Austen retelling of *Pride and Prejudice*.

"I've been meaning to ask you." Hayley looks up from the computer where the library's catalog is glowing on the screen. "Can you call me at exactly 7:10 tonight?"

"That's a really specific time. What would happen if I called at 7:09 or 7:11?" My fingers graze the zipper of my skirt, which has scooted to its current and erroneous position in front of my hip bone. Taking the waist, I rotate the material an inch to the left to put it back in place.

"I might either be the victim or the perpetrator of a murder." Hayley spins the desk chair to face me.

The bookmarks by the checkout area are askew, so I reach over and fix the stack. "If you think you might be murdered, then don't do whatever it is you're planning on doing. Same advice if you think you might be the one on the other side of the trigger."

"Or—" she draws the word out—"you can call me at exactly 7:10 like a good friend and citizen. Really, Evangeline, you might be considered an accessory if you don't make the call. Sheriff Jacobs is just looking for a good bust on which to build his new reelection campaign."

"And arresting a couple of small-town librarians will give that to him?"

"I don't know." She winks. "I heard a rumor that librarians have a wild side."

At this my composure cracks and I let out the small laugh I'd been holding back. "Let me guess, another first date tonight?"

She nods, her thick bangs bouncing a little with the motion. "I need a way-out call. 7:10 is the perfect time. We're supposed to meet at the Tasty Tortellini at 6:30. That gives a ten-minute buffer if he's running late, plus thirty minutes to order and deduce if he's some weirdo who collects his own toenail clippings in a jar or Chris Hemsworth's equally hot but less famous long-lost brother. The food comes, I take a couple delicious bites of their portobello ravioli in Parmesan cream sauce, then you call. If the date is going horribly, then I pretend you're having an emergency and I have to leave right away—taking my meal to go, of course. *But* if the date is going well, then I'll tell you I'll see you at work tomorrow and then give you the juicy details in the morning."

"He's going to know exactly what you're doing," I warn.

Hayley shrugs. "So what? If I leave, I won't care if he does. If I stay, then he knows I'm interested. Win-win, if you ask me." She leans forward and captures my hands, begging over them. "Please? I promise I'll return the favor next time you go out on a first date."

I snort. "You know I don't date."

"Then I promise to feed your cat the next time you go home to see your grandparents."

Kitty Purry is rather independent, and I can leave her with some extra food and water over a weekend, but she did give me the stink eye last time I came back from a visit home, hiding under the bed for two days at the perfect distance where I could almost reach her but not quite as punishment. "Fine."

Hayley springs from the chair. "You're the best!"

See? Sidekick material.

3

Instead of waiting at home until the appointed time to call Hayley, I decide to head to the Tasty Tortellini. I've been thinking about their roasted garlic gnocchi ever since she mentioned the restaurant, plus I feel more comfortable being onsite for her blind date. The location is public and the restaurant draws a decent dinner crowd, so she should be safe, but a girl can never be too careful. Most of the residents of southeastern Tennessee are exactly how you'd expect them to be: generous, hospitable, and overly friendly. Fast to smile but with a slow southern drawl.

But then there are the occasional nutcases like Eric Rudolph, the Olympic Park Bomber, who managed to evade law enforcement for years by hiding out in the mountains of Appalachia. In case Hayley's date tries to slip her a roofie so he can haul her back to his corner of the hollow, I'll be here to stop him.

I'm seated at a small table near the middle of the dining room with a clear view of the front door. So far, Sheriff Jacobs has come in with his wife. He's out of uniform and off duty, but if Hayley's date has any nefarious tendencies, the sheriff will be close at hand for backup.

Dalton Matthews came in and picked up a to-go order. His

Carhartt dungarees and plaid flannel shirt had a thick layer of sawdust clinging to them. Probably taking a break from the chainsaw sculpture he's working on just long enough to get a bite to eat. Everyone in town is dying to see the top-secret art installation he's been creating in the town square over the past couple of weeks, but not a single person besides Dalton has laid eyes on it.

The front door opens, a sliver of early evening sunlight shooting through the space and tracking across the wide-planked floors. A bouquet of white gladiolas sitting in a vase along the half wall separating the hostess stand from the dining room hinders my immediate view of the newcomer. I tap the screen of my phone. 6:18. Unless Hayley and her date are early, it's not them.

"Right this way." The hostess's sweet soprano voice floats across the distance. She sashays around the half wall with a menu tucked against her body.

I blink at the man stepping around the partition. What are the odds that in a small mountain town I would run into a man twice in one day whom I previously had never laid eyes on?

An uncomfortable feeling in my diaphragm, a unique concoction of shame, embarrassment, and guilt, makes me shift in my seat. It's the same feeling I'd get as a kid when Granny would catch me being particularly naughty. I send up a silent prayer that Tai Davis hadn't seen me staked out on the other side of the bookshelves. I doubt he'd be any more understanding of my vigilante bent toward book protection than my coworkers are.

My phone screen lights up at the same time the ping of a text notification sounds. Relief washes over me. I can bury my face in my phone and ignore the world and possibly the accusing glare of the man who—my stomach dips—is currently being seated at the table in front of me.

Because of course he is. There are exactly nine vacant tables, seven of which aren't in my direct line of sight, but he has to be seated at the one in front of me, in a chair facing me, with no centerpieces or obstructions to hide behind. If he noticed me at the library, then his subconscious is likely to poke at him until he can place my face.

He sets a book on the table before picking up his menu.

Ping.

I unlock my phone with Face ID and open the text message from my sister, Penelope.

> Penelope
>
> Granny and Grampie's fiftieth wedding anniversary is coming up in a few months. We should do something special for them to celebrate.
>
> Any ideas?

I sit and ponder.

My brain is . . . blank. I've got . . . exactly nothing. My thumbs hover over the screen as I wait for inspiration to strike. This shouldn't be this hard. A celebration of fifty years of love and commitment. Of doing life together. Through highs and lows. Good and bad. But always together. While my love for romance is unrequited, my grandparents have the real deal.

My phone starts ringing, and I jolt, tapping the accept button with my thumb.

"You were taking too long to respond." My sister forgoes any greeting to get straight to the point.

"I was thinking," I explain, careful to keep my voice quiet so I don't disturb any of the other diners. "Plus, I'm at a restaurant. Can we talk later?"

A server stops at Tai's table. He turns his head, his neck elongating as he looks up, the rose tattoo unfurling above the collar of his black shirt.

I've never been much of a tattoo person, really. Maybe because of lack of exposure? Maybe because of the undertones in which they were talked about around me? I grew up in the Bible Belt, attending both church and church schools. If someone did have a tattoo, it was in a location easily hidden, not paraded about. So, maybe *that's* why this tattoo in particular has me hypnotized every time I see it—the allure of the taboo.

Tai hands the menu to the server. He's shed his leather jacket, and for the first time, I get a glimpse of his arms. His golden skin gleams under the restaurant's hanging lights, the silhouette of strong muscles pushing against the confines of the fabric of his tee. Color and black lines wrap around one of his limbs, disappearing under the hem of his shirtsleeve and illustrating his arm to the wrist.

I swallow, trying to add moisture to my suddenly dry mouth. My granny's voice in my head tells me not to stare. To mind my manners. Be a good girl.

"I think we should throw them a big party." Penelope ignores my request that we talk later. She's a corporate manager for some tech company in Chattanooga, so she's used to bossing people around—and getting her way. "Give them a second wedding reception, so to speak."

I twist in my seat and stare at a painting of a provincial Italian alfresco bistro. Tai Davis's body art is out of sight, out of mind.

"And who would we invite?" I know the answer, so I'm not sure why I'm asking. Maybe holding on to that teeny-tiny sliver of hope that my only sister wouldn't ask me to—

"Everyone," she says with the finality of a nail driven into a coffin.

Everyone encompasses the one person I have no desire to ever lay eyes on again.

The server approaches my table with a steaming plate of potato dumplings with roasted cloves of garlic in a brown butter sauce. The smell arrives before the plate is even set, making my mouth water. I pull the phone away from my ear. "Thank you so much." The server dips her head in acknowledgment and heads back to the kitchen.

Taking a sip of water, I begrudgingly return to Penelope. "How about we do something small and intimate instead?" I should save my breath, I really should. My sister has already made up her mind, so no matter what I say, she's not going to budge. But I plow forward anyway.

"A candlelit dinner in the backyard, hundreds of tealights flickering against the night sky. I'll cook something really special, or we can order from one of your fancy-schmancy restaurants that you take clients to. We can serve them like we used to do when we were kids. You can even serenade them on the violin. It'll be romantic."

"Hundreds of candles sounds like a fire waiting to happen, and I haven't played the violin in ten years. My screeching would be far from romantic."

"But—"

Penelope's sigh is a bucket of water on my protest. "You know exactly how we can get away with not inviting him, Evangeline." Her frustration is evident in the tightness of her tone. She's probably pinching the bridge of her nose right now, staving off the headache I'm causing.

This is a conversation we've had more than once. Even though I told my big sister the whole messy truth about why Brett had called off the wedding, and she's had a front-row seat to witness the depths of my pain and the scars that are still trying to heal, I've kept the sordid details hidden from my grandparents. Brett's grandparents are my grandparents' best friends and have been for at least thirty years. It's how Brett and I met. We grew up together. The friends-to-more story everyone loves.

Because our two families are so intertwined, I didn't want to do or say anything to my grandparents that could potentially jeopardize or ultimately end their friendship. I was already dealing with so much; I couldn't add the guilt of killing a decades-long relationship too. Penelope understood my reasons, but she's also been vocal about her disagreement. She thinks I'm excusing Brett's behavior by keeping quiet. She also thinks I'm not giving either set of grandparents enough credit, assuring me Granny and Grampie are capable of not throwing out a bushel of apples because of one bad fruit.

The front door opens, and Hayley's laugh tumbles into the restaurant.

"I really have to go, Penelope. We can discuss their anniversary another time."

"I want to get this pinned down. We need to—"

We probably need to do a lot of things, according to my sister, but this time I don't stay on the line to hear the itemized list of responsibilities she's going to delegate to me. I hang up, grimacing as I do so. My phone immediately starts ringing, and I wince again as I send the call to voicemail. That's going to be one angry message, but I just can't right now, and I tried to tell her, but she wouldn't listen.

Hayley's eyes widen at me as she follows the hostess into the dining room. *What are you doing here?* she mouths.

I pick up my fork and take a bite, thankful to finally be able to eat my dinner and that it's still warm, smiling pointedly at her as I chew.

She nods in understanding, then with her eyes she gestures to the guy behind her and gives me a small thumbs-up tucked close to her body so her date can't see.

I don't recognize the man. I'm not sure if he's a native of Little Creek or a resident of one of the other small towns lining Highway 411 or even if he made the trip from Cleveland or Chattanooga, but he looks nonhomicidal. Which, on a first date from an app, is pretty much the best you can hope for.

He's basketball-player tall with a willow-like build and what appears to be an easy smile. All in all, her type. Personally, I prefer not to have to crane my neck to look a man in the eyes or to feel as if I can beat him in an arm-wrestling contest.

I give Hayley a little wave as she and her date are seated in the corner before taking another bite of my meal. Why is Italian food so yummy? I stifle a groan of pleasure as I chew. Gnocchi are little heavenly potato pillows, and I can die a happy woman right now.

A chuckle has my eyes popping open. Funny, because I hadn't even realized I'd closed them. I blink, the man sitting across from me coming into focus.

Tai Davis is smirking in a knowing way, staring at me as if he's privy to a secret no one has let me in on.

Oops. The plan had been not to draw attention to myself. Not to give him a reason to think he'd seen me before.

Also, what does he know that I don't?

I dab at the corner of my lip with my napkin.

"I think I need to change my order and get what you're having." He grins. "You seem to be really enjoying it."

I place my napkin back in my lap. "I am," I say primly, hoping to erase from his mind whatever sound of enjoyment I'd made that probably wasn't all that appropriate in public.

My response fuels his amusement for some reason, and his smile grows.

This is the first time I've really gotten the chance to look at him outside of profile. His eyes have the most interesting shape, and when he smiles, it's like the ends of his lips reach up and tug at the corners of his eyes, cajoling them to join in on the fun. He doesn't just smile with his mouth. He smiles with his whole face.

"I'm Tai Davis, by the way."

I nearly say *yes, I know* but catch myself just in time. If I acknowledge I know his name, then he'll wonder how I know it, and I'll have to admit to finding his information in the library system. "Evangeline Kelly."

I lower my attention back to my food, hoping he'll lose interest in our exchange. I don't want to risk there being a moment of recognition because I don't want to have to explain my earlier stalking. Although I stand by being a literary crusader, I'm not above feeling embarrassed by my tendency to go overboard.

"Evangeline." He says my name like he's tasting each of the syllables, savoring the feel of them on his tongue.

An involuntary shiver shoots down my spine, and I stiffen against my body's response. How is it possible that he makes the simple act of saying my name sound so intimate? Feeling exposed, I reflexively touch the base of my skull. My lungs deflate in relief as my fingertips come in contact with my wig.

This interaction, brief as it's been, is quickly draining me on multiple levels. I need to find a polite way to close the conversation so I can recover. I offer him a small smile, then pick up my fork and resume my meal. There, that should do it.

"It's a pretty name."

I lower my fork and take a sip of water. "Thank you." Polite. Succinct. No invitation to continue our little tête-à-tête.

"Do you go by Evangeline or a nickname? Evie or Linny, perhaps?"

I look up at him. He's still grinning at me. Still has that secret-knowing smirk in place.

I don't want to appear rude, but I'm running out of ways to graciously extricate myself from this conversation. "Evangeline," I say, tight-lipped.

And Penelope is Penelope, not Penny. Granny overheard us trying out nicknames once and immediately shut that down. She said our names are one thing our parents gave us. That if they wanted us to be called Evie and Penny, they would have done so, and that using the names they'd given us was one way to honor their memory and feel closer to them. As far as I know, neither of us have allowed anyone to use a shortened version of our names ever since.

"Good." His pronouncement, said in such a final and authoritative manner, as if his opinion matters in any way possible, makes me raise my eyes.

But as I'm lifting my gaze, he's lowering his and directing his attention to the open book in front of him.

My shoulders hit the back rest of the chair as I sigh in relief at the reprieve from being the center of his attention. Anxiety unwinds from my muscles. I must be better at the sleuthing thing than I thought. My lips tip in self-satisfaction.

A server arrives at Tai's table with a steaming plate of spaghetti and meatballs. Tai moves his book—still open—to the side to make room in front of him so she can set down the plate.

I wait. Surely he's going to put the book away. Close the cover at least. It's a hardback with a protective jacket, so as long as the book is closed, the cover and pages within won't get ruined. A wet wipe will clean any food that might splatter.

He picks up his fork. Twirls spaghetti noodles on the tines.

I picture a meatball falling from the utensil. Red sauce splattering over the pages. Stains. Smears. Carnage.

"Wait!"

He stops moving. The fork in the air, his mouth open.

I clear my throat. What's a polite way to tell a person to cease and desist committing crimes of a bookish nature? "Um. What are you reading?"

He lowers his fork and picks up the publication, showing me the cover. "*Unbroken* by Laura Hillenbrand." He moves to set the book back on the table.

"Can I see it?"

One brow slowly rises. "You haven't read it?"

I have. And seen the movie. But if I admit that, then there's

31

no reason for him to hand me the book where I can keep it safe from marinara sauce and flying meatballs. But good southern girls don't lie. At least not outright. I settle for a smile instead.

He looks to the left, at something over my shoulder, and his brows collapse above the bridge of his straight nose. "I think someone's trying to get your attention."

Dagnabit. I've totally forgotten about Hayley. I tap my phone screen as I turn. 7:25. Hayley's eyes are wide and accusing. *Sorry!* I mouth and quickly click on her name in my contacts. Ringing sounds through my phone and trills in the corner of the restaurant. Hayley picks up.

"I'm sorry. I lost track of time."

"What? Oh no. Don't worry. I'll be right there." Her voice is full of forced fake concern. Guess her date wasn't exactly her type after all.

A few seconds later, she marches out of the restaurant, throwing a glare over her shoulder in my direction. I stand to follow her out, needing to apologize again, and give my half-eaten dinner a final mournful look. The sacrifice of uneaten gnocchi should be penance, but I'm not sure Hayley will see it that way. Maybe I should snag Sheriff Jacobs for protection just in case she's not yet in a forgiving mood.

As I pass Tai's table, he grins at me. "See you later, Miss Marian."

It takes a second to catch his reference to *The Music Man*, but when I do, my step falters. Curse my inability to channel the essence of Nancy Drew with any amount of success.

4

The conversation from last night replays through my mind like a piece of dialogue highlighted on my Kindle and posted to Goodreads. A bag of English breakfast tea steeps in a mug of hot water, the steam rising and filling my nostrils, gently coaxing me into a state of remembrance.

"After some stewing, I've decided we're even," Hayley had offered magnanimously.

"What do you mean?" I'd expected her to be exasperated with me for longer than a hot second. I hadn't come through for her with the phone call on time, and she'd had to endure an extra fifteen minutes listening to a man who thought talking about his irritable bowel syndrome was a great conversation topic for a first date.

"Well, I kind of pulled a tiny, harmless prank on you." She'd shot me a glance to gauge my reaction at this admittance before plowing forward. "I'd say I more than paid my penance by enduring Dean's commentary on flatulence for ten minutes straight."

"What kind of prank?"

She'd looked at me without a hint of chagrin. "Tai's my cousin."

"Your cousin?" I'd blinked in confusion. "But you guys—"

"Look nothing alike, I know."

Not that cousins necessarily resembled each other. But they did usually have some sort of genetic similarities. Hayley had hair the color of watered-down strawberry wine and a freckle-kissed complexion that was allergic to the sun. Tai's skin, on the other hand, appeared to have been touched by Midas, and he had a head of thick ebony layers of hair.

"My aunt was adopted from China."

I nodded, scrunching my nose. "Then why'd you—"

She'd waved off my question before I could even get the whole thing out. "A girl has to amuse herself somehow in a small town, doesn't she?"

Kitty Purry headbutts my ankle before slinking herself in a figure eight between my slippers, pushing herself against my legs. She looks at me and lets out a plaintive meow.

Bending down, I pick her up and cradle her in my arms, scratching her under the chin. "Do you think they were playing me? Seeing if I'd go all ninja to save an open book beside a plate of pasta?" Which, I admit, isn't too farfetched. I'd been half a second away from diving for the book and then primly letting Tai know he could have it back when I could trust him with it.

Kitty Purry meows again, caring less about the events of last night and more about the fact that I haven't yet fed her breakfast. I set her down and scoop a portion of food into her bowl. Daintily, she lowers her elegant gray head into the dish and extracts exactly one piece of kibble, nibbling on it with the manners of a southern belle. I give her another scratch between the ears, then leave her to her meal.

Collecting my perfectly steeped cup of tea and my phone from the kitchen counter, I amble to the tufted settee in the living room and plop down, tucking my legs under me. My sister's voicemail glares accusingly from the icon on the bottom corner of my screen, but I'm not ready to listen to her incrimination yet. Instead, I open my web browser and click on the tab to the *New York Times*, forgoing the news portion and heading straight for the word game. Six attempts to guess a five-letter word. Vocabulary with at least three vowels are always good starters, which proves to be true when I guess the day's puzzle in three tries.

I set my empty teacup on the coffee table and sigh. No more procrastinating. Time to face the music. Bracing myself, I click on Penelope's voicemail.

"Did you seriously hang up on me?" She sounds stunned. And angry. Stangry—if that was a real word. Her huffed-out breath creates static on the line. "Real mature, Evangeline. But don't think you're going to get out of this party by simply refusing to take any of my calls."

She pauses, then sighs again, this time more gently. More compassionately. "Listen, I get why you don't want to see Brett. *I* don't want to see Brett. What he did to you . . . that's unforgivable. My offer to slather him in honey and stake him to a fire anthill still stands. You just name the day. But we have to invite him to Granny and Grampie's anniversary party if you continue to refuse to tell them the whole story. I know it sounds like I'm being the bad guy here, but you hold the cards, sister mine." She sounds like she's Smokey the Bear, but instead of telling me only I can prevent forest fires, she's telling me I have the power to incinerate the last of my dignity and good will in my hands. "Just . . . call me back so we can hash out the details and get the ball rolling, okay? I love you."

I release my pent-up breath as soon as the call ends. She's right. If I won't tell Granny and Grampie the way that man hurt me, then they'll definitely question his absence at their party. He's been in attendance at our family's events, big or small, since I can remember. It was over the course of those years that I slowly fell in love with him. He went from the annoying boy with the gap-toothed smile to the man who could coax a laugh out of me with his dry humor. He had, in hindsight, shown his true colors during high school when he'd spent more time trying to get the pretty, popular girls' attention than studying chemistry, but I'd chalked that up to hormones and convinced myself that he'd grown out of that superficial stage. There were so many other good qualities to him, besides. He had a generous and hospitable nature . . . or so I'd thought.

Anyway, it seems I have three options, two of which end in my sweet, innocent grandparents getting hurt and one with me *dealing with it* for a few hours. My head hangs in defeat. No matter how hard I've tried to run away from my past, it still manages to come back and haunt me.

I'd moved to Little Creek for a fresh start. No one knows me here. No one knows that I'm bald. No one stares at me in the produce section while I check to see if the kiwis are ripe. No one clucks their tongue in pity or mistakes me for a cancer patient, assuming my hair loss is from chemotherapy. No one hushes their kids or whispers in a too-loud voice to their offspring how it's impolite to stare and point, but then won't look me in the eye. No one knows my fiancé had stopped finding me attractive. Had stopped loving me. Had left me.

One would think it would be easier to disappear in a city than in a small hill town in the mountains, but even though Chattanooga is fairly large for Tennessee standards, my family's personal circle is relatively small. Every time I'd turned around, I'd been met with a look that had changed with my relationship status. I'd been suffocated with *"you poor thing"* and *"bless your heart"* until I was afraid one day I'd lose control of my Southern upbringing and scream in public.

Now I have to go back. To the stares and thinly veiled pleasantries masking curiosity as polite concern. Not that I haven't been back to Chattanooga since I moved. I have. But I've always planned my visits at times when I know I won't run into anyone I don't want to see. Which is basically everyone beside Grampie, Granny, and Penelope.

To ensure such results, I make a casserole and bring it with me so we eat at home instead of going out to a restaurant. I show up after church with an excuse about how I have to be back before my own congregation's evening service to help with the youth so I'm not wrangled into attending vespers with my grandparents. A carefully laid out plan can save a person from heartache.

Except I can't plan my way out of this one. Not if I want to spare my grandparents' feelings.

I tap open the camera roll on my phone and scroll back to the picture I took the last time I'd been home for a visit. Grampie had hooked his arm around Granny's hips as she'd made to pass him, tugging her down onto his lap. I'd snapped the picture as she'd lovingly called him an old coot and swatted his shoulder playfully. He'd responded by saying he still found her as irresistible almost fifty years later as he had on the day they'd met.

For them, I'd do anything. Sacrifice anything. After all, they've been doing just that for Penelope and me since before I can remember. After our parents tragically died in a plane accident, they took us in and raised us. While their friends retired and traveled the world in their golden years, Granny and Grampie were going through a second round of elementary school plays, dance recitals, and sleepover parties. I owe them so much. Much more than enduring my ex-fiancé's presence for an evening.

Kitty Purry slinks her way into the living room, primly sitting by the fiddle-leaf ficus soaking up the early morning rays by the window, then raising a paw to her face before giving it a few good swipes of her tongue. She looks at me with impatience in her yellow eyes.

"Okay, Your Highness. Let's go." I stand and so does she,

following me down a short hallway to the single bedroom of my little cabin. She jumps on my bed as if it's her throne and she's presiding over court.

I rummage in my closet and pull out a bright red pencil skirt, holding it in front of me. "This one?"

She bats the air with her right paw.

Her Highness has spoken. Red it is. I lay the skirt on the bed and turn to the other side of the closet. I pull the faded *Reading Rainbow* tee I usually wear with that skirt off the hanger and toss it on the bed. Kitty Purry bats at it until it falls to the ground in a crumpled heap.

"What? You don't think they go together?"

She stares at me, unblinking.

"Okay, okay. Sheesh. I'll pick something else." I collect the offending garment and rehang it, choosing a black tee with white lettering along the chest that says *Bookmarks are for Quitters*. "Is this better?"

Kitty Purry lifts her paw like the maneki-neko cat that sits beside the register at my favorite sushi restaurant. I guess she approves.

Before my hair started falling out, I wasn't much of a skirt or dress girl. Overalls were more my thing. But when I no longer had what people call "a woman's crowning glory," I also started to no longer feel very feminine. A bald head is so inherently masculine. Add the loss of eyebrows and eyelashes . . . yeah, I started searching for other ways to feel my femininity.

Enter the pencil skirt.

Stretchy enough to still be comfortable but with distinct lines that enhance the female form. I feel womanlier in a pencil skirt, so I wear them every day, paired with a bookish graphic tee and a pair of high-tops for comfort and practicality. Heels may be fundamentally feminine, but I'm likely to twist an ankle if I try to balance on them, and there is nothing graceful or ladylike about limping.

I dress, and Kitty Purry follows me to the bathroom, jumping on the vanity and positioning herself by the sink. Some people may find it weird, but my cat thinks she's human—a queen, really—and therefore does her grooming in the bathroom like every other diva. As I layer on foundation, she licks at her paw and rubs the limb over her ear.

My temporary eyebrow tattoos are still very much intact, so after I apply the normal makeup (foundation, blush, lipstick), I reach for the false eyelashes, glue, and tweezers. The learning curve to applying false lashes is steep, but I've been doing it every day for so long now that the movements of swiping the glue brush along the edge and then having a pair of tweezers so close to my eyeball is second nature. I don't even flinch anymore. Kitty Purry doesn't try to bat them off the vanity anymore either.

I blink a few times and inspect myself in the mirror, turning my head left and right to view from profile. Profile is always the worst. I can't ignore the roundness of my crown or the bump off to the side near the top of my head that hair used to cover. I can't help but be reminded of the early nineties film *Coneheads*, although the shape of my cranium is more asymmetrical than exaggeratedly pointed.

My wig sits on a faceless mannequin bust on the corner of the vanity. The first time I'd stepped foot in a wig shop, I'd had no idea what I was doing. Granted, I hadn't known that I'd need the equivalent of a master's degree to buy a wig, but you don't know what you don't know. It took about three seconds to realize I should've done my research first. The attendant tried to be helpful with her questions—Did I want a lace front, full lace, or cap wig? Real hair or synthetic? If synthetic, then did I have a preference on fiber types like polyester, acrylic, Kanekalon, or polyvinyl chloride?

I'd almost run out of the store but instead forced my feet to stay put as I politely told the clerk I'd just look around on my own. The price of the real hair wigs made me choke, especially when I learned that they only lasted about a year before needing replacement. One decision down. The full lace and lace-front wigs were beautiful, the hairs individually hand-tied into a thin, almost invisible lace material that made the hairline and part look the most natural. Honestly, in the display pictures, I couldn't even tell the models were wearing wigs. But those came with a pretty steep learning curve. Depending on the wig, I'd have to pluck or bleach some of the knots, and with all of them, I'd have to trim the lace around my face without ruining anything as well as learn how to apply an adhesive to get the wig to stay in place.

One day I may feel confident enough and have the budget to try a lace-front or even a full lace wig, but I was so overwhelmed that day at the store. I just needed something I could put on and not be able to screw up. That's when I tried on *my* wig.

I lift the synthetic hair from its stand and shake out the strands that feel nothing like my hair used to. Even though the strands' texture is thick and coarse to my touch, it isn't too bad. I set it on my head, adjust it just so, and look at myself in the mirror.

The first time I'd seen myself wearing this wig, it was like I'd found me again. The best way I can describe it is from a scene in the movie *Hook* with Robin Williams. Peter Pan/Robin Williams returns to Neverland as an adult and the Lost Boys don't recognize him because he grew up. One little boy starts inspecting Peter Pan's older and wrinkled face, smooshing it this way and that, then he pushes Peter Pan's cheeks into a wide smile and says in recognition, "Oh, there you are, Peter."

When I'd put this wig on in the store and looked in the handheld mirror, I'd said to myself, "Oh, there you are, Evangeline," even though the cut isn't one I'd ever had before and the color is a light shade of almond, at least three gradients lighter than what I'd been born with. The curtain bangs hide the abrupt hairline of the machine-made piece while also framing my face and drawing attention to my cheekbones. The rest of the hair in the wig is pre-styled in shoulder-length beach waves that hold their shape with minimal effort from me. No one has ever commented on the fact that I wear my hair the same way every day (the wig is an easy wear-and-go but not really that versatile, so I can't change the style that much), but I figured if anyone ever did, I'd just brush it off by saying that the style is my signature look.

Finally transformed into the Evangeline Kelly that everyone in Little Creek knows, I gather my purse, plant a begrudgingly received kiss atop Kitty Purry's head, and lock my cabin door behind me. I stop by Mimi's Bakery to purchase some baked goods for the human story visiting the library today and any of the patrons who want to check her out.

The idea of a living library originated in Denmark in 2000 with a model of borrowing a person instead of a book in a means to challenge stereotypes and prejudice through dialogue. It also bridges generational gaps, broadens perspectives, and celebrates the oral traditions of long ago that have been lost by so many. Mrs. Miriam Goldmann was supposed to visit our branch a few weeks ago as our first living book to be checked out—just in time for Valentine's Day, as the subject of her story is marriage from a Jewish perspective—but she'd developed a nasty cold and had to reschedule.

I balance the boxes of pastries in one hand as I unlock the library door, step in, then reengage the lock. The lights are turned on, so either Hayley or Martha is already here.

"Do I smell donuts?" Martha sets down a crate of craft supplies. Every Tuesday, she spearheads a crafternoon around a beloved children's book. Last week, kids made bear paws from paper bags and drew maps on butcher block paper all

41

the while chanting *"Can't go over it. Can't go under it. Oh no! Got to go through it!"*

"Cronuts." The marriage of a croissant and a donut made the most delicious offspring. "And chocolate croissants. And a few other pastries thrown in for good measure."

"From Mimi's?" Martha licks her lips.

"Of course." I set the boxes down and retrieve some paper towels from the supply closet.

A couple of hours later, a woman in her eighties, white hair braided into a loose, low-hanging bun and wearing a bottle-green dress and matching overcoat, walks into the library, supported by a cane.

"Mrs. Goldmann?" I approach her with a smile.

She smiles back, watery eyes bright with enthusiasm. "I'm Miriam Goldmann. It's been a few years since I've been *checked out*"—she winks—"but I'm ready for the opportunity for it to happen to me again."

I lead her to the sitting area and offer her a baked good from the box. She selects a croissant and puts it on a small plate. A college-aged young woman approaches and asks to hear Mrs. Goldmann's story, taking out a notebook and pen as she does so.

"You know the song in *Fiddler on the Roof*? It goes 'Matchmaker, matchmaker, make me a match'? Well, a Jewish matchmaker is called a *shadchanit*, or a *shadchan* if the matchmaker is a man, and that's where my love story starts."

As Miriam Goldmann continues to speak and share about the great love of her life, an idea begins to form in my mind. It's hazy, the outlines not yet well defined, but I smile. With a little fleshing out, this may just be my best idea ever.

5

This wasn't the first time Hayley had talked Tai into doing something he normally wouldn't have, but it was the first time he thought about thanking her for it.

He'd definitely not considered gratitude the time she'd persuaded him to play the game Chubby Bunny with habanero peppers instead of marshmallows. Nor the time she'd convinced him to yell out a random word starting with each consecutive letter of the alphabet on Thanksgiving when he was eight. The first had sent him into an asthma attack that had made his already overprotective mom hover even closer, while the second saw him meeting with a psychiatrist because that same helicopter parent was convinced he'd developed Tourette's Syndrome.

Then again, Hayley probably wouldn't thank him for the time he'd dared her to only speak in pig latin for a whole day. The same day the most popular guy in school had asked her to go with him to the winter formal. The quarterback had quickly changed his mind when she'd responded with "Esyay! I'd ovelay otay ogay ithway ouyay!"

Tai shook his head at the memory, a wry grin tilting the corners of his lips. They'd been playing this game with each other for years. Twenty-four, to be exact. He still remembered the first dare she'd ever issued him. He'd been moping around his room when he was five. His mom had just pulled him out of T-ball after he'd collapsed between second and third base, coughing and clutching his ever-tightening chest in an effort to drag in a full breath. He had no idea what asthma was at the time, nor how much it would change the rest of his life. He only knew his mom was being unfair and that he wouldn't be able to grow up to be like Derek Jeter if she made him quit T-ball.

Hayley had marched into his room and looked around, an expression of disgust on her preschool face. "Don't you have any pictures on your walls or anything?" she'd asked.

Earlier that day, his mom had taken down the shadow box of baseball memorabilia, along with shelves that had displayed his Hot Wheels cars, muttering something about dust like it had committed the most atrocious of crimes. He'd merely shrugged in response to Hayley, too upset to say anything out loud.

She'd frowned at him. "My dad painted a rainbow on my bedroom wall. It makes me smile. I bet if you had a painting on your wall, you'd smile instead of looking like Oscar the Grouch."

He'd just stared at her.

She'd poked one of his four sad, empty white walls and issued her first challenge. "I dare you to paint a picture right here."

Tai knew he'd get in trouble. That his mom would be furious. But he didn't care. He was mad at her anyway. Turned out, that was the start of his and Hayley's challenges to each other as well as the beginning of his love for art.

Hmm . . . Maybe he should thank Hayley for more than one dare after all.

Tai climbed out of his Dodge Challenger that took the corners of the country roads in the Cherokee National Forest like a dream—or a nightmare, if anyone asked his mom, Missy Davis. Or listened to her scold him at family dinners. Which he didn't. If she had her way, he'd be living his life in a bubble. He'd taken a needle to that balloon a long time ago, and he wasn't about to let her shove him back inside a safe little box ever again.

He opened the door to the library, the biography he'd checked out earlier that week tucked under his arm. A grin spread across his face as he imagined what Evangeline's reaction would be. No doubt she'd immediately retrieve the book from the return receptacle and inspect each page to make sure he hadn't ruined the book in some way.

At first, he hadn't understood Hayley's dare. Returning a book she'd checked out under his account with a bunch of dog-eared pages didn't make a whole lot of sense. Until he'd done it and then noticed he was being followed around the library by the world's least stealthy librarian. That was when Tai realized Hayley had only used him to poke at Evangeline.

His cousin had been talking about her newest coworker ever since Evangeline had arrived in Little Creek, which happened to be only a few months after his own reappearance in his hometown. He'd heard whispers that his being back was like the prodigal son returning, but he'd yet to see any fatted calf killed on his behalf in celebration. More like a small uproar that his presence and his newly opened business were going to bring riffraff to their peaceful corner of the world. He figured time would prove them wrong, so he didn't plan to waste his energy trying to change anyone's opinion.

He chuckled to himself, remembering the way Evangeline had tried to hide behind a large tome on the life of Sir Isaac Newton. The only thing she'd managed to conceal had been her pert little nose and her rosebud-shaped lips. Her wide expressive eyes, however, had been impossible to miss. Even if he hadn't seen her, he'd have been alerted to her presence by the steady weight of her gaze, which he felt on his skin as keenly as if she'd touched him.

Hayley might've orchestrated his encounter with Evangeline because of the dare, but now that he'd met her, he found himself thinking about her more than Hayley might have intended. Or maybe not. A part of him wondered if her dare had been twofold—mess with Evangeline while also attempting to set Tai up with her. If that were the case, Hayley could be two for two.

There was something about Evangeline that intrigued him. Something different about her that he couldn't quite put his finger on. He'd noticed immediately she was a list of walking contradictions. Perfectly poised and tightly controlled on the outside but a current of live wires just waiting to spark underneath. Her mouth said one thing while her eyes spoke something entirely different. But it wasn't the juxtaposition of her that he couldn't pinpoint. While she was like two sides of a color wheel, opposite and yet alluringly attractive, there was also something . . .

Something.

Like he'd said, he couldn't put his finger on what that was. He just knew it was there and that he couldn't stop thinking about the anomaly. About her. He needed to study her more. Figure out the mystery or the hidden piece of the picture that she presented. It was just an added bonus that she was easy on the eyes and that getting her decorum to slip a bit, letting what she tried to hide on the inside shine through, was the most fun he'd had in ages.

Hayley stood behind the information desk, pecking away at the keyboard. She looked up with a smile of greeting on her lips as the front door slid shut behind Tai. When she registered it was him, she tilted her chin in a signal for him to come over.

"I thought you were loyal to your Kindle," she said as he approached, an undertone to her voice that made him wonder if she suspected he had ulterior motives in showing up at the library.

He held up the book in his hand. "I have to return this."

"Oh." A hint of disappointment in her tone made him feel like his suspicions weren't off base.

"Why? Did you think I stopped by for a different reason?"

She plucked the biography from his hand. "Of course not." She scanned the barcode and returned the title to the system. "There. I'll see you Friday night for dinner at your parents' house."

He hooked his thumbs through the belt loops of his jeans and leaned a hip on the desk. "Any particular reason you're trying to get rid of me?"

She cocked her head and narrowed her eyes. "I thought you said you only needed to return the book. Well, it's returned." She paused, her gaze turning calculating. "Why? Is there some other reason you might need to linger?"

The way she watched him was telling. He wasn't mad at her meddling, but he also didn't mind messing with her either. "Yes, actually, there is."

Hayley straightened, almost surprised but certainly delighted. "Really?"

Tai nodded.

Hayley's grin spread across her face like a river after a rainstorm. "I knew it." She began to throw a fist in the air in victory.

"I need another book."

Her hand made a sudden detour to smoothing her hair. She cleared her throat, trying to look with all her might like his response was the one she'd expected. "I knew it. I mean, what other reason is there to come to the library, right?"

Tai pointed to the pods of computers to the left, smashing his lips together to keep from grinning. "I could have needed to print something."

Hayley scowled but waved her arm toward a mural of kids

reading under an oak tree. "Or wanted to get a head start on making Lorax trees from pipe cleaners and pom-poms? You're a few hours early for crafternoon."

"Pity."

"Isn't it just."

Tai stared at his cousin. Hayley stared right back.

"Hayley." He tried for a serious tone, hoping she'd crack and confess to her interference.

The problem came when one's cousin was more like one's sister and could still remember the days of watching cartoons together in their superhero and princess pajamas. Serious tones didn't lead to pressure-induced confessions.

The corner of Hayley's lips twitched, but her laser beam eye contact never broke. "Tai."

Laughter erupted from the sitting area in front of the multimedia section. Both Hayley and Tai's heads swiveled in the direction of the sound. A little old lady with the style of the late Queen Elizabeth sat in a wingback chair, presiding over her court of a half dozen rapt listeners.

"What's going on over there?" Tai asked.

"It's a new program that Evangeline established. Mrs. Goldmann is the first living library book that patrons can check out and listen to her tell her story."

Tai felt his brows rise. He'd never heard of such a thing. Being able to check out a person at the library? Definitely a new concept. Although by the spellbound look on the five patrons' and one librarian's faces, the idea held a lot of success.

Tai let his gaze settle on the niminy-piminy woman perched on the edge of a folding chair, the eraser end of a sharpened pencil lightly tapping against rose petal–pink lips. Evangeline's posture was one any beauty pageant contestant would be proud of. He had a feeling that the word *slouch* wasn't in her vocabulary.

Her skirt hugged her thighs, her legs pressed together and slanted at an angle until her toes touched the floor, the epitome of ladylike decorum. What would it take for her to lose her tightly bound control? To give in to the hint of free spirit she showcased with the graphic tee and canvas high-tops?

"I think I might need help finding a specific book," Tai murmured without taking his eyes from Evangeline.

"What's the title? I can look it up in—"

But Tai didn't wait for his cousin to finish offering her help. When it came to librarians, there was only one who could give him the assistance he was looking for.

He approached Evangeline, loving the way her eyes rounded the moment she spotted him advancing in her direction. She stood, pressing the notebook she'd been writing in close to her middle, as if it held her deepest, darkest secrets.

Her throat worked as she swallowed, then she gave him a practiced, polite smile. "May I help you?"

He looked pointedly at her notebook, grinning as she pressed it even more tightly against her stomach, her arms crossing over the cover. When he lifted his gaze to meet her eyes, her chin rose in a defiant tilt.

The change in position gave him the perfect angle to inspect her features. There was symmetry to her heart-shaped face. Her green eyes were evenly set. A proud turn to the slope of her jaw and the elegant angle of her neck flowed into a stark contrast with the sharpness of her collar bones. Her skin was smooth, with three small freckles in a tiny triangle on her right cheek. What some may call an imperfection only added allure and character in his opinion.

That niggle he couldn't place came back to him. The feeling that he was missing something right in front of his eyes. But what?

"Mr. Davis?"

Evangeline's voice made him blink, and he focused again on her eyes. "Tai."

She tucked her chin a notch to let him know she'd heard him.

"I'm looking for a book."

One corner of her mouth twitched in a barely there smile. "Then you've come to the right place. Any specific title that you're looking for?"

Hayley had been right when she'd said he preferred reading on a Kindle. However, with art books, he liked being able to closely inspect each stroke and study the craft of the artist, and that was better done on printed pages than pixels. "Henna art."

Evangeline pursed her lips in thought. He could imagine her brain riffling through a mental card catalog.

"I think we have a couple that might interest you." She turned, an unspoken invitation for him to follow.

They passed a few shelves before stopping in the center of a nonfiction aisle. Evangeline grazed a finger along a row of spines, then stopped at a thin hardback and tugged the book from its cozy spot wedged between a treatise on watercolor and a how-to for pen and ink.

"Will this work?" she asked as she handed him the book.

Tai opened the cover. He paged through the history and culture of henna, slowing to take in the tiny details, scrollwork, and symmetry of the designs. Yes, this would do nicely for his purposes.

"This is perfect, thank you." He looked up and smiled.

But he found Evangeline's focus decidedly lower than his eyes—on his rose tattoo, to be precise. He tucked his chin to give her a better view, then leaned in slightly.

"You know, I'm not one of your living books," he whispered.

She startled, her gaze finally rising to meet his. "Pardon?"

He grinned. "You were checking me out."

"I wasn't . . . that's not. . ."

He laughed as her cheeks reddened to a deep rosy hue.

"Thanks for the book." He winked and left her sputtering on the spot.

6

Tai had only a few more minutes to put the finishing touches on the design he'd worked out for his seven o'clock appointment. Transferring the intricate details of the lacelike mandala with jeweled edging from the flat surface of his tablet to the rounded contours of Darla Shapiro's head would take skill. Especially since he'd have to freehand the design instead of use a stencil like he usually did for his tattoos.

"Tai, your seven o'clock is here," Maggie shouted back at him from the reception area.

Tai added the last teardrop to finish out the symmetry of the mandala, then saved his design in his drawing software. He kept the document open so he could show Darla and get her approval before he got to work applying it on her skin. Tucking the tablet against his side, he made his way to the front of the shop and smiled when he saw the woman in her midfifties he'd met the week before when she'd come in and shared her vision with him.

"Good to see you again," he said with a warm smile. Some of the first-timers were nervous when they walked through the doors of a tattoo shop. Needles tended to do that to people. Not that she had that particular concern today. "Want to come on back?"

"I'm really excited to see what you came up with." Darla followed him to his station, then took a seat in the chair that resembled something you'd see in a dentist office.

Tai dragged over his rolling adjustable stool and sat beside his client, turning the tablet around so she could see the screen. "What do you think? Let me know if there are any adjustments you want to make."

A telltale sheen washed over her eyes as she stared at the picture he'd created. "This is perfect." Emotion clogged her throat as she handed the tablet back to him.

"A headdress fit for a warrior princess." He held her gaze a few moments so she'd know he meant what he'd said. People like Darla held a hidden strength that he could only imagine.

Customers came into the parlor for many different reasons. Tattoos were personal and permanent. Most patrons took a lot of time to decide what they wanted forever inked into their skin. Sometimes a person wanted to memorialize a lost loved one in a piece of art, or a couple wanted a lasting symbol of their relationship, or someone wanted a quote they could look at and be reminded of in moments of doubt or weakness.

Darla, however, was a fighter. And the dye he would put to her skin was an outward representation of that fighting spirit she carried within.

"Are you ready?" He didn't want to rush her. There was a lot of emotion surrounding what they were about to do.

She looked at him and smiled. "I'm ready." Reaching up, she grazed her fingers at the hairline above her forehead. A second later, her hair slid off her head, revealing a bald dome the wig had previously covered.

Tai blinked. That was it. How could he have missed it before? The *something* that always niggled at him whenever he looked at Evangeline. The wavy curls framing her face were part of a wig. Was she locked in a similar battle as Darla? The thought caused an ache to bloom behind his breastbone. Evangeline wasn't anyone to him, but he hated the thought of her going through such a fight.

Beside him, Darla gave a nervous chuckle, snapping him out of his dazed epiphany.

Right. The woman he should be focusing on at the moment. He set his tablet on a mount, then pulled on a pair of medical-grade disposable gloves. He'd already prepared the henna the day before, per his research, mixing the henna powder with lemon juice, sugar, and tea tree oil, and letting the paste rest to release the dye.

"You said you've never done this, right?" Darla's voice didn't sound nervous, just matter-of-fact.

Tai turned from the equipment to face her. "Henna, no. Although I did practice and I have done my fair share of mandalas, so you needn't worry on that account."

She leaned back in the chair. "I'm not worried." She rather looked like she was ready for a day at the spa. Speaking of . . .

"Were you able to exfoliate the skin within the last three days like we discussed?" For the tattoo to last longer, the dead skin needed to be scrubbed off so it wouldn't fall away, taking the dye with it.

"My daughter gifted me with a sugar scrub that smelled divine."

"Good." He moved to stand behind her. "I'm going to touch your head now and get a feel for your skin and the contours of your skull."

"Go right ahead."

He ran a hand over the top of her head, noting that she'd already shaved the area.

He stepped back in front of her. "I'm going to get started, but tell me if you need a break or, well, if you need anything at all." There wouldn't be any needles involved. No pain to take a break from. But still. He wanted to put that out there just in case.

She eyed him behind squinted lids. "I promise you, I won't break."

He smiled at her softly. "No. I imagine you're made of stronger stuff than that."

"I've got to be, don't I?" She repositioned herself in the chair. "Besides, I plan to walk into that first chemo treatment with my chin high and shoulders back. I'm not going to let cancer make me tuck my tail between my legs."

Thus the reason behind the henna and not the needles and ink. Permanent tattoos left open wounds that needed time to heal and, quite frankly, a strong immune system to back it up. With Darla going in for chemo, her immune system was about to take a major hit.

Tai quickly cleaned and dried Darla's head, then transferred the henna paste into the special plastic bags he'd purchased for the occasion. When he'd practiced, he'd felt a bit like a baker piping and decorating a cake. He had to squeeze the henna paste out of a cut coned edge, paying particular attention to the pressure he applied to the bag. How hard he squeezed correlated to the line weights he needed to make the design come out the way he planned. Less paste resulted in thinner lines. More paste meant thicker lines. He had a few bags with different sized tips to help with the weight of the lines as well.

"Can you tilt your head to the side for me, please?" He positioned himself to her left. It would be best to work from one side of her head, across the top and back, then finish on the other side.

Darla bent her head so her opposite ear nearly touched her shoulder. "So, how did you get into tattooing?"

Tai hovered the bag near her scalp, careful not to let the edge of the cone touch her skin to prevent any scratchy marks. He squeezed the bag, pulling the string of henna paste to form a delicate scallop design around the curve of her ear, leaving the dark paste on her scalp much like puffy paint.

"I mean, I'm not sure I've ever met a kid who said, 'When I grow up, I want to be a tattoo artist," Darla continued.

Tai chuckled. "When I was a kid, I wanted to be a professional baseball player."

"A baseball diamond is a long way away from needles and ink."

"You're telling me." The thing with mandalas was that to make them look good, you had to have precise symmetry. Tai concentrated on his lines, glancing at the tablet screen every now and again to reference his design. Most people were chatty in the chair, however, so he was used to having a conversation while he worked. "Art kind of rescued me, though."

"How so?"

"I was a bit of a sickly child. Fairly severe asthma, and my mother in particular worried about me a lot. I had to stay inside most of the time. Art became my escape. My way to express myself. Even an avenue to experience the world."

"What do your parents think of the tattoo thing? Are they supportive, or do they wish you'd gone a direction without as much stigma to it?"

Tai readjusted the bag. "My mom, being the worrier that she is, is happy that I have a job that's inside instead of out in the elements and that doesn't make me exert myself physically."

"Has the asthma not gotten better as you've gotten older? I thought a lot of kids outgrew it."

Tai's lips twisted in a wry grin. "It's a lot better and more manageable now. In fact, it hardly ever bothers me. Okay, you can straighten your head now. Do you need to take a break to use the restroom?" Tai shook out his hand. He was used to holding the tattoo machine for hours, but that was all vibration and didn't require his grip to constantly tighten. He was starting to get a small cramp near the base of his thumb.

"I'm good." Darla crossed her ankles.

He didn't know much about chemo, but he imagined it required long stints sitting in a chair, hooked up to an IV. Darla was going to be a pro.

"Can you lean forward a bit for me?" He gently nudged her shoulder.

She did as asked, her eyes wandering around the studio. "It's a nice place you have here."

"Thank you."

"I'm surprised you get enough business in this location."

Tai smiled ruefully. Even though his shop had been open less than a year and was off the beaten path, he was booked out for months.

He worked for a few moments in silence, but Darla Shapiro apparently wasn't one to stay quiet for long.

"Can I admit something to you?" she asked, her voice not quite as strong as it had been before.

Tai didn't answer. The question seemed rhetorical, and he figured Darla was going to share either way. That she needed to.

"This"—she waved her hand to indicate the artwork he was applying to her head. "It may look like I'm brave, but inside I'm really scared."

Tai lowered the henna bag and walked around to face Darla once again. Her chin wobbled in a show of vulnerability. He picked up her hand and ran a thumb along her knuckles. "Bravery isn't the absence of fear."

"No?" Her eyes watered. "What is it then?"

He squeezed her fingers. "Bravery is just the voice telling fear he can't win today."

Darla took in a deep breath and nodded once, resolution hardening the set of her jaw. "Not today."

Tai let go of her hand but didn't resume the tattoo. It wasn't his place, but . . . "Miss Darla, do you have someone going with you to chemo? If not, I could—"

Darla shook her head as she managed a trembling smile.

"Oh, honey, does this town have you pegged wrong. You don't have a single bad bone in your body."

"I don't know about that." He winked at her, cloaking himself in the outward appearance of how he knew many still saw him. The shadow of teenage rebellion and poor decisions was long.

"Mm-hmm." She looked unconvinced. "But don't worry about me. My sweet husband will be by my side."

"Good."

He finished the tattoo, then let it dry for thirty minutes. To get the best color, he mixed lemon juice and sugar and applied it to the design with a cotton ball, wrapping Darla's head with plastic wrap to keep the henna paste safe as she let it set into her skin.

"Keep this on until tomorrow. The paste will flake off after you remove the wrap. If the color isn't what you expected right away, don't worry. It takes a little while for the dye to darken in color on your skin. Keep away from water and soap for at least twenty-four hours, and if you need to use a moisturizer, then coconut oil or olive oil will work better for the longevity of your tattoo than conventional moisturizers or creams."

Darla stood. "Thank you so much. You don't know what this means to me." She gave him a hug, then picked up her discarded wig.

Seeing the long strands of synthetic hair immediately made Tai think of a certain librarian. What exactly was Evangeline Kelly's story?

7

"Stavors likes to swing left, so get ready, Davis." Burke, Tai's teammate, warned as a man with the build of a steam train stepped up to home plate, a metal bat resting on his shoulder.

Tai bent at the knees, his fingers flexing in his leather glove. The sun warmed his back, and the scent of fresh-cut grass attested to the beginning of spring, as did the hints of blue along the fence line where the landscapers missed Weedwacking the first crocuses of the year.

Dalton Matthews wound up on the mound, brought his arm behind his head, then let the ball fly from his hand like David's stone from a slingshot. Hopefully his fastball would make the Goliath of a batter fall after three strikes.

Stavors swung.

Crack!

The ball lifted into the sky like a rocket. To the left, just as Burke predicted. Tai squinted, thankful the sun was behind him, and calculated the trajectory.

"I got it!" he called as he sprinted backward, afraid that the left fielder would collide with him and they'd lose an easy play. He brought his glove up, cradled his other hand behind the worn leather, and closed his glove around the catch.

His teammates whooped as they jogged to the dugout. That made the third out. They were now heading into the ninth and last inning. It would be nice if they could add a few more runs to the scoreboard, but as long as they didn't allow the other team any, they'd still win the game.

A couple of his teammates slapped him on the back as they passed him to take a seat at the long bench under the lean-to that served as the dugout. He grabbed his water bottle and squirted a long spray into his mouth.

"Okay, Burke, you're up first. Matthews, you're on deck." Pepé was the team's unofficial manager, coach, and captain. Really, he was the one who filled out the paperwork and submitted it to the county. Plus, he really liked a clipboard.

A sharp whistle came from the bleachers as Burke walked out onto the field. His wife never missed a game and had the enthusiasm of a Little League mom.

Tai scanned the risers behind home plate. Sure enough, a petite woman decked out in their team colors stood from the top, waving a pair of pom-poms in the air. A familiar bent head caught his attention. If Tai hadn't recognized her by the hair that had captivated his curiosity more than he cared to admit, then the T-shirt sporting a Brachiosaurus carrying a huge tower of books the height of its long neck would pinpoint her identity in a second.

What was Evangeline doing at the game?

A stack of papers rested on top of her thighs, and in one of her hands were three highlighters of different colors. She riffled through the papers, pulling one out and setting it on top. With her teeth, she uncapped one of the highlighters, then made some marks on the paper.

She appeared to be studying something, but why study at a baseball game?

Her head lifted, and her gaze settled on Dalton in the on-deck circle, who was taking a few warm-up swings. She thumbed through her papers again and pulled out another sheaf, settling this one beside the first. Her eyes moved between the two, and she traded her highlighter for a pen, then made a few notes in the margins.

Tai looked at Dalton, trying to figure out what in the world Evangeline was up to and what it had to do with the town's chainsaw sculptor. The most obvious answer would be that she was romantically interested in the man, but what woman appeared to be studying for a test when watching the guy she liked at a sporting event? Unless she knew nothing of baseball and the papers she poured over were the rules and regulations of the game? It was a possibility.

But for some reason, that answer didn't sit right with Tai.

The crack of connection between bat and ball rent the air a second before Burke's wife's screams of enthusiasm did. The bat clattered to the ground, and Burke took off to first base, a cloud of red dust behind his cleats.

Evangeline looked up again from her papers, but her focus wasn't on the game. She was still peering at Dalton. Scrutinizing him, more like.

So, yeah, her presence had nothing to do with the game.

She'd proven herself a bit of a stalker (and a bad one, at that) in her overzealous crusade to protect all things published. Was she there to present Dalton with some type of summons or fine on behalf of the library?

Again, a theory that seemed highly unlikely—not that Tai wouldn't put it past her to attempt such a thing. She sure had appeared to be ready to read him his Miranda rights when he'd dared to open a book anywhere near the vicinity of marinara sauce.

Dalton walked toward home plate while Rickers moved from the dugout to the on-deck circle. Tai looked back at Evangeline. She was nibbling on the capped end of her pen, deep in thought. Nothing at first glance would give anyone the idea that the woman was mysterious. Yet here he was again, trying to figure her out.

A gust of wind picked up, causing a swirl of dust on the baseball diamond but wreaking even more havoc in the stands. Evangeline's neat pile of papers on her lap decided it was a perfect time to make a break for it. With the gusto of a classroom of kids being let out for recess, the papers flew in every direction, cackling with laughter in the breeze as Evangeline made futile swipes to bring them back under control.

Tai's turn in the batting rotation was pretty far down the list. Pepé might not even call his name before it was time to go back out and play third base.

"I'll be right back," he said to no one in particular before jogging out the side entrance of the dugout toward the grassy section between the fence and the parking lot.

One of Evangeline's papers rolled like a tumbleweed across the short blades of grass. He bent down and picked it up. Another rode the wind like a magic carpet, it's getaway coming to an abrupt halt when it collided with his chest. He peeled the paper off the T-shirt the county distributed as jerseys.

Evangeline was scrambling to retrieve her wayward pages. Her apologies as she climbed over legs and tried to keep from stumbling into the other spectators reached him even from this distance. Two more of her papers were being pressed into the fence behind home plate as if by gunpoint.

He'd help her get the rest. But not before he snuck a peek.

Glancing down, he quickly scanned the printout. His brows pulled together over his eyes. He was holding a copy of Dalton's library check-out history in one hand and Stacey Lawerence's in the other. *A Christmas Carol* by Charles Dickens had been highlighted in red on both papers, which Tai could understand, but then *This Road We Traveled* by Jane Kirkpatrick was highlighted in yellow on Stacey's history while *Back to Basics: A Complete Guide to Traditional Skills* was highlighted in the same color on Dalton's. Tai had no idea what those particular books had to do with the other.

His gaze flicked up. Evangeline was collecting the runaway papers pressed along the fence. He had a few more seconds. Looking back down, he squinted to read the tiny handwriting on the side.

Similar interests:
Classics
Love of Christmas
Simple living/pioneering

What in the world was the woman up to?

The papers were snatched from his hands with such force that the corner he held with his right thumb and forefinger remained in his grip, a ripped edge attesting to how much Evangeline didn't want him snooping.

From the look in her eye, she'd like to take a similar bite out of him.

Tai rocked back on his heels and gave her a lopsided grin in hope of disarming her. He didn't necessarily want to defuse the situation entirely since he kind of liked the spark in her eye. Even if (or especially if?) said spark was directed at him. "Hello, Miss Marian."

Evangeline took in a long breath through her nose, visibly trying to compose herself. "You know that is not my name."

He took a half step forward and bent his head toward her as if imparting a secret. The faint scent of books and ink mixed with a delicate femininity filled his nostrils. "It's something people like to call a nickname."

Their faces were close, and he could see her throat work as she swallowed, but she didn't take a step back.

She did, however, hold her papers a bit closer to her chest. "No one calls me by a nickname."

Tai paused. He liked her name. It fit her. But it was also a mouthful. He couldn't imagine it had never been shortened before. "No one?"

"No one." She said the two words with finality.

Well, that settled that. Everyone needed a nickname at some point in their life. "I can't say I've ever been called a no one before, but today's as good a day as any."

While her lips pressed into a firm line, his curved even more. "But if you're going to get your first nickname, maybe we should ease into it a bit more. Something a little closer to what's on your birth certificate."

She sputtered. "Mr. Davis, I hardly think—"

"Tai, if you please. Even southern manners will allow you to use my first name." He plowed on when she opened her mouth to protest, tapping his chin as if giving his words a great deal of thought. "Now, see, Tai can't really be shortened since it's already one syllable—"

She mumbled something under her breath.

"What was that?"

She sighed. "I just said, it could be shortened to the first letter of your name. People could call you *T*."

"Now you're getting it." He grinned at her in encouragement, then had to bite the tip of his tongue to keep from laughing when she rolled her eyes. "But back to you. You have a name that is practically begging to be shortened."

Her gaze skittered away for a brief moment. "My mother gave me the name Evangeline."

"Well, I didn't think it was bestowed upon you by Rumpelstiltskin."

She let out a disgruntled sound at the back of her throat.

Which he ignored. "We've established no one has given you a nickname. We've established I am no one. We've established

64

what your mother calls you. What we haven't established is what *I* will call you."

"Mr. Davis—"

"You know, the more you say my name that way, the more I like it." Tai let his voice take on a husky, seductive tone.

Evangeline's face mottled.

Tai swallowed his laugh.

"Tai—"

"That's good too," he practically purred. He had no idea where this flirtatious nonsense was coming from, and he was sure his mom would box his ears if she overheard how he was behaving at the moment, but he couldn't seem to stop himself. He was quickly becoming addicted to seeing the effect he had on the woman. "My name on your lips is like hearing it for the very first time."

Evangeline blinked at him, her mouth agape.

He winked at her for good measure. "But back to the topic at hand. A nickname for you." He studied her.

She studied him right back, an almost-challenge in her eyes. It was probably only manners that kept her from turning on her heel and storming off. But whatever kept her standing in front of him, he was enjoying every minute of their exchange.

After another moment, the perfect name came to him. The muscles in his face softened. "Angel," he breathed. "Because I can't imagine anything in heaven could be lovelier than you."

She flushed and looked away. "While this has been highly . . . enlightening, I must be going." She rushed past him, her head down, cheeks pink, and muttering to herself in a low but strident tone.

He watched her go with a grin, then turned back to the dugout, only just remembering he'd never asked her what in the world she was doing with those library check-out histories in the first place.

8

If I'd had a question before as to what casting category Tai fell under, our conversation at the baseball field cleared that up. The man is reprehensible. Incorrigible. He is absolutely without shame.

My cheeks heat just thinking about the things he'd said. The way he'd said them. How his eyes had lingered. Studied. Probed. I'd felt almost naked under that gaze and had fingered the collar of my shirt to assure myself that, yes, I was in fact fully clothed.

I shake my head. Tai Davis is nothing more than an insatiable flirt. An unequivocal rake.

Rakes make the best husbands.

A choking sound emits from the back of my throat. I don't believe the claim, even if certain historical romance authors have tried to lure unsuspecting wallflowers into crediting the farce. And while I adhere to the notion that there is a lot of truth within the stories of fiction, especially pertaining to the human condition, on this particular trope I call malarky.

Do I love a reformed rake as a literary device? Absolutely. But in real life? A girl needs to see what's in front of her face. If he moves like a rake, talks like a rake, and flirts like a rake, he's a rake. He's not going to all of a sudden have a Cinderella moment and turn into Prince Charming to sweep you off your feet into a happily-ever-after.

Not that it matters what Tai Davis is or isn't. Not to me, anyway. For all I care, he could be an undercover heir to the throne of an obscure European country (another unbelievable yet indulgent trope). Then again, that would literally make him Prince Charming.

Well, he is a charmer.

I roll my eyes at myself. *Focus, Evangeline.*

Not Angel. Not Miss Marian or Madam Librarian. Evangeline Victoria Kelly. I give my head a single perfunctory nod.

The only reason I'm thinking of Tai in the first place is because I wonder how much he saw when he was in possession of my printouts. I shouldn't be worried, though. Even if he had a good, long look, there isn't any way that he'll figure out what I'm doing. The papers are only checkout histories from the library.

Except they are so much more. To me, anyway.

And to Dalton and Stacey, although the two don't know that yet. But they'll thank me later. After they walk down the aisle toward blissful wedded happiness.

"White chocolate mocha for Shannon," Stacey calls out from behind the counter of Cotton-Eyed Cup of Joe.

I watch from the corner table, my place of reconnaissance this morning. So far, I've learned that the citizens of Little Creek have a serious caffeine addiction. Which, to some degree, has been to my benefit. I've been able to observe Stacey interacting with a lot of different people. From the impatient businessman who barely looked up from his cell phone to the haggard mother with a toddler in tow, one who'd put dozens of sticky fingerprints all over the glass display showcasing the coffee shop's pastry selection. Stacey had greeted and dealt with her customers with a smile and grace.

Like now. She holds out the disposable to-go cup to a

woman presumably named Shannon, a warm, easy smile on her face. Her rich brown hair hangs over one shoulder in a loose braid, the end swishing against the name tag pinned to her barista apron.

When I had been listening to Mrs. Goldmann tell her story at the library, an idea had sparked. She's experienced over sixty-two years of marital bliss. Sixty-two years that didn't even start with her or Mr. Goldmann. A love story that began . . . with a matchmaker.

My own history with romance leaves a lot to be desired and is more a cautionary tale than an advertisement for love, but if the old adage that "those who can't, teach" is true, then the same logic leads me to believe that being unsuccessful in my own relationship makes me the perfect candidate to set up other people to find their happily-ever-afters. I will be Jane Austen's Emma but with better results for those I match and no Mr. Knightley in sight for me.

Which is fine. Really.

Unlike Mr. and Mrs. Goldmann's matchmaker, however, I don't have the benefit of being able to interview my potential couples. I don't have a list of characteristics and attributes they're looking for in a partner or even what they bring to the table themselves. Shoot, I don't even have their permission to insert myself in their love lives.

Then again, I've heard it's better to ask for forgiveness than permission.

I hide a grimace because I know for a fact Granny would disapprove of such a sentiment, shake her head, and comment on how she'd taught me better than that.

It's true. She did.

But the ends will justify the means. Everyone needs love in their lives. I'll just get my dose of romance secondhand. Besides, I'm *helping*. And what Dalton and Stacey and the other potential couples on my list don't know won't hurt them. And if everything goes according to plan, they won't know. They'll never know. They'll believe that things like fate and destiny brought them together.

I study Stacey some more. She and Dalton will make a cute couple. She can indulge her fascination with pioneer living (she's checked out two books set on the Oregon Trail and three more with a plot centered around either the transcontinental railroad or the Homestead Act just this month alone) with a little vegetable garden where she can imagine she's living off the land like Laura Ingalls Wilder. Which Dalton will be all for, considering his interest in an off-grid way of life and getting back to a symbiotic instead of parasitic relationship with nature (that was the subtitle of the last book he returned).

I'm confident in my first pairing. These two appear compatible on paper and yes, by *on paper* I mean their literary interests. Look, you can learn a lot about a person by the kind of books they read. Is their reading eclectic or genre-specific? Strictly fiction or nonfiction or a variety of both? Do they only check out an occasional book or are they voracious in their consumption of the written word?

I've done my homework. Dalton and Stacey have similar interests. They'll be able to bond over commonalities. Plus, there aren't any children linked to their accounts, nor have they ever come into the library with little ones in tow, so I don't have to worry about either of them being single parents. I may be bold and presumptuous in what I'm doing here, but I do have boundaries.

Besides, my observations of Stacey and Dalton around town lead me to believe that both are genuinely nice people—I'd never forgive myself if I inevitably matched a hero or heroine with a villain. I'd decided to match Stacey first because, unlike the majority of Little Creek residents, she's someone I feel I can call an acquaintance because of our interactions and short conversations at both the library and here at the coffee shop.

The last time I came in to get tea, we commiserated over our history of bad dates, so I know that she's single and looking. Dalton I don't know as much about personally, but he doesn't wear a wedding ring and I've never seen him with anyone in the whole time I've lived here, so it goes to reason that he's unattached as well.

Now, the million-dollar question is, How am I going to arrange for them to *accidentally* bump into each other? Their story needs a meet-cute, and it's up to me to write it for them.

"Is this seat taken?"

A familiar voice drags my attention away from Stacey at the espresso machine while simultaneously kicking my pulse into overdrive.

I attribute the reaction to being startled. To being caught, yet again, with the evidence of my well-meaning plans in front of me. Reflexively, I close the cover of my manila file folder, then slide it off the table. Out of sight, out of mind.

Except when I raise my eyes, masking my face in careful innocent serenity to offset any suspicions, I'm met with just that. A quirk of a brow. A lopsided tilt of the lips. An air of danger wrapped in a leather jacket. Individually not intimidating, but the combination of the three leaves me wanting to squirm guiltily in my seat.

Bad boy. Rake. Reformed. Husband.

The words fly through my mind like arrows, landing a bull's-eye that makes my breath hitch.

Lies. Lies. Lies. Stop telling lies, all you romance authors.

"What have you got there?" Tai presses his palms into the back of the chair and leans toward me.

I scoot forward, even though his view of the file folder is already obscured by the table. "Nothing."

He doesn't say anything, just peers at me knowingly. There's no way he can know, and yet the way he's looking at me makes me feel exposed. An uncomfortable bead of perspiration forms under my wig, and I want to swipe at it, but of course I can't. No one in Little Creek is aware of my condition, and I plan to keep it that way. I don't need to be the sideshow of yet another town.

"If you need the chair, go ahead and take it." *Please. Take it. Forget all about this conversation and what you think you saw. Forget all about me.*

"Thank you, I will." Instead of dragging the chair to one of the other tables, Tai plops down across from me and grins. "You're up to something, Angel."

I tense at the nickname. I should remain loyal to my dead mother's memory and hate it, but I've always secretly wanted a nickname. Nicknames are a symbol of acceptance and belonging, and I find the only thing I'm hating is having to steel myself against secretly liking the two syllables coming out of Tai's mouth.

All the vertebrae in my spine align as I sit as straight as a compass needle pointing north. "I'm up to the same thing everyone else who comes to Cotton-Eyed Cup of Joe is up to." Reaching out, I grab the mug of black plum tea in front of me and take a swig. It's long since turned cold, and a layer of honey coats the mouthful I force down my throat.

His eyes spark as if he knows how awful that tasted and is amused by my attempt to appear otherwise. "Good?"

"Delicious," I croak.

"Mm-hmm. I bet."

Why am I still sitting here? I've gotten the information I need. I've seen what I need to see. My stakeout is essentially blown. There's no reason for me not to gather my stuff and go.

"Look, I know I didn't make the best first impression. Do you think we could maybe start over?" Tai rests his forearms on the table and gazes at me with open earnestness.

"Why?" The question is out of my mouth before I even realize my lips have formed the word. But, really, it's an honest question. I feel like I've been trying to figure the guy out since the first time I laid eyes on him. I finally think I've gotten a handle on his character, but here he is, throwing me for another loop with his apparent sincerity.

His head tilts. A beat passes. Two.

I try not to squirm as he seems to see beyond the constructed façade I've worked so hard to build around me. I want to say something to deflect his intuitive gaze, wondering how he's turned the tables so fast. Too bad my brain is stalling worse than an old car with engine problems.

"You're very guarded, aren't you?" he asks softly.

I snort and look anywhere but at him. "This is not when you ask who hurt me."

"I'm sorry?" His brows draw down in confusion. He leans forward, his expression turning serious, almost angry. "*Did* someone hurt you?"

My breath gets caught somewhere in my throat. Oh no. I'd said that as a joke. He wasn't supposed to get protective. The way he's looking right now, thunderous and like Brett should be worried to ever meet him in a dark alley . . . That wasn't supposed to happen. And, dear heavens, I wasn't supposed to *enjoy* this type of reaction.

I lick my lips and force a breathy laugh past the constriction in my chest, waving my hand in the air for reasons I'm unaware of but hope looks like I'm brushing away his concern. "It's a book trope—who hurt you. Sorry. Occupational hazard."

He sits back, his face clearing and returning to its usual jovialness. "Is that why you moved to Little Creek?"

I'm taken aback by the direct question and turn in conversation. "What?"

"Why you moved to Little Creek. Sometimes people move to start over. Is that what happened? You were hurt and wanted to start over someplace new?"

My mouth opens. Shuts. Opens. Shuts.

He smiles the tiniest bit. "I'm going to take that as a yes."

"I didn't say that," I sputter a little too loudly. The people at the table beside us turn to stare at my outburst. I lean in and repeat myself more quietly. "I didn't say that."

Tai shrugs, unconvinced and unbothered.

I worry my lip. I don't owe him an explanation. Even so, I feel pressure building behind my ribs to say something. Maybe I could let a pinprick of honesty out? Just a little. Not enough to reveal anything too personal that will ruin the haven I have here in Little Creek but enough to appease him so he won't make any other too-close-to-the-whole-truth assumptions.

"Have you ever . . ." I start, pause, then start again. "Have you ever reached a point where you couldn't bear to see the way people look at you anymore?"

He considers my question, and I'm taken aback yet again by how serious he's being right now. Until today, our interactions have been him teasing me and amusing himself at my expense.

He nods slowly. "I'm pretty sure there are some people in town that think I must have a Marauder's Map on me."

"Because you solemnly swear you're up to no good?"

He dips his head. "Thank you for catching my reference."

"It was an easy lob to field."

"Anyways"—Tai grins, his usual carefree expression back in place—"I may have made some poor decisions with some cans of spray paint and a few buildings along Main Street in my youth. Pair a small town's long memory with the fact that when I came back after a few years away looking nothing like their idea of a clean-cut, respectable young man, and you can imagine some of the looks I get."

"Is that how you got your reputation?"

He gives me a look that I think is supposed to be an impersonation of Johnny Depp in *The Pirates of the Caribbean*. "So you have heard of me."

I laugh in spite of myself. "Not really, no. I just assumed you must have one in some circles."

At this, he mock-pouts, and I laugh again.

What are you doing, Evangeline? a little voice in the back of my mind accuses. I freeze. Dagnabit. What *am* I doing? I wasn't . . . oh heavens . . . I wasn't *flirting back* with Tai. Was I?

Oh no. This isn't good. I should leave. Right now. Before I do or say anything else I shouldn't.

My gaze flicks to Tai. He's back to regarding me with a singular focus that creates a phantom shiver that tracks down my spine.

I bolt to my feet, picking up the folder I'd momentarily forgotten about and pressing the front and back cover in a vise grip to ensure that none of the pages escape again.

I give Tai my practiced, polite smile. "Well, I really have to go now. I hope you have a nice rest of your day."

He seems bewildered by my abrupt departure but recovers quickly. "I'll see you around, Angel."

An innocuous salutation that anyone would give, but coming from Hayley's cousin, I can't quite figure out if I should take it as a threat . . . or a promise?

9

"ou've got plenty of food and water in your bowls to last you until I get back."

Kitty Purry ignores my comment like I'm beneath her notice. She knows I'm leaving and wants to make sure I'm aware of her displeasure. Her Highness is keenly offended that I expect her to consume kibble that's been put into an automatic feeder instead of being served to her. Not to mention the fact the food will not be one hundred percent fresh. Just who do I think I am?

I collect my purse and the lasagna from the kitchen counter, then slowly approach my cat. Her tail flicks the closer I get. She waits until my hand is a breadth away from giving her a scratch on the head before she saunters out of reach, an air of offense following in her wake.

"I'll see you when I get back," I call to her as I open the front door. Once she forgives me and deigns to allow me back in her presence, that is.

The morning is crisp, and I take in a lungful of fresh air as I walk to my car. I'm looking forward to seeing Grampie and Granny, but not so much the congestion of the city. Chattanooga is by no means on par with New York City or Chicago, but I've been living in a small town with only three traffic lights in the whole municipal limits for a hot minute now. I've gotten used to raccoons as my neighbors and being woken up when they decide to have a party at my trash cans, rather than the traffic noises of I-75 or the loud music my neighbor liked to play until one o'clock in the morning.

A northern bobwhite calls out in its distinct two-whistle pattern. I pause at the side of my car and peer into the underbrush of the woods around my cabin. The small quail is easily camouflaged among the foliage. Without him whistling out his own name—*bobwhite!*—I'd never know the fowl was even there.

He calls again, but I can't see him, so I go ahead and open the car door, set the lasagna and my purse on the passenger seat, and slide behind the wheel. I plug my phone in so that CarPlay will connect, then open the audiobook app and click the green triangle to start playing the epic fantasy I'm in the middle of.

The drive to Chattanooga is along a windy two-lane highway that hugs the mountains. Caution signs for rockslides are posted along the road as well as plenty of pullouts for slower vehicles or those wanting to rest and take in the breathtaking view of the Cherokee National Forest.

The scenery opens up along with the lanes as I descend into the valley. Before long, I see the city sprawl on the banks of the Tennessee River, Signal Mountain on one side as sentinel and Lookout Mountain on the other. The mountains are rich in Civil War history, one being an important communication spot of Union troops, while the other was the setting of a skirmish known as the Battle Above the Clouds. Now, however, they are both popular destinations for tourists and locals alike. Signal Mountain has a gorgeous vista of the Tennessee River Valley that excites hikers, while Lookout Mountain is known for its incline railroad, a 145-foot waterfall inside a limestone cave called Ruby Falls, and See Rock City, one of the only places in the United States where you can see seven states from one vantage point.

The narrator of the audiobook has a slight British accent, making me wonder if the fictional kingdom of Lilyra was inspired by that great island. Probably a far cry from the backwoods or even the big city of the Volunteer State. Although, with how often Lilyra is on the brink of war with the neighboring northern kingdoms, she could use an ally in a nation nicknamed for its eagerness to step forward in times of war.

I increase the reading speed to 1.5 on the app, then reach up and slide the wig from my head. I'm far enough away from Little Creek that I'm safe from anyone in my adopted speck of a town finding out about my secret.

While the wig gives me a measure of comfort and security, it also seems to take a little bit of me away as well. Which makes no sense, I know. How can something make me feel both more like me and less like me at the same time? I can't explain it. Probably because I don't understand it myself.

All I know is, it's nice to be able to take the wig off every once in a while. The synthetic hair isn't necessarily uncomfortable to wear (although it is a little itchy), but not having to worry about the wig slipping or someone discovering I'm hiding something is a bit freeing. I can just be me. Who I am now. No pretenses. Nothing fake. No hiding.

My skin prickles as I pass the exit to the Walnut Street Bridge, and not just because of the coolness of the car's air conditioning. The iconic blue-trussed walking bridge that suspends over the Tennessee River used to hold many happy memories for me. Brett and I went on our first official date to the Tennessee Riverpark at the foot of the bridge. We got scoops on cones at the Ice Cream Show and then leisurely strolled across the bridge, stopping to peer down at the flowing current below us and cheer on a group of kayakers who were training for an upcoming race. We laughed together as our ice creams melted in the warm summer heat and dripped onto our hands. Brett had even gently wiped a smudge of smeared chocolate from the corner of my lips for me.

I accelerate, putting distance between the bridge and my memories until they're only dots in my rearview mirror. One day, maybe this beautiful city won't have the power to dredge up a painful lump that sits behind my breastbone. Until then, I focus my mind on the reason I endure the unpleasant walk down memory lane in the first place: my family. I can come and soak up the love they have for me, then retreat to my little cove in the mountains. I just have to ignore the reminders that my life isn't turning out like I'd planned.

But that's okay. I have a new plan. I may be officially off the marriage mart (why, yes, I did just binge a regency series), but now I'm the respectable chaperone introducing potential couples to one another at a ball (I'm speaking figuratively here) and watching with the overwhelming satisfaction that only a meddling mama can have when interest sparks during a waltz.

Granny and Grampie's townhouse comes into view, and I pull in behind their car in the driveway. Penelope's little Volkswagen Beetle is parked in front of the house. I'll have a reprieve from her badgering me about the anniversary party while our grandparents are near, but I have no doubt she'll devise a way to get us alone so she can hound me again.

Granny is standing in the doorway with a welcoming smile on her lips when I trudge up the front steps, balancing the lasagna in my arms.

"Oh, sugar, it's good to see you." She steps aside, beaming at me as I walk into the house, then follows me into the kitchen, where I set the casserole dish on the counter. As soon as my arms are free, she wraps me in a warm hug smelling of the Chanel No. 5 she always puts on before church. A wave of nostalgia washes over me, and I squeeze her just a tiny bit harder.

"There now," she says as she pulls away enough to get a good look at me. "It's good to have my baby back home."

"I'm twenty-seven, Granny. I haven't been a baby in a long time." This is a script we've been performing ever since I can remember.

The lines on her face deepen as she smiles. "Doesn't matter how old you are. You'll always be my baby." She squeezes my hand again, imputing all her love in the small gesture.

I look around the kitchen and into the great room. "Where's Grampie and Penelope? I saw her car out front."

Granny rolls her eyes. "They're down in the basement working on one of their models."

Grampie had built both Penelope and I wooden dollhouses when we were girls. Penelope's had been a miniature model of a Victorian home complete with gables and cornices on the outside and handcrafted furniture pieces that were exact replicas of the time period as well. Mine had been a New England cottage with a lighthouse attached to it, but instead of making it a family home, I'd talked him into converting the inside into a bookstore.

"Since when did Penelope start building with him?" My sister isn't exactly very handy when it comes to tools or construction.

Granny gives me a look I can't quite decipher, then motions me toward the stairs that lead to the basement. "I forgot you haven't been down there the last few times you've visited. Just be prepared that it may be different than you remember." There's part humor, part pride, and part exasperation in her voice.

The last time I'd been down to Grampie's hobby area, he'd been in the middle of constructing a replica of a colonial house someone would have seen at Jamestown. I'm not even sure who he was building the dollhouse for, just that he likes to spend hours tinkering on his model projects now that he's retired.

"I think it needs to go a little bit more to the left." Penelope's voice drifts up the stairwell as I make my way down.

"Are you sure?" Grampie doesn't sound convinced.

"Yes. Here, listen again."

I step down the last riser and wait at the bottom of the stairs with Granny. Penelope and Grampie have their backs toward us, heads bent over something on Grampie's worktable that I can't see because their bodies are blocking anything from view.

"Because of the blood splatter on the walls, the police think the suspect faced the victim at an angle, standing just slightly to the victim's right." Penelope presses pause on her phone. "See?"

"I suppose you're right. So about here do you think?"

"Huh-hem." Granny clears her throat.

Both Penelope and Grampie spin around, the former pressing a palm to her chest. "You scared me," she accuses on a panting breath.

Granny grins wickedly, which makes me wonder how many times she's snuck down here just to give one or both of them a fright. "Evangeline wants to see your new project."

Grampie hustles over in his uneven gait and pulls me fiercely to his chest in a crushing hug while being careful not to get the tiny paintbrush pinched between his fingers anywhere near my clothes. Even with his eightieth birthday behind him, he's still a strong man, and I love that his hugs squeeze the air from my lungs.

Grampie kisses my bald head, and I try not to be self-conscious of the action. There's not a hint of disgust on Grampie's face when he pulls back, his eyes twinkling with energy and mischief. "Come see. You're going to love this."

I follow him over to the table where a boxlike structure

sits. Instead of a full house, it appears he's working on a single room. There are only three walls, with the fourth and the roof missing. Better to see inside. Although, as I look closer and my stomach spins in on itself, I'm regretting the easy view.

"What is it?" I ask in horror. This isn't one of the sweet, innocent dollhouses I'm used to seeing Grampie working on. No. This is a macabre horror show of a child's nightmare come to life.

"Isn't it great?" Penelope is staring down into the box with a look of awe and wonder on her face.

My decorous and genteel sister, her long chestnut hair pulled back in a stylish low ponytail with the ends curled to perfection, is wearing a dress that would command a conference room of her male counterparts. She gazes at a miniature replica of a gruesome crime scene with the same expression other women bestow on baby bunnies.

"They started listening to a true crime podcast a couple of months ago and one thing led to another. Now they re-create murder scenes—"

"One foot to one-inch measurements," Grampie interjects, making sure Granny gets her facts straight.

Because that's what's important here. Obviously.

Granny shakes her head. "Anyway, they build these tiny crime scenes based off the podcast descriptions and then they try to see if they can solve the murder."

Grampie dips his paintbrush into a small container of red paint. Ever so carefully, he moves his hand into the scene and hovers the bristle beside the wall to the left of the victim. "About here?" He looks at Penelope for confirmation.

She studies the angle carefully before nodding. "I think that's about right."

Then I watch something I never thought I'd ever see in my life: my eighty-year-old grandfather meticulously creating believable blood splatter on a dollhouse wall.

"All right, Rizzoli and Isles, time to come upstairs for lunch. Evangeline brought lasagna." Granny clutches the railing leading to the main floor with her blue-veined hand and leans heavily on the support as she makes her way up the stairs, confident we will obediently follow in her wake.

Penelope peers down at the gruesome scene she and Grampie must have spent hours re-creating, a disappointed pout pursing her lips. It's like she's eight again and Granny has just told her to put away her Barbies.

Grampie reaches for a ratty old dishcloth, then cleans the brush he'd been using. "The blood needs to dry anyway. Besides, we can work on it again after lunch. Maybe Evangeline will want to help out." He looks at me, his watery eyes hopeful.

I don't want to disappoint Grampie.

I also don't want to have nightmares tonight.

While the majority of people in this country seem to have been bitten by some type of true-crime bug, I'm much more comfortable with the fictional variety. After all, I can console myself that the twisted mind of the killer is just a figment of an author's imagination. With true crime, I have to face the fact that there really are warped and evil people in the world doing heinous things every day. It's not a comforting thought to try to fall asleep to, let me tell you. Every whistle of the wind outside my bedroom window has me conjuring images of a serial killer about to make me his next victim.

I forcibly lift my attention away from the crime scene, which had held me in some sort of trance, only to meet Penelope's smirk and an expression I can only describe as *older sister*.

"I don't know, Grampie. Evangeline looks a little green around the gills already, and she hasn't even heard the details of the murder yet."

Grampie puts the tiny brush back in the Mason jar with the other ones. He turns to me and pats my shoulder a couple of times. "Don't worry, sweetheart. This particular murder happened five years ago."

"So they've caught the woman's killer?" I'm going to need to triple check my locks tonight. Maybe watch *The Sound of Music* before bed in an attempt to whitewash the mental image this scene has seared into my brain. Maybe then I'll be able to sleep.

Penelope smirks louder. Yes, louder. Her body language is at a deafening decibel at the moment. "Nope. They never could figure out who shot her or why. Isn't it fascinating?"

"Not the word I'd use," I mumble, though not quietly enough that Penelope doesn't hear me.

"You want to see some of the other scenes we've built?" Grampie grins like a little kid in a candy store.

I don't have the heart to refuse him, which is how I find myself staring at a shelf of death. "Wow. You guys have been busy." I try my hardest to sound impressed and not ill. It *is* impressive. But mostly it's disturbing.

I turn to Grampie and force a bright smile on my face. "Well, should we go upstairs now? Granny's sure to get cross with us if we stay down here any longer."

Grampie pats his belly. "I'm getting hungry anyway. And you know how much I love your lasagna."

I'm a decent cook, but Grampie would say that even if the noodles were crunchy and the cheese on top burnt.

Penelope lingers beside me as we let our grandfather mount the steps ahead of us. Both Granny and Grampie are in good health for their age and don't have any issues with mobility, but we still worry about one of them tripping and falling.

"You were supposed to call me back," Penelope whisper-hisses out of the side of her mouth.

"I've been busy," I whisper back.

"Too busy for them?" Her arm flings out to indicate Grampie, who's made it perfectly fine to the top of the stairs and to Granny, who we can hear puttering around the kitchen above us. *You're too busy for the two people who raised you?* she implies. *Too busy to give back to the two people who sacrificed so much for you? Too busy to honor the two people in the world who love you no matter what?*

I cringe at her silent accusations. "That's not fair and you know it."

Penelope sighs. "We need to hash out some details. Today. Before you leave, okay?"

"Fine."

While Grampie had been opening my eyes to the turn his hobby has taken, Granny had reheated the lasagna, put together a salad, and set the table. She's setting the steaming casserole dish on crocheted hot pads when Penelope and I finally emerge from the basement.

"Don't forget to wash up before you sit down."

Doesn't matter that Penelope and I are both adults now. Granny will be reminding us to wash up before a meal for the rest of our lives. We head down the hall to the bathroom.

Granny and Grampie are already seated at the formal dining room table when we return. Honestly, this is one of the things I miss most, gathering with my family around this scarred table with a trove of memories. Growing up, we were never allowed to eat in the living room in front of the TV like my friends said they did, and I'd thought it was totally unfair. Now, I can appreciate my grandparents' unbending rule about the sanctity of family meals.

Grampie places his hands on the table, palms up. Granny slides her fingers between his on one side as I clasp his hand on the other, completing the circle by also grasping Penelope's.

"Dear Lord, for this food we are truly thankful. For this family, we are truly blessed. May we always recognize your workings and sustenance in our lives. Amen."

"Amen," we chorus.

Grampie looks up and smiles warmly at Penelope and me. "So, girls, how have you been? Fill your granny and me in on your lives."

Granny uses a spatula to serve squares of lasagna. "Thank you," I say as she hands me a plate laden with cheesy and saucy goodness.

"Well—" Penelope wipes her mouth with a napkin before settling the paper back onto her lap under the table—"I was just named lead on a new project at work."

"Congratulations." Granny beams. "We're so proud of you and your accomplishments."

Penelope glows under their praise.

Grampie turns to me, his fork poised in the air. "And what about you, Evangeline?"

Granny's looking at me, her eyes wide in expectation. I love that they automatically assume I'll have great news to share like Penelope does. But, really, what can I say? That I've decided to be a matchmaking librarian because I just can't give up on the idea of romance altogether, even though it's given up on me? Yeah, that wouldn't go over well.

Instead, I do the one thing that has worked since the beginning of time.

I change the subject.

"I'd rather talk about you. Your fiftieth anniversary is coming up soon. Any special plans?"

Penelope kicks me under the table. Hard. It's a challenge to keep the pleasant smile on my face and not flinch. About as challenging as ignoring her tight expression and narrowed gaze. I'm not looking at her, but I can still see it out of the corner of my eye.

Granny looks at Grampie and visibly melts in her chair. "Fifty years. Can you believe it, Ron?"

He leans over and presses a kiss to her cheek. "It's only the beginning, if I have any say in the matter."

Granny blushes as if she were a new bride and playfully swats at his arm. "Oh you. You always have been a charmer."

Seeing their interactions makes me think of the trouble I've been having figuring out a way to set up a meet-cute between Stacey and Dalton. Fictional romances have been helpful up to a point. I mean, authors seem to really like their heroes and heroines to literally stop in their tracks by physically running into each other. Aside from shoving Stacey at just the right moment so she stumbles and falls into Dalton's waiting arms, that option doesn't seem very logical for an orchestrated romantic moment.

Some other alternatives I've gleaned from perusing the romance display at the library:

- They meet when he accidently locks himself out of his apartment. For some reason, he's only wearing a towel.
- They meet at a coffee shop and both go to the counter to collect their drinks after the barista calls out the name. Wow, they share a name. What else could they share?
- It's Christmas and they are both shopping for the same rare-to-find toy. And, of course, there's only one left on the shelf.
- She accidentally takes his suitcase at baggage claim instead of her own.

None of these will work for staging a moment in which Stacey and Dalton—who, let's face it, in a town the size of Little Creek probably already know each other—can have their first meeting.

Maybe I need some real-life inspiration. I lay my fork down on the side of my plate. "You know, I don't think you've ever told Penelope or me how you two met or fell in love."

Grampie's brows jump to his receded hairline. "We haven't?"

I shake my head. "You used to tell us how Mom and Dad met at a baseball game. They were fan rivals sitting beside each other. She was cheering for the Atlanta Braves while he was a die-hard Mets fan. The kiss cam zoomed in on them. At first, they shook their heads and tried to wave the camera away, but when the crowd started chanting *kiss, kiss, kiss,* they both sort of laughed, shrugged, and leaned in for a peck. Which turned into a whole lot more." I grin. I can't help myself. I love that story so much. I used to ask Granny to tell it to me every night for a whole year. "But I've never heard your story."

"Your grandfather used to write me the sweetest, most romantic notes and then somehow sneak them into my bag or somewhere else he knew I'd find them." Granny is talking to me, but her focus is fastened to Grampie. "He never signed his name, though. He always ended the notes with *eternally yours, a secret admirer.*" She laughs. "It nearly drove me insane not knowing who was writing me such lovely things. By the time he finally confessed it was him, I was already head over heels for him from his penned words."

They lean toward each other for a sound smooch.

"Did you keep the notes?" Penelope asks.

"Of course I did. A girl doesn't throw away sentiment like that."

Love letters. My mouth parts in a smile. Completely feasible and the perfect way to get Stacey and Dalton to realize they are a match made in heaven. Roxane fell in love with Cyrano's words though he signed Christian's name, didn't she? I rub my hands together under the table. This is going to work.

10

Writing a love letter to someone you don't have any romantic feelings for and don't really know while also pretending the sender is someone other than yourself is harder than I thought it would be. Go figure, right?

I stare down at the empty sheet of paper, the pencil in my hand poised for inspiration to strike. Why is this so hard?

You're overthinking it. Dalton isn't a closet Lord Byron. What would a flannel-wearing chainsaw artist write to his secret barista love?

I press the tip of lead to the paper and write.

I like you a latte. Let me espresso my feelings for you.

I move the pencil away and read the sentences again. Then immediately groan. Stacey and Dalton are supposed to fall in love. A few punny pickup lines isn't likely to set off wedding bells.

I scratch out the sentences and try again.

To the woman I can't stop thinking about,

Okay, yes, this is already a better start. I glance up and look around the library. It's raining, and there aren't many people willing to brave the elements to drop off or pick up a book. Apart from the homeschool mom who always brings her two kids every Tuesday at this time and the man working on his

88

résumé at the bank of computers, the walkways between the rows of shelves are deserted.

My chin dips back toward the paper. What would make my heart skip a beat if I was the one to receive an anonymous love letter?

Please don't consider me a plagiarist, but I must borrow a confession from a classic and say that you have bewitched me, body and soul. Your sweet smile lights up the room and

"Whatcha doing there, Angel?"

"Eeee!" A startled cry launches from the back of my throat, and on reflex I swipe the paper off the desk and watch it float down to the floor while my heart thuds against my ribs.

Tai grins at me from the other side of the counter.

My palm is pressed against my sternum as I will my pulse to return to normal. "You shouldn't sneak up on a person like that."

He leans an elbow on the desk, the epitome of casual relaxation, while I'm over here recovering from a mini heart attack.

"Who said anything about sneaking? You were so engrossed in your writing that you didn't notice me walk in." He leans forward a bit more and tries to peek over the counter. "What had you so enthralled anyway?"

Uh-uh. No way will Tai Davis be getting a peek at that paper. I take half a step to the right and cover my handwriting with the sole of my high-top. "I'm not sure what you're talking about." I neatly fold my hands in front of me and give him my most serene smile.

Amusement flashes in his dark eyes, reminding me of stars at midnight. "Sure you don't."

"Is there something I can help you with, Mr. Davis?"

"I really do love it when you call me that." His smile simmers, causing heat to climb into my cheeks.

Do not react, Evangeline. It'll only encourage him. I toss a thick lock of synthetic hair over my shoulder and rotate toward the computer, resting my fingers on the keys. When I look back at him, my face is void of any emotion. At least, that's what I'm attempting. Hopefully it's working. "Can I look up a book for you, perhaps?"

He pushes off the counter. With our similar height, our faces are closer than I'm used to. The lack of distance is disconcerting. Intimate somehow, and I find myself easily staring into his eyes without even meaning to.

I blink, clear my throat, and force myself to look at the computer screen.

"I'm not here for a book today." His voice is soft and low. Hayley would call such a tone smooth as butter, although she might not use the saying on her cousin.

Even though it's true.

"I came to ask you if you'd like to join me for dinner sometime."

My head whips around so fast I might need a chiropractor later. I reach up and finger my wig, thankful that I hadn't displaced it. "Excuse me?"

"Dinner." He gives me that smile that engages his entire face, practically radiating carefree, confident charm. "You know, the meal people eat in the evening. Or maybe you call it supper?"

"I know what dinner is." My surprise makes me snippy before I remember my manners and repeat myself a second time in a more controlled tone of voice.

He shrugs, then casually stuffs his hands in his pockets. "You sounded confused."

"Not about the definition of *dinner*."

If possible, he's grinning even more now. "Oh? Is there something else about my invitation I need to clear up?"

I can feel my irritation rising with my suspicion. I don't know if I should try to push the feelings back down or wrap them around me like some sort of defensive armor.

"Yes." My voice is clipped, so I try to modulate the next words out of my mouth. I cannot let him see that he is affecting me in any way. "Like why you asked me to dinner in the first place."

He looks me straight in the eye. No provocation. "Angel, I'm asking you out on a date."

He's not laughing. At this point, he's no longer even smiling. *Are you serious? Why are you asking me out?*

He smiles again now, this time softly. "I'm asking you out because I like you and I want to get to know you better. I want to spend more time with you."

My eyes widen as my hand darts to hide my mouth. "I said those thoughts out loud?"

"Yes." Mirth is a dancing flame behind his expression. "But I'm glad you did. Now you know the answer."

I blink, wishing there were a cosmic pause button I could push right now so I could have just a few moments to sort out this massive tangle of knots that has become my thoughts and feelings. Seriously. My brain currently resembles a ball of yarn after Kitty Purry has gotten her claws in it. This is a plot twist that I hadn't seen coming.

Tai Davis is interested in me? He wants us to go out on a date? I'm inputting the data, but my mind is still shooting out *does not compute* messages.

I glance up at him through my false eyelashes. He *looks* sincere. His hands are in his pockets, and he's regarding me with a half hopeful, slightly amused expression. More like he finds the fact that I'm dumbstruck endearing and less like he's having a laugh at my expense or considers me a toy he's just playing with to pass the time. I know I've classified him as a modern rake, but is there a chance I might have misjudged him?

I nibble on the inside of my lower lip. There's a humming below the surface of my skin. A thrill of possibility sending up flares of endorphins that's getting increasingly harder to wade through with logical thought. I admit there's a part of me that wants to say yes, to throw caution to the wind and jump on the slim chance that maybe the love of a man could be in my future. That someone could still want me or find me desirable.

But that part of me is the naïve optimist. The little bit left that hasn't shriveled and died to let cynicism—or reality—take its place. Even if Tai is sincere now when he doesn't know how I truly look, how long will that interest last? Until he sees me without any makeup and no eyebrows or eyelashes? Or maybe when he realizes I'm balder than a newborn baby under this wig?

I'm not ready to risk going through that again. I'm not ready to possibly watch the interest die from another man's eyes when he looks at me without a wig or makeup. Brett had promised to protect my heart and he'd shattered it when I needed him most. That wound is still fresh and raw, the pain still aching. Maybe one day the injury to my heart will be healed enough to risk getting hurt again for a chance at love, but I'm definitely not ready now.

"No," I say, shutting him—*this*—down before it can even get started.

He blinks, clearly expecting my answer would be different. "No? May I ask why not?"

Why not? Umm. I didn't think he'd come back with a follow-up question or for me to lay out my reasons. Can't no just be no? Again, where's a pause button when you need one?

I rack my brain, trying to think on my feet. I need a reason good enough that he won't ask again. In my mind, I know that allowing any sort of romantic doors to open right now is a bad idea, but my chest aches with such a yearning to be loved and accepted that I'm afraid I could be persuaded to make a wrong choice in my current state of vulnerability. Between my head and my heart, my heart is the bigger bully of the two. In a street fight, it will win every time. If Tai were persistent in his pursuit, he could possibly wear down my head's resolve, my heart possibly ending up in more jagged pieces than it already is.

I cross my arms over my chest and tilt my chin, hoping my determination is enough to keep my pathetic need for romantic love in place. "You have trouble written all over you, and I'm not looking for any."

He opens his mouth to protest, but I hold my hand in the air to stop him, wincing that I've used what he told me in the coffee shop about his reputation against him.

"I'm not interested in becoming a cautionary tale or the next tidbit in small-town gossip. Besides, I don't date. But even if I did, I would only go out with someone who is sincere and committed, not someone who flirts with every woman he meets and only sees them as a game or a challenge or a means to pass the time."

His face tightens. He looks as if he wants to say something, but then he just shakes his head. He opens his mouth, closes it, then finally turns and walks away without a word.

I watch him go, my chest caving in on itself. I'm still looking out the front glass door when a black Dodge Challenger zips out of the parking lot. I hate myself a little bit right now, and the feeling of guilt unsettling my stomach isn't helping either. I don't think I've ever spoken to anyone the way I just spoke to Tai. I hope I never do again.

I sigh and bend down to pick up the paper with the beginning of a love note on it. A dirty print of the sole of my shoe mars the surface. I'll have to start over. But not right now. For some reason, I'm not really in the mood to pen a fake love letter anymore.

11

The frigid spray of water coming over the bow of Tai's kayak from the white crests of the Ocoee River did little to cool the heat of blood pumping through his veins. He dug the blade of his paddle into the living beast of a river below him and pulled the shaft, his muscles bulging as he simultaneously fought and worked with the swirling, churning rapid that would enjoy nothing more than chewing him up and spitting him out.

Kind of like Evangeline had done earlier.

The river roared in his ears, but neither the low din of thousands of gallons of water breaking on rocks nor the high shrieks of fear mixed with enjoyment coming from the group in the large raft from a local adventure company could drown out the echo of Evangeline's pronouncement. He'd been a bit taken aback and more than a little disappointed in her assessment of him.

"You have trouble written all over you."

While body art didn't hold quite the same stigma it once had, there were still some people who looked at him warily or with a quiet judgment in their eyes. He was mostly used to it and didn't really care that much. Life was too short to live confined to other peoples' expectations and opinions. He'd done too much of that growing up—first by trying to appease and lessen his mother's fears, but no matter what he did, how small and restricted he made himself, she still worried. That had led him to rebel when he'd gotten a bit older, trying to break free of the confines of her anxiety.

He'd admittedly made some bad choices in his teen years, which had consequently soured the town's opinion of him. When he'd left for college, it had been that reputation that had kept him away for so long. It had only been relatively recently that he'd come to a point where he realized he couldn't let what other people thought of him dictate his decisions. He'd much rather enjoy every moment he had on this planet than worry about what went on in someone else's head. That was their problem, not his. Besides, it was totally out of his control anyway.

He hadn't thought Evangeline had seen him in the same narrow-minded way others had, though. She'd shown interest and curiosity in his body art, not judgment or scorn. Could he really have been that mistaken? It seemed so, based off her reasoning for rejecting him.

Tai dipped the paddle blade into the water on the right side of the kayak's stern to steer around a protruding rock. The rapid shot him out of the section of white water and into the calmer swirls of a slower current. He laid his paddle across the cockpit of the kayak and let his head fall back to feel the sun on his face.

Kayaking had been one of his first *rebellions*, as his mother liked to call his more thrill-seeking interests. She'd railed on him after she'd learned he'd joined a group heading down the river with one of the tour companies. He'd grown up only hours away from multiple rivers people far and wide traveled to experience: the Ocoee, the Nantahala, the Nolichucky, and the Pigeon, to name a few. Right in his own backyard but never allowed to so much as put a toe in the water.

"What if you have an asthma attack?" his mom would say. It was too dangerous to put himself in situations that required physical exertion and were so far away from medical help. What if help didn't come in time? It was too dangerous.

He'd lived with those words and fears drilled into his head. He tried to understand why she was so hypervigilant and worried about him at every turn. He could imagine how she must have felt those times she'd had to rush him to the emergency room because his airways were closing, his lips turning blue. How helpless and scared she must have felt. But the longer he lived in the shadow of her fear and hovering, the harder it had been for him to breathe. It hadn't been the asthma that suffocated him—it had been existing under the weight of ordering his life with the consideration of what she would think of each of his decisions.

When he'd finally shucked off the yoke of caring what his parents or his hometown or anyone for that matter thought about him was when he was finally able to take a full breath.

He recognized a similarity in Evangeline. Granted, he didn't know much about her and hadn't really spent a whole lot of time in her company, but he saw the shadow of it darkening her countenance. Beneath the cordial exterior, she was drowning just as much as he'd been suffocating.

Tai picked up the paddle and, with smooth strokes, steered the kayak to the pullout along the bank of the river. He unhooked the spray skirt from the cockpit and stood. The boat wobbled under him before he stepped out, hooked his hand in the opening above the seat, and flipped the kayak over to drain the small amount of water that had leaked in from the rapids. He hefted the kayak onto his shoulder and marched up the knoll to the parking area where Hayley waited for him.

She pushed off the side of her yellow Jeep Wrangler when she saw him. "Good run?"

He nodded. "Just what I needed." He fastened his kayak to

the roof of her vehicle, glad she'd let him talk her into buying her a rack for this reason. She'd take him back upstream to where his own vehicle was parked.

"How was your day?" He unclipped his life vest and tossed it into a crate in the back of the Jeep. He grabbed the zipper string dangling down his spine and pulled, his wetsuit opening at the back.

Hayley's mouth pinched to the side as she considered. "Good, I guess. Evangeline was acting weird earlier, though."

Tai peeled the wetsuit from his chest and arms. "Oh? Weird in what way?"

"I don't know how to describe it exactly. She kept muttering to herself under her breath. Usually she's this unflappable, happy-go-lucky person, but today she had something stuck in her craw."

Interesting. Could she be feeling off-kilter because of their conversation earlier? He turned his head so Hayley wouldn't see his smile. It was silly, this hope that began to inflate in his chest. Evangeline had laid some harsh accusations at his feet that he didn't deserve, including questioning his sincerity in asking her out, but if she'd truly meant and believed everything she'd said, why had she been affected by the conversation for the rest of the day?

There was something else she'd said that was driving him a little crazy. That she didn't date. Why? He had a feeling the answer to that was also the answer to the other questions that had crossed his mind since their exchange. Now, though, he'd settled on one thing. The door that she'd tried to slam in his face had bounced off the frame, leaving just enough room for him to try to walk through again.

"You ready to go?" Hayley asked as she opened the driver's door and slid in behind the wheel.

Tai shut the back of the Jeep and walked to the front. A towel covered the passenger seat, and he made sure that it didn't slide too much as he climbed in. He hadn't run the whole river, so it didn't take long for Hayley to drive him back to the old beat-up truck he used whenever he needed to haul his recreation equipment. The Challenger was fun to drive on the windy roads, but the truck worked better when he was going out kayaking or spelunking in the area's limestone caves.

"I'll see you later at your parents' house." Hayley waved before driving away.

Tai had just enough time to go home, put his gear on the racks to dry, take a quick hot shower, and change before heading out again. His parents lived in the same house that he'd grown up in, a turn-of-the-century ranch-style home at the end of a steep drive on top of a hill covered in pine, fir, rhododendron, and mountain laurel. There wasn't a backyard to play in or really any grassy area because of the pitch of the land, but he and Hayley had had fun playing hide-and-seek among the wild, overgrown bushes in the summer and then building mounds out of fallen leaves in the autumn to jump in—when his mom wasn't looking, of course.

As soon as he killed the engine, his mom swung open the front door to the house and stepped out onto the porch. She was a diminutive woman in stature, but she made up for it in presence. Even on the other side of fifty, there were hardly any wrinkles on her face. Tai wondered if there was some sort of magic in their genes since her forehead should have deeply etched worry lines by now, given how much she fussed over everything.

He climbed out of the car and walked up the steps of the porch, pulling his mom into a snug embrace when he reached her. Her head fit under his chin, and he breathed in the scent of her secret mac and cheese recipe clinging to her cardigan.

When people first met Missy Davis and were invited to her house for a meal, they thought they'd be served fried rice and dumplings and were usually surprised to find a spread of southern comfort in the form of collard greens, pimento cheese, and fried chicken. She may have been adopted from China, but she was Southern through and through.

His mom pulled out of his arms, and Tai stood tall, ready for her inspection. A thorough looking-over always came before he was allowed inside to eat. He held his arms out to his sides and smiled down at her. "Do I meet with your approval?"

She narrowed her eyes at him, then pinched his waist. "You're too skinny. Are you eating enough?"

He let his arms drop. "Yes, Mama. I eat plenty."

"How are your lungs? Are you breathing okay? Do you keep your inhaler with you at all times?" She peered at him with the same narrowed expression.

He dug his inhaler from his pocket. "Right here. Happy?"

She wagged a finger at him. "Don't get sassy with me, young man."

"Sorry, Mama. But I'm in perfect health. Would you like a note from my doctor stating such?"

"There goes that sass again." Her face softened as her gaze roamed over him again. "Good. I'm glad you're okay." She breathed in deeply then exhaled as if taking her first full breath of the day.

"Missy, are you done examining our boy yet?" his dad called from inside the house. "I'm starving."

"You're always starving," she yelled back, then turned to Tai. "I know for a fact he's stolen at least two cornbread muffins, so he's not wasting away." She rolled her eyes, but the small upturn to her lips belied her feigned annoyance. "And he says I'm the dramatic one."

Tai followed his mom into the house. Family members rose from lounging on the furniture to greet him as soon as he stepped into the foyer. His aunt and uncle each gave him a quick hug, while Hayley's younger brother, Elliot, held out his knuckles for a fist bump.

"Good to see you, son." His dad slung an arm around Tai's shoulders. "Can we eat now, Missy?"

She shook her head at her husband but directed everyone to the table where dishes of food sat with tea towels over them. With a flick of her wrist, she removed each cloth. Steam rose in aromatic waves over crispy fried chicken, golden yellow mac and cheese, cornbread muffins, and tomato casserole.

"Everything looks delicious, Aunt Missy." Hayley pulled out a chair and sat down.

"Did you use Mom's recipe for the casserole?" Aunt Bonnie slid her napkin off the table and set it on her lap.

Missy finished putting the serving spoons in each dish, then took her seat. "No, I—"

"Before we get into who makes what dish better, let's pray so I can eat while you hens cluck." Walter Davis bowed his head.

Hayley caught Tai's eye as his chin dipped. *Hens? Really?* she mouthed with a look of exasperation on her face.

Tai shrugged but closed his eyes as his dad said a blessing over the food.

Thankfully, the conversation turned to other topics instead of a sisterly disagreement about cooking.

"So, Tai, Hayley tells me you were hoping to get to Telluride to do some skiing before the season ends," Uncle Bob said before biting into the drumstick clutched between his fingers.

Tai glanced at Hayley, who mouthed *sorry* as she winced. The sound of silverware clattering against a plate crashed down the table. Tai sighed but turned in that direction. There was a reason he hadn't let his parents know of his trip.

"Skiing? Really, Tai?" His mom's disapproving tone filled the dining room like it was another member of the family. Which it might as well have been. He'd lived with that disappointment enough growing up that the sentiment should probably have its own room in the house.

"Yes, Mama. Skiing. One more trip before the season ends." Tai kept his voice modulated. He was an adult. If he wanted to go skiing, he'd go.

"Why? The cold, dry air, all that continuous activity . . . you know that combination is the worst thing for your lungs."

"I'll be fine."

She clucked her tongue. "'I'll be fine,' he says. You don't know that. Not when you put yourself in these dangerous situations. Why do you have to worry me like this? Don't you care that I'll be a ball of anxiety every second that you're away?"

"Of course I care." He didn't like seeing his mom when she got worked up, but he couldn't let that dictate his decisions either. "I'll be perfectly safe. My asthma is no longer the same issue it was when I was a young child. I'm not going to let it control my life."

"You may not have a life anymore if you keep engaging in these risky adventures!" she cried.

"Missy." Walter covered his wife's hand with his own. "You can't helicopter parent the boy." His tone was more comforting than rebuking, and he met Tai's gaze with a sympathetic look.

"Well, you stuck your foot in it, didn't you, Bob?" Aunt Bonnie said in a stage whisper to her husband.

Awkward chuckles sounded as the family picked up their forks and resumed eating. His dad and mom were speaking quietly at their end of the table while Aunt Bonnie and Uncle Bob did the same. Elliot had his eyes glued to his lap, where Tai guessed he was scrolling on his phone under the table.

Hayley turned to Tai, speaking low. "Were you at the library this morning?"

"Yeah. Why?"

She contemplated him over the rim of her water glass. "I've just been wondering if you're the reason Evangeline was acting out of sorts earlier."

He tried not to show any outward reaction. "Why would you think I was the culprit?"

Hayley snorted. "Oh, please. Like I haven't noticed the way you've been flirting with her any chance you get."

He couldn't defend himself by saying he acted that way all the time because it wasn't true. Honestly, he wasn't usually flirtatious. He was cordial and friendly, but nobody would lay the moniker of lady's man at his feet. Only Evangeline had brought out that side of him. More playful and carefree. Her buttoned-up persona made him want to push those buttons and glimpse the spark in her eyes. There was attraction there. Definitely on his side, without a doubt, but he had a feeling she was struggling against the pull toward him as well. He hadn't been oblivious to the overlong looks she'd cast his direction. Before she shuttered her reaction behind a wall of perceived misconception, he'd witnessed a certain level of captivation when she looked at him. He just needed to get her to stop stifling that response and be willing to explore it instead.

"I might have . . ." Tai pulled a hand across the back of his neck, unsure why he was confessing this to his cousin. "I might have asked her out."

Hayley's eyes widened, and she shoved lightly on his shoulder. "Shut up! What did she say?"

She must have seen the answer on his face because the hand on his shoulder turned to a conciliatory pat. "Turned you down, huh?"

Tai shoved half a cornbread muffin into his mouth in response.

"Well, my advice is to not give up too easily. Evangeline keeps her cards close to her chest and swears up and down that she's not interested in dating, but I don't believe her for a second. She's the most in-love-with-love person I've ever met. Definitely a hopeless romantic." Hayley took a sip of her water.

"If I had to wager a guess, though, I'd say she's been hurt pretty badly before and is scared of getting burned again."

"Hmm," Tai murmured as he chewed. He'd asked her that very question, if someone had hurt her. She'd appeared uncomfortable and had laughed the whole thing off as a silly book trope.

But maybe some tropes were based more on reality than people gave them credit for.

12

The door to Cotton-Eyed Cup of Joe opened as Sheriff Jacobs exited with a cold brew in his hand.

"Afternoon, Sheriff." Tai dipped his head in greeting and caught the corner of the door before it could close.

"Tai," Sheriff Jacobs responded in kind. "How are things going over at Inked by Design?" The uniformed man stepped out of the way to let an out-of-town couple bustle into the coffee shop.

"Business is good." It was actually more than good. He was booking out months in advance thanks to word of mouth and the explosion of followers on his social media pages. Before he'd decided to open his own place, his industry friends had warned him that Little Creek may not have the population to support such a venture and was too remote to be convenient for even those in the surrounding areas. Thankfully, people didn't mind traveling once they saw pictures of his work.

Sheriff Jacobs nodded distractedly. Some concerned citizens had sent the man out to the shop when it had first opened, afraid the tattoo parlor would attract a certain variety of riff-raff and crime in their little town would skyrocket. Tai had been happy enough to show Sheriff Jacobs around the place. He'd walked the lawman through the safety precautions artists in the industry used, assuring him the needles and ink were completely safe.

He also let the police officer flip through his printed portfolio. If his art didn't relieve any misgivings, Tai wasn't sure anything he said would. The thing was, he limited the designs he put on people's skin. If someone wanted a grotesque or demonic tattoo, they'd have to go elsewhere. Tai was aware that tattooing could have a dark side—everything on the planet could—but he was only interested in creating things that were uplifting and light.

"Stay out of trouble." Sheriff Jacobs gave a two-fingered salute and walked toward his squad car.

"Always do, sir," Tai said to the man's retreating back before striding into the coffee shop.

He had even less time now to get a strawberry banana smoothie before the game. Thankfully, the line to the register wasn't long. He took his place and waited, looking over the room. His internal system received a jolt when he noticed Evangeline over by the table of straws, napkins, and add-ins such as cinnamon and nutmeg. Just seeing her brought a smile to his lips. He was about to step out of line and head over to talk to her, willing to forfeit his smoothie to have a few minutes in her company, when she peeked over her shoulder and quickly looked around.

Nothing necessarily out of the ordinary about her actions, but a radar went off inside Tai just the same. Call it a sixth sense where Evangeline Kelly was concerned. His gut told him the woman was up to something, and he planned to stay put and watch it pan out.

Evangeline furtively glanced over her other shoulder. She was clearly on the lookout to see if anyone was paying any attention to what she was doing so she wouldn't be caught in her mischief. Not unlike a burglar right before they picked a lock.

She slipped her hand into her pocket as she looked back over her shoulder yet again. Amusement ignited a warm glow inside Tai's chest. He'd thought her stalker abilities subpar after her attempt to tail him at the library, but now he knew she was equally bad at any endeavor that required even the most minimal level of covertness. Whipping her head around every two seconds to make sure no one was watching was like a neon sign drawing everyone's attention.

She pulled out an envelope, reached forward, and placed the white rectangle between the napkin and straw dispensers.

She was hiding a letter as if the coffee shop were some kind of drop-off location? Why? Who was the letter for? Why not just mail it? A dozen questions zipped through Tai's mind.

"Iced chai latte for Morgan," Stacey called out from the other end of the counter.

Evangeline startled, her hand darting out to reclaim the letter she'd only set down a second earlier.

"Oh, Stacey." Her voice was half an octave higher than normal.

Yeah, no one would be recruiting her to work for a government agency anytime soon.

"This has your name on it." She handed the envelope to a confused Stacey.

"What is it?" Stacey's brow wrinkled.

Evangeline shrugged. She tried to hide her excitement behind a faux innocent expression, but the way she slightly bounced on her toes gave her away. "I don't know. I found it on the table over there." She waved behind her.

Found it, hmm? More like planted it. Tai dug his hands into his pockets and forced his body to remain relaxed. Evangeline was oblivious to anyone in the coffee shop except for Stacey and that envelope, and he didn't want to do anything to draw her attention to himself. Not yet, anyway. Thankfully the person in front of him ordered a drip coffee instead of an espresso or he might not have been able to eavesdrop on the conversation.

Stacey opened the envelope and withdrew a folded piece of paper. Tai swung his gaze back to Evangeline as the barista silently read. Evangeline had let a smile slip onto her lips. She knew exactly what the letter said.

"You found this?" Stacey looked up, a mixture of bewilderment and badly suppressed wonder on her face.

Evangeline quickly dampened her telling grin. She widened her eyes the same way Tai remembered Hayley doing to convince her parents of her guiltless status after she'd managed to dye their cat blue with Kool-Aid. "Yes. It was wedged between the napkins and straws."

Stacey peered around Evangeline to study the spot. She chewed on her bottom lip. "You didn't happen to see who left it there, did you?"

Evangelina tugged her own lips down into a frown. The little minx. "No, I'm sorry. Why? It's not bad news, is it?"

"No, it's . . ." Stacey let out a breathy little laugh. "It's a love letter from a secret admirer."

A secret . . . Tai buried his mouth in his shoulder just in time to stifle the sound of his cough-covered laughter. Looked like some poor sop had talked Evangeline into being his messenger à la middle school. The guy probably should have picked someone who wasn't so obvious if he wanted to keep the whole thing a mystery.

"What can I get for you today?" The other barista behind the counter drew Tai's attention, taking his order and money, then measuring out fruit and ice and dumping them into the Vitamix beside the espresso machine. The blender drowned out any other conversation, and Tai missed what Evangeline said to Stacey before she turned on her heel and almost skipped out the door.

Stacey pivoted and noticed him there, her steps faltering. She hesitated but then seemed to come to some sort of decision. Her mouth firmed as she approached him. "Hey, Tai."

"Stacey."

"I have a weird favor to ask you."

"Go for it."

She fiddled with the paper in her hand, then held it out to him. "Does this handwriting look familiar to you?"

He studied the script as he quickly read the letter. Wow. Someone had bared his soul and laid it on thick.

Then again . . .

He started once more from the top.

A niggle of *something's not right* scratched at his brain. Not the words themselves—although he certainly had thoughts about those—but the penmanship. He often tattooed inspirational words or phrases, so he was familiar with different fonts and styles. He'd even copied the handwriting of loved-ones onto skin. Men tended to write with more blocky letters and sharp corners, pressing down hard on the pen. Women's writing was a bit neater, with more curves and softness to their letters. If he had to guess, he'd say Stacey's letter had been written by another woman.

Evangeline hadn't . . .

She hadn't written the letter herself, had she? The evidence pointed to that conclusion, but . . .

Man, was that woman twisting him up inside. He didn't want to sound like a narcissistic egomaniac, but he hadn't been imagining the chemistry sparking between them, and it *wasn't* one-sided. She said she didn't date, but if that was the case, then why in the name of Sam Houston was she writing love letters to Stacey?

Nothing added up.

He lifted his head and handed the letter back, trying to appear nonchalant. "Sorry. Doesn't look familiar."

"Yeah, not to me either." She tucked the letter into her apron pocket. "Not knowing is going to drive me crazy."

You and me both. "Not a big fan of the secret part of having a secret admirer?"

"I'm flattered, but . . ." She gave a nervous chuckle. "I don't know."

Tai took his smoothie, wished Stacey good luck, and headed toward the baseball fields, his head spinning the entire time. He somehow managed to arrive before the umpire called "Play ball!" Their team was up to bat first, so he took a seat next to Dalton on the bench in the dugout. The big man stared in the direction of the pitcher's mound, but he seemed a million miles away.

Tai finished off the last of his smoothie and set the plastic cup beneath the bench under him. "What's up with you?"

Dalton didn't move. He hadn't seemed to have heard Tai at all.

Tai bumped him with his shoulder. "What's up, man? Head not in the game already? We just started."

Dalton blinked and turned toward him. "Sorry. Something on my mind."

"Want to talk about it?"

He started to shake his head, then snorted. "Why not? Lord knows I haven't been able to figure it out."

Tai prepared himself for a hard punch of news. Hopefully he'd have some nuance of wisdom to help his friend.

A familiar-looking envelope fluttered onto Tai's lap. A sense of foreboding twisted his insides. He slipped his finger under the flap and pulled out a sheet of paper, unfolding it. The same neat, rounded handwriting marked the page that he'd seen only a little bit ago.

Relief punched out of his lungs, but he covered the quick exhale of breath with a cough. Granted, there could be more than one explanation. Yet even as he tried to think of other possibilities, he knew what he held in his hand and he knew where it had come from—or rather, whom. What he didn't know was why. Why was Evangeline writing love letters to both Stacey and Dalton?

His mind flashed back to the last game. To the papers she'd been pouring over in the stands as she'd observed Dalton on the field. The paper that he'd gotten a glimpse of when the wind had torn it from her possession. Book checkout histories with handwritten notes in the margins. Hadn't made any sense to him at the time, but now . . .

A groan and a laugh battled their way up his throat. He shook his head at the evidence in his hand. That meddling, matchmaking, adorable woman. And she'd called *him* trouble.

"Where'd you find the letter?" Not that it mattered, but Tai was curious.

"In my shop. Sitting pretty as you please in the middle of the sculpture I'm working on for the town square."

"You don't happen to have any security cameras in there, do you? Then you'd know who left it."

Dalton shook his head. "Haven't needed any cameras before. My place isn't exactly the most accessible, you know. I kind of live out in the boonies."

That was an understatement. Evangeline must've had quite the undertaking to find Dalton's property. Without four-wheel drive, she'd have had to abandon her car and make the trek on foot.

"It doesn't make sense, though. When could anyone develop feelings for me? I'm in my shop working most of the time, and when I do venture into town, I keep to myself. Besides, everyone knows I'm engaged to Rachel." He groaned, his head hanging low. "What's Rachel going to think when I tell her about this? She's going to jump to conclusions, isn't she?" He lifted his head, his hands reaching out and fisting into Tai's shirt with desperation. "I swear I'm not leading any other women on. I love Rachel."

Tai gently removed Dalton's hold on him. "Everyone knows you love Rachel. No one is going to think you've been cheating, least of all her."

Dalton gave him a relieved, hope-filled look. "Really?"

"Really. The letter came to you, not the other way around. Knowing Rachel, she'll probably find the whole thing funny."

Dalton sighed, and his shoulders relaxed for the first time. "What should I do about that?" He tapped the letter.

Tai folded the paper and put it back in the envelope. "If you want, I can take care of it for you."

"You can? Really? That would be great, man."

"Don't worry about it. I think I know just what to do."

13

"Umm, excuse me?"

I turn away from the cart I'd been placing returned books on and face the grandfatherly gentleman on the other side of the welcome desk. His faded, oversized dungarees are barely being held up by the suspenders slung across his shoulders, under what Grampie would call a *dunlap belly* (because it done lapped over his belt buckle).

"Can I help you with something?" I smile at him sweetly, praying under my breath that the clasp holding up the left side of his pants will keep its grip. It wouldn't be the first time I'd been mooned at the library, but that's an experience I don't particularly want to repeat.

"There are some strange noises coming from the book return receptacle outside. Sounds like maybe a critter has got himself stuck inside." He hooks a thumb toward the exit door.

I shudder. Again, not the first time. "Thank you for letting me know."

The man shuffles off, hiking his pants up as he goes.

I really don't want to play Ace Ventura at the moment. Sometimes snakes or lizards crawl through the slot for books, looking for shelter or whatever reptiles look for . . . their cousin the bookworm, perhaps?

I snicker at my own joke, then remember I have to go evict the creepy crawly creature and a shiver runs down my spine. Maybe I can talk Hayley into doing it instead.

"Oh Hayley," I singsong as I enter the breakroom. She's scrolling on her phone with one hand, a fork raised to her mouth with the other. "How much do you love me?"

She eyes me warily as she swallows a bite of her lunch. "By the look on your face and the sound of your voice, not as much as you want me to. Why?"

"Something's got itself stuck inside the return box again."

She points at her food with her fork. "I'm on break."

"Please." I clasp my hands in front of me and beg. "Pretty, pretty please."

"No dice. It's your turn. Remember?"

"Rock, paper, scissors?"

She rolls her eyes. "Fine."

We both hold out a fist in front of us and chant "rock, paper, scissors, shoot." I keep my fist there in the hopes she throws scissors, but her hand comes down with her flat palm facing the ground.

"Paper covers rock. I win." She takes another bite of her lunch, and I turn, grumbling.

"Oh, Evangeline?"

I look back at her. "Yeah?"

"Red touch black, safe for Jack. Red touch yellow, kill a fellow."

My expression goes bland. "Yes, because I'm going to stand there long enough to figure out the color pattern on a potentially venomous snake. Why don't we call animal control for these things again?"

"They take forever to get here. Just open the back and step aside. The animals usually leave on their own. Eventually."

I never thought snake charmer would be a part of the job description when I'd decided to become a librarian, but here

I am. Walking as if someone is behind me with a gun pointed at my back, I approach the waist-high drop-off box against my will, pausing when I'm about ten feet away. Huh. I don't hear anything. Maybe the creature has already crawled out on its own somehow. I take another tentative step forward, freezing when I hear it.

Chomping. Chittering. Scratching.

Scratching? Snakes can't scratch. At least I no longer have to worry about figuring out if red touches black or yellow before I die, but—

Purrr.

I stop in my tracks. Purring? How in the world did a cat get itself stuck in the return receptacle? I imagine a tiny little furball helpless in the metal box.

All my anxiety leaches out of my tight muscles. "It's okay, little guy," I coo. "You poor thing. You must be so scared in there. Don't worry. I'm going to get you out." I continue my calming monologue as I slip the key in the lock and turn the mechanism. "There you are, you—"

Beady eyes stare at me, sharp teeth bared as the not-tiny-little-fluffy-kitten hisses menacingly. I stumble backward, my breath catching. "Well, this is a first."

There, sitting on a pile of books, is a bandit-faced racoon with . . . I squint at what he has clutched between his little paws. "Just had to read a John Grisham novel, did you?" Although the title *A Time to Kill* is a little ominous.

"If you would kindly leave the book and be on your way, Mr. Raccoon, I'd be forever grateful." I make a shooing motion with my hand.

The raccoon doesn't budge. He stares me down as if taunting me to make him. Then he does something even worse. He lifts the book toward his open mouth.

"Don't eat it!" I screech at him.

He hisses, then takes a bite.

We've had to replace books that dogs have chewed on, but this will be the first time I'll be putting *eaten by a raccoon* in the description area in the library's software while ordering a new copy.

I slowly take a step closer. I need to get the animal out of the box and away from the other books, lest he destroy them all. Maybe if I bang on the side the noise will scare him into running away. I keep my eye on him in case he decides on any other funny business.

Wait. My eyes narrow. The raccoon isn't gnawing on the pages of *A Time to Kill*. He's eating . . . Is that . . . bacon? "Seriously, people? Food is not an appropriate bookmark!"

I take out my phone and snap a picture of Mr. Raccoon eating his bacon brunch served on a platter of John Grisham. I've read some pretty ridiculous signs before because of the general public's lack of common sense—a tag on one of my shirts says *Do not iron while wearing shirt*—but I never thought I'd have to create one about what is and is not suitable bookmark material. Food, no. Always no.

I bang on the side of the metal receptacle, but the racoon doesn't seem to care about the racket I'm making.

"This is not what I expected to see when I came out here." Hayley laughs as she shoves a Cheeto in her mouth, watching me as if I'm the main attraction in a traveling vaudeville show.

I march over to her and snatch the bag of junk food out of her hand.

"Hey!" she protests.

I fish out a Cheeto and wave it in front of Mr. Raccoon. "Yum. See this? You want this."

He perks up, his nose twitching as he smells the processed goodness in my hand.

"That's right. Come and get it." I set the Cheeto on the ground about three feet away. Mr. Raccoon inches forward. I set another one farther away. I am luring a wild animal out of a library book return box with a trail of Cheetos. Not sure if this should make it into my résumé or not.

Led by his stomach, Mr. Raccoon takes the bait. By the time he scampers off library property, the fur around his mouth is coated bright orange. Maybe I should contact the people at Frito-Lay. Fodder for their next Super Bowl commercial right here in Little Creek.

"You owe me a bag of Cheetos," Hayley says when I press the empty snack bag back into her hands.

"Add it to my bill."

She mimes writing something on an invisible piece of paper, and I roll my eyes with a chuckle. I go to walk past her toward the entrance, but she stops me with a hand to my arm.

"Hold on a sec. I came out here because I wanted to talk to you real quick."

"About what?"

"About Tai asking you out and you turning him down."

My head whips back in surprise. "He told you?"

"We're very close." She walks past me to the drop-off box and closes the back door, locking it with a twist of the key. When she turns, she studies me for a moment.

I lift my chin. Then lower it again because I realize how defensive the gesture is.

Hayley sighs. "Look, I don't know why you've pulled a 1990s Joshua Harris, but you should give Tai a chance."

"What in the world is a 1990s Joshua Harris?"

"You know, the guy who wrote the book *I Kissed Dating Goodbye*? Never mind. The point is, since you never talk about it, I've assumed some jerk broke your heart and you're still not over it yet. But Tai is a good guy."

I snort because I have to respond somehow and admitting the truth isn't an option.

Hayley's face pinches and starts to turn an alarming shade of red. I hold up my hands, placating her before she gets too hot under the collar. "Look, I'm sorry. Maybe he is a nice man. I don't know him very well so I can't really say, except he did dog-ear almost all the pages of that book. But the fact remains that I'm not looking for a romantic relationship right now."

Hayley wrestles with what I'm saying. I can see she wants to argue but ultimately she decides against it. Instead, she shakes her head in disappointment. "It's your turn to take a lunch break." She pivots, stopping when she reaches the door. "Just so you know, he didn't dog-ear the pages. I did. The book was going to the Friends of the Library book sale anyway so I bought it. The whole thing was just a joke, Evangeline." With that, she marches back into the library.

I turn to follow but pause when the sound of a V8 engine pulls into the nearest parking spot. My shoulders sag. This day keeps getting better and better.

Tai steps out of his car. "I need to talk to you."

"Can it wait? I have a lot of work to do." It's the truth. But so is the fact that I won't be getting to that work until after I've taken my lunch break.

Tai thinks for a second, then nods. "Meet me at the gazebo at seven after you lock up."

"Fine," I say just to get him to leave. I can think of an excuse later as to why I wasn't able to show up.

He opens his car door and turns back toward me. "Oh, and Angel? Please don't stand me up. You may be putting me off now, but you won't be able to avoid me forever."

14

The library is quiet when seven o'clock rolls around, not a patron in sight. Which means I don't have an excuse to keep Tai waiting. Although inconveniencing him with my delayed arrival is the least I want to do. I'm irrationally upset. I know he hasn't really done anything to deserve my ire, but that's what the word *irrational* means—not logical or reasonable.

I just wish he'd stop being there every time I turn a corner. Six months of coexistence in the same town without laying eyes on the man and now he seems to be everywhere. Showing up with his ready smile and easy manner and silver tongue. Asking me out and flaunting the chance of a future that I'm—

Well, let's just say it out loud, shall we? A future of love and acceptance and companionship that I so desperately want but am too paralyzed with fear of the past repeating itself that I . . . that I . . .

Argh! He should be a gentleman and stop harassing me!

He's not harassing you. He said he needed to talk to you. That's all.

We have nothing to talk about.

You don't know that until you hear what he has to say.

I guess there's at least one part of my brain that's being

rational tonight, and it seems like it's finally winning its argument.

I turn the key to lock the library and deposit it in my pocket. The sun has wholly disappeared behind the hills, casting the ridges in a dark blue silhouette, the sky behind them a vibrant sea of cascading colors. Already the chill of the approaching twilight has chased away what warmth the sun had left behind, causing me to pull my jacket closed around me and zipping the fleece material up to my throat.

There's a footpath from the library to the small community park next door. The town uses the grassy space for Fourth of July picnics, and parents rent out the area for their children's birthday parties. Now, however, the park is quiet and serene. I'd enjoy the setting, the picturesque gazebo standing innocently in the middle of the lawn, were it not the backdrop for a conversation I don't want to have.

The warm-lighted, old-fashioned streetlamps lining the path turn on as the sky's pallet mutes. A man leans against the support post to the gazebo's entrance, ankles casually crossed and hands shoved in pockets as his shoulder rests against the wood. He appears as if he doesn't have a care in the world. The blackguard.

He pops himself off the post and stands straight as I approach, watching me in an unsettling way.

"Angel." He grins at me.

"You wanted to talk about something?" I walk past him and take a seat on one of the six benches lining each side of the hexagon.

"I've discovered your little secret."

My heart plummets to my feet before shooting straight into my throat, my pulse so loud I can feel the beat between my ears. I seal my eyes shut. Behind my lids, my future here in Little Creek plays out, an encore to how it was in Chattanooga before I moved. The stares and speculations. The pitying glances or *you poor dear* consolations from those who think I have cancer. The inner battle of simultaneously remaining polite while explaining myself to strangers to whom I owe nothing while also wanting to scream. I'll no longer just be Evangeline Kelly, the local librarian. I'll be the bald woman. My lack of hair becoming my sole identity in everyone else's eyes.

I open my eyes to find Tai's gaze roaming my face. Starting at my chin and moving slowly up my jawline toward my brow, his look feels like a physical touch, igniting a path of shame that slices through the thin veneer I've managed to encapsulate my heart with. Is he picturing me barefaced, stripped of makeup, no fake eyelashes or temporary eyebrow tattoos? Is he mentally removing my wig, dethroning my crowning glory of womanhood and leaving me in an unnatural state of nakedness?

"There's a pop-up restaurant near Athens this weekend. Go with me."

I blink against his unexpected change in conversation. The formation of his words makes his sentence declarative instead of interrogative, but I hear the question in the cadence of his tone. I blink again. Is he . . . mocking me? He now knows I lack some of the fundamental physical attributes that make a person attractive and he's still asking me out. Why? I shake my head to clear the cobwebs and try to align the new information being thrown at me.

"I see," Tai says softly. Regretfully. He's taken the shake of my head as a response of no to his invitation. Which, I mean, he isn't wrong. I won't go, but that's not what I was saying no to.

He leans against the back of the bench and extends an arm over the top until his hand lands near my shoulder. His thumb and forefinger gather a strand of my hair between the pads of his fingers. He stares at the tresses, entranced, as he pulls out an envelope from the inside pocket of his leather jacket. "I think this belongs to you."

I reflexively take the envelope, staring at it uncomprehendingly. What?

Oh!

This is the love letter I snuck into Dalton's workshop. Does that mean the secret Tai knows . . . isn't my alopecia? He doesn't realize the hair he's running his fingers through isn't my own but a wig?

A twisting sort of sensation happens beneath my ribs.

Relief. The feeling is relief. Not disappointment. Not even a little. Because why would I be even a little bit disappointed that my most-hidden secret is still safe? That I'm still invisible—I mean, *anonymous*—in this town? That the obvious attraction in Tai's eyes would still be there even after he'd discovered the truth about me. Which, it turns out, he hasn't. Or at least not *that* truth.

"At first, at the baseball game, I wasn't sure why you had their library book checkout histories with you. You have to admit, it's an odd thing to take to a sporting event. But I thought maybe you were killing two birds with one stone. Getting some work done while supporting your favorite local team. But then Stacey showed me a love letter she'd received from a mysterious sender. And lo and behold, Dalton had a similar letter written by the same person. Which, not so coincidentally, were the same two people's information you'd been studying so intently at the game."

I swallow past the lump in my throat that's been lodged there since hearing the words *"I've discovered your little secret."*

"How do you know the letters were written by the same person?" I ask.

He gives me a crooked smile. "You write your capital *S*s and lower case *B*s in print while every other letter is written in cursive. In both notes."

It's probably pointless to try and refute his claims at this point, but that irrational side of my brain is starting to speak again.

He only has conjecture. Don't unwittingly give him more evidence against you and seal your own fate.

I seal my lips together instead.

He continues to play with the ends of my hair, watching the way the length falls through his fingers. Can he feel the synthetic fibers of the strands? Realize by the texture alone that the weave is machine made? I want to snatch the hair away from him but force myself to be still. An overreaction will draw more attention.

Out of the corner of my eye, I glance down to where he's touching me. The tendons along the back of his hand flex and bunch with the movement of his fingers, his veins pulsing with life and vitality. Dark black and various shades of gray color on the skin at his wrist disappear under the cuff of his jacket.

My finger twitches on my lap. I want to run the tip over the lines, trace the stroke marks and become intimately acquainted with the artwork. If our bodies are a temple, then Tai Davis's is like the Sistine Chapel, every inch covered in a tapestry of art.

Is every inch covered? What masterpieces are being hidden by his clothing?

Embarrassment heats my body and chases the chill of the evening air away.

"I know you're the author of the letters for another reason as well."

Tai's words snap me out of my trance, and I flick my gaze back to his face, hoping he can't read the thoughts that had been skipping through my mind.

"Everyone in Little Creek—that is to say, anyone who's lived here longer than six months—knows that Dalton is engaged to Rachel Belvedere."

"Dalton is . . ." The blood drains from my face. Did I really try to matchmake an already engaged man?

Tai nods. "Taken. Spoken for. Affianced."

My spine sinks into the support of the bench.

"Don't worry. I didn't tell either of them that their secret admirer was the town's new romantically inclined meddling librarian."

"Thank you," I sigh. There isn't a point anymore denying I penned those letters.

Tai laughs at my visible relief.

"I'm glad one of us thinks this is funny," I grumble.

"Oh, Angel, I can almost promise you that one day you'll find the humor in this situation as well."

"Not likely."

He shrugs, unperturbed. "The way I see it, you need my help."

I jerk, my shoulder bumping the back of the gazebo's bench. "Excuse me? Why would I need *your* help?"

He gives me a look as if to say *Isn't it obvious?* "You did just try to set up a man about to be married with a woman not his fiancé. That's pretty disastrous, don't you think? And who's to say the next time you attempt to matchmake that the people in question aren't also in a relationship you don't know about? Or related? I mean, I know Appalachia has a reputation in other parts of the country, but we really aren't keen on dating our relatives."

My mind immediately goes to Tai and Hayley and the fact that I never knew they were cousins. I blanch. Tai's right. I stand by my belief that book preferences are a great way to see if two people are compatible, but I made a huge mistake not factoring in more personal information. Like if they were engaged. Or related. Or had been in a previous relationship with each other that ended badly for one reason or another.

Good gravy there are a lot of scenarios I didn't take the time to consider before bulldozing ahead in my excitement to have a part in the act of falling in love again.

I eye Tai warily. "And you're willing to do that? Help me with the personal information so I don't make the same mistake again?"

He nods. "I am."

My shoulders sag with relief once again. "Thank you."

"But I want something in return."

My spine snaps back to its rigid position.

"In exchange for helping you with this matchmaking scheme of yours, which I feel I need to go on the record as saying is a bad idea—" He pauses as if giving me time to respond. Which I don't because I never asked nor wanted his opinion on the matter.

When I don't say anything, he continues. "In exchange for my help, you agree to accompany me to different outings and events of my choosing at prearranged times."

I blink at him. He can't be serious. "Let me get this straight. You're blackmailing me to go on dates with you?"

He winces, looking away from me. "Not blackmail. We're . . . striking a bargain." He pulls his gaze back to mine. "You need something from me and I need . . ."

You.

He doesn't finish the sentence, but that's how it would've ended. I need *you*. Because he's not asking me *for* something. Like house-sitting when he goes out of town or helping him with a DIY project or looking up books at the library to help him trace his genealogy. He's asking for *me*. My side of the bargain would be *me*.

My breath is punched out of my lungs.

"It's a gray area," he mumbles under his breath.

Who is he trying to convince, me or himself?

I stare at him. A bargain like this doesn't help me figure out his protagonist/villain role at all. His morals might be as gray as this bargain of his.

"So," he asks uncertainly, "do we have a deal?"

I chew on my bottom lip, thinking. I had a little hiccup with Dalton and Stacey, but I can do better. I *know* I can make a successful love match. Spending more time with Tai goes against every grain of self-preservation I have within me, but if I don't agree to his proposed arrangement, then I risk doing more harm than good with the hearts of the people of Little Creek, and I can't have that on my conscience.

The only other person I could question about fellow towns-people would be Hayley, but she'd get suspicious real quick if I asked if a specific man was single, especially since I've made a stink about not dating anyone. My friend would hound me until I cracked, and I'm just not ready to unpack my baggage in Little Creek yet.

I hold out my hand for Tai to shake. "Deal."

15

I owe it to Stacey to find her another match. She already thinks there's someone secretly in love with her. If she only gets the one letter and then communication from her admirer stops suddenly, she'll take it as a rejection. That's something I can't allow to happen.

Printouts from the library's recording software are scattered over the surface of my bed—my very own bibliophile dating profiles. But instead of name, age, and hobbies, I have something better: their nonfiction intellectual interests combined with their fictional escapes. Of course, there's the pesky problem of knowing if each person is actually single and looking to mingle. A very important point that I should've considered more carefully before getting myself into the mess with Tai.

Kitty Purry jumps onto the bed and walks across the papers I've divided into categorical stacks. Her tail flicks as her paws dislodge the top pages, making a disarray of my organization system. She lowers her head and nudges the largest pile with her nose before slinking her body to sprawl on top of it, rolling in a way that mixes the pages together.

"Kitty!"

She blinks her yellow eyes at me as if to say, *Yes, peasant?*

I reach forward to pick her up, but she anticipates my movements and launches herself into motion, a whirling tornado running a tight circle over the top of my bed before stopping and sitting primly on my pillow. She peers at the scattered papers on the bed, on the floor, and wafting in the air, and then looks at me. I swear one of her brows (do cats have brows?) arches condescendingly as if the mess is somehow *my* fault. Then she curls up into a tight ball and closes her eyes, dismissing me entirely.

"You really are a diva, you know that?" I snatch a paper out of the air. Now I'm going to have to start the process of separating interests based on genres all over again.

I peer down at the list in my hand. Might as well start somewhere.

Westward Expansion: A History of the American Frontier
The Worst Hard Time
The Pioneers

My gaze jumps from the nonfiction historical titles to the name of the patron at the top. Caleb Chapman. I read the list of books he's checked out again. Seems like Mr. Caleb Chapman is a fan of American history. And who else is a fan of American history, albeit of the fictional variety? None other than the woman of the hour, that's who.

"I think I've found a match, Kitty Purry."

My cat ignores me, her breathing even.

Now all I need to know is if Caleb is romantically unattached and not in any way related to Stacey.

Do you know Caleb Chapman?

Henry Crawford
Is that your next victim?

I'd edited Tai's contact information the night before. If he can give out nicknames willy-nilly, then so can I. And what better moniker than a character of Jane Austen's who's vibrant and alluring while also being morally ambiguous? It's a good reminder to myself to stay on guard around him.

> I think you mean beneficiary.

Henry Crawford
> If you say so, sweetheart.

I ignore the term of endearment. This is the South. Everyone is sweetheart; it doesn't mean anything.

> Can I safely assume you know him?

Henry Crawford
> Since second grade when he moved here so his dad could take over being principal at our elementary school. Caleb is single and ready to mingle.

I ignore the fact that Tai uses the same exact phrase to describe Caleb's relationship status that I had. It doesn't mean anything except that rhymes are catchy.

Henry Crawford
> Is it my turn to ask some questions now?

> I have a feeling you'd ask even if I said no. Or find a way to coerce me into answering if I declined the first time. Is that not your modus operandi?

Henry Crawford
> I guess you won't find out since you didn't say no. Here's what I want to know: What life lesson have you learned the hard way? Do you enjoy being yourself? What would you do differently if you knew nobody would judge you?

"What?" I stare at my phone. I'd been expecting some flirty innuendo or something better left in the archives of a middle school Truth or Dare game. Honestly, that would've been easier to roll my eyes at and brush off than these out-of-the-blue deep questions.

Henry Crawford

Don't answer now. Think about it. You can tell me on Thursday when I pick you up for our date.

I toss the phone onto the mattress faster than a medal-winning Hot Potato player. Kitty Purry lifts her head and glares at me.

"Sorry, Kitty."

She stands and stretches, then climbs into my lap, demanding attention. I pet her between the ears absentmindedly. I think I might have underestimated Tai and the level of danger he poses. The flirty comments and constant attention are bad enough, but now he wants to get to know me on a deeper level?

Be strong, Evangeline.

Categorizing Tai is supposed to make things easier. If I can pin a bookish archetype on him—cinnamon roll, grump, alpha, etc.—then I can better prepare myself for my interactions with him. But bad-boy rakes are supposed to be shallow, up for quick debauchery with anything in a skirt. They aren't supposed to ask meaningful questions that allow them to get to know their conquests on a deeper level. He's throwing me a curveball I'm not prepared for.

I survey the sheets of paper still littered over the surface of my bed. If I'm up to bat, I might as well get my three swings in before I'm called out.

I lower my head and groan into Kitty Purry's fur. "Since when have I started to use baseball analogies, Kitty?"

Kitty Purry twists and paws at my face as if to say *snap out of it.*

I sit up. "Thanks. I needed that."

I swear her feline eyes roll as she looks at me, and she meows her displeasure at the human race—or me as its representative—before jumping off the bed and striding out of the bedroom.

"Right. Okay. Let's see who else is booktastically compatible." I retrieve two sheets of paper. The person in my right hand seems to consume a steady diet of adult epic fantasy. They like to escape into a world of fairies and magic and fights against good and evil. The person in my left hand—I quickly read down their booklist—oh, they seem to only read highbrow literary fiction. Probably not the best of matches. I pick up two more papers, consider them, discard them, then pick up two more. Finally, I settle on another couple I think could really hit it off.

My phone rings from where it's slid under my thigh. Retrieving it, Penelope's name lights up my screen.

"Hello, sister dearest," I say.

"Sorry I'm calling later than expected. I got stuck in a meeting." Her voice is agitated and clipped.

"Everything okay?"

She takes in a long breath and exhales slowly. "Fine as frog's hair, as Grampie would say." The false cheeriness she's coating her words with sticks about as well as wet paint in a rainstorm.

"Want to talk about it?"

"Not particularly." She pauses. "But I swear if one more guy tries to mansplain something to me, I'm going to knee him right in said manhood."

I grin. "Tsk-tsk. What kind of genteel ladylike behavior is that?"

"I'm sure Scarlett O'Hara would approve."

A very *un*ladylike snort escapes my lips. "Yes, because she's the gold standard."

"Don't let Granny hear you imply otherwise."

"Never."

She chuckles. "Okay, speaking of Granny and Grampie. You evaded me on your last visit, but we really need to pin down some specifics for their party."

"I was thinking . . ." I hedge.

"Out with it."

"What if we find the love letters that they wrote to each other and incorporate those in some way?"

Penelope doesn't respond immediately, and I hold my breath. I really do think it would be special for Granny and Grampie to revisit the written words that ignited their love in the first place. It's personal and special and celebrates them in a non-generic way.

The fact that the letters may be useful in my own matchmaking is icing on the cake. And what's cake without icing?

"What would that look like? Lay it out for me."

"Well . . ." I draw the word out, scrambling to come up with some specific ideas. "First off, we can commission a wax seal to be made with their monogram and then seal the invitations like the aristocracy used to, a nod to when letter writing was the main avenue of communication. To continue with the love letter theme, we can have Granny's antique desk set out as a note station. Guests can use the desk to write personal messages to Granny and Grampie, expressing their well wishes and felicitations."

"In lieu of a guestbook."

"Exactly."

"Okay, I like that idea."

I smile, gathering steam. "For decorations, along with flowers and candles and such, maybe we can make or commission a custom backdrop with one of Grampie's letters written in calligraphy on a large piece of fabric. We could hang it either behind the cake table or behind where Grampie and Granny will sit."

Penelope is quiet as she seems to digest my suggestion. "It's a good idea, Evangeline. Let's do it."

"Great!"

"Do you think you can be responsible for the backdrop and the wax seal? Actually, can you just take care of the decorations and sending the invitations out? I'll help you with the guest list, of course, and I'll find a caterer and uncover where Granny keeps the letters stored without her knowing."

"I can do that."

"Thanks. I also wanted to ask . . ."

The I'm-stepping-on-eggshells quality to her voice instantly puts me on guard. "What?"

"Well, it's just that I was wondering . . ."

"Spit it out, Penelope."

"Fine." She blows out a breath. "I was just wondering if you've reconsidered telling Grampie and Granny how much of a jerk Brett was to you."

Not this again. "You know my stance on the subject."

"Fine. If you are choosing to continue to be a martyr, then I was wondering if maybe you should bring a date to the party."

My head rears back. I wasn't expecting that. "A date? Why? You know I'm not dating anyone right now." Or anytime in the near future.

This bargain with Tai doesn't count.

"A friend. I should have said a friend. But . . . a guy friend?"

"Again, why?"

"Well, Brett will be there, and I thought you might want some . . . you know . . . backup or emotional support or something." She rushes on. "Obviously I'll have your back, Evangeline, but I'll also be busy with the other guests and making sure everything runs smoothly. I don't like the thought of you having to face Brett alone because I'm occupied with something else, so I just thought . . ." She trails off.

A date. To my grandparents' fiftieth wedding anniversary. Celebrating their lifelong love where my ex-fiancé, the man who broke my heart and shattered my self-esteem, will be. A mental image of Tai materializes in my mind. Followed by one of his fists smashing through Brett's weak jaw.

I smile despite myself, then wipe the expression off my face. My mind should not automatically jump to Tai when the word *date* is bandied about, even if it is to fantasize about him punching Brett.

My lips begin to curve upward again.

Nope. Nuh-uh.

Going out with Tai is *his* part of the bargain, not mine. And I will *not* renegotiate our terms. End of discussion.

16

An inkling of regret tugged at Tai's conscience as he mounted Evangeline's front porch steps. The word *coercion* didn't have a nice ring to it, especially in the context of getting a woman to go out with him. But motives and intentions outweighed means in situations like this, didn't they? And his motives and intentions, if not completely unselfish, at least came from a good place.

Yes, he wanted to get to know Evangeline better and perhaps have her see past what Hayley called his "wolf's clothing," whatever that meant. But that truly was secondary. What he really wanted and hoped to achieve was for her to get to know *herself* better because he truly suspected she'd somehow forgotten who she was deep down inside, letting how others saw her distort her self-image. Chalk up the insight to like calling to like or a sixth sense, but he recognized the signs of lost identity in her because he'd traveled down that road himself, first believing he was weak and sickly because of his mom's view of him, and then that he was the black sheep and not someone to be trusted based on the town's verdict. It was only recently that he'd been able to get out from under other people's perceptions, and he wanted that same type of freedom for Evangeline.

Tai lifted his fist and knocked on the storm door, taking a step back to wait for the entrance to swing open. He was under no false impression that Evangeline would like this corner that he'd painted her into, and while the front door swung inward, the storm door's hinges opened the other way, and he wouldn't put it past her to *accidentally* use the frame to bludgeon his nose.

The lock mechanism clicked, then the front entrance opened, revealing one scowling librarian and an owl-eyed feline at her feet. Only one of them appeared as if she wanted to hiss and scratch at him . . . and it wasn't the cat.

Tai grinned at Evangeline, then ignored her completely, lowering to his haunches so he could address the cat at her level. "Hello. Who do we have here?"

"This is Kitty Purry, and she doesn't take to strangers," Evangeline said from above him.

Tai lifted his gaze, a sardonic half smile tipping one side of his lips as he held out two fingers for the cat to sniff. "Kitty Purry?"

"It's a perfectly acceptable name for a cat."

Said cat, the one who supposedly didn't like strangers and had been named after a pop star, headbutted Tai's hand, demanding to be petted.

"Is this when I hear you roar?" He chuckled as he scratched between her ears.

"Out of frustration," Evangeline mumbled.

Tai suppressed a chuckle. That inkling of regret he'd felt earlier? Yeah, it had completely vanished. Amusement replaced any sort of contrition that had been weighing him down.

He tickled Kitty Purry under the chin one more time then stood, addressing his date for the night. "You ready to go?"

"A deal is a deal." She met his gaze head-on, a wry slant to her pretty mouth.

Tai searched for anything that would make him call the

bargain off. He wasn't above a little arm-twisting (although a few days ago he wouldn't have believed it about himself), but he drew the line at *really* forcing his company on a woman.

She lifted her brows in challenge.

Nope. Tai didn't have anything to worry about on that front. Evangeline may have clouded herself in an air of provocation and offense at his heavy-handedness in getting her to agree to these dates with him, but any sign of wariness or trepidation had been replaced with a defiant tilt to her chin.

"Let me get my jacket." She turned and walked farther into the house.

Tai watched her retreat. He'd half expected her to answer the door in old, stained sweats, her wig unbrushed, and perhaps food in her teeth for good measure. Would have served him right, although the efforts would also have been in vain. There wasn't anything she could do to change her physical appearance that would make him find her unattractive.

Although, admittedly, he was glad she'd chosen a flattering dress that hugged her upper body, then flared out over her hips, hitting just above her knees. The skirt swished about her legs as she moved, almost like a hypnotist's pendulum.

He blinked out of a trancelike state. "You look very nice this evening," he said as she stepped through the front entrance and locked the door behind her.

She turned to him after putting the house key inside her purse, her hand punched to one hip and her jaw set again at a defiant yet elegant angle. "This isn't a real date, so you can save the false flattery for someone who'll fall for it hook, line, and sinker. This fish isn't biting." With that, she marched past him and down the steps.

"You're wrong on both accounts." He raised his voice toward her back as he hurried to catch up to her and open the passenger door before she could reach for the handle. "This is very much a real date, and there was nothing false in my statement. You must know you're beautiful."

Looking less sure than she had moments before, she avoided his eyes, chewing on her lower lip as she rounded the opened door.

Tai put out a hand and settled his palm on her upper arm, stopping her from climbing into the car. Reluctantly she turned but still refused to meet his eyes.

She couldn't really . . . could she? But . . . why not? His brows tugged to the middle of his forehead. The realization that she had no idea how beautiful she was surprised and confused him. Did she not own a mirror? Had no one ever told her before?

"You don't know. How can you not know?" He said this last part more to himself than to her. As far as he was concerned, he'd stumbled upon one of life's greatest mysteries. Or tragedies, really. One he had to rectify immediately.

Lifting a hand, he crooked two fingers under her chin, turning her face so that she could see the sincerity in his eyes as much as hear them in his words. "Angel, you're beautiful."

She swallowed hard, the muscles in her throat giving her away. After a moment, she dipped her chin and pulled out of his grip, lowering herself to the leather bucket seat. Tai stayed rooted to the spot. She'd heard him, but he rather thought she hadn't really *heard* him. Finally, he roused himself, sighed, shut the door, rounded the hood, and climbed behind the wheel. He wouldn't press. Not now. But this was a conversation he would circle back to in the future. It was too important not to.

"Just so you know." Evangeline's voice was thick. She spoke but kept her eyes focused on a spot outside the car's front windshield. "This isn't going to be some *Beauty and the Beast* thing."

Tai started the ignition, the power of the engine causing the car to rumble and vibrate under them. "Of course not. One,

I'm not keeping you hostage in an enchanted castle. Two, and you must concede this point, I'm much better looking than Prince Adam in either his human or beast form." Tai hooked his arm over the top of the steering wheel and waggled his brows at Evangeline.

She peeked at him, her lips twitching as she tried valiantly to hold back her laughter.

Tai redoubled his efforts, hooking one side of his lips high on his face and dipping his head in her direction as he pointed finger pistols at her. It was an Elvis Presley/Flynn Rider/Danny Zuko mash-up meant less for a real smolder effect than to get her to let loose her laughter.

And it worked.

She rolled her eyes even as a mellifluous sound escaped her pert lips. "Whatever that is"—she waved a hand at him—"it needs to stop."

Tai grinned. "What? Can't handle my charms?"

She snorted. "Charms. Right. Okay." She shook her head, taking a moment to compose herself and hide all evidence of amusement from her face. "I *meant* I'm not going to ignore the fact that I'm here for no other reason than to hold up my end of the bargain, and I'm definitely *not* going to fall in love with you like in some fairy tale."

"At least not before the last petal on the rose drops." Maybe most guys weren't familiar with Disney princess classics, but most guys were allowed to spend their childhood outdoors playing sports and getting into mischief. His mom had preferred him in front of the TV where she could keep an eye on him and make sure he was safe.

"Stay delusional if you want, but I warned you." She let herself relax against the seat, then a second later sat bolt upright, her eyes huge as she frantically looked around the inside of the car. "Wait, what kind of vehicle is this?"

Tai followed her gaze around the interior of the car but

couldn't see anything that would cause her the distress that made her muscles tighten like guitar strings. "It's a Dodge Challenger, why?"

She groaned, closing her eyes. "Please tell me you aren't some kind of *Fast and Furious* wannabe."

He smirked at her while the car idled in her driveway. At this rate they'd never get on the road to the restaurant. Did he care? Nope. The date hadn't even officially started, and he was already enjoying himself more than he ever thought he would.

"Why, Miss Kelly, are you intimidated by the horsepower under my hood?"

"Why, Mr. Davis, are you trying to parse a double entendre to overcompensate for something?" she fired back.

Tai laughed and reached for the shifter to put the car in gear.

Evangeline covered the stick with her own trembling hand. "Seriously, though." The banter had vanished from her voice. A real fear had entered her eyes. "You aren't going to drive irresponsibly in this thing, are you?"

Tai studied her. "Would you be more comfortable if you were the one behind the wheel?" No one ever drove his car but him. For her, though, he'd make an exception. Especially if doing so evicted the trepidation from the contours of her eyes.

Her fingers flexed on the shift. "Honestly, yes, but I don't know how to drive a manual transmission."

His lips pulled down. Everyone should know how to drive a stick shift. He let his thumb trail over the hills and valleys of her knuckles in a touch of comfort. "I promise I always drive responsibly, and this car is safer at taking these mountain turns than top-heavy vehicles are." He waited while she seemed to be weighing his words in her mind. "So, are we good to go?"

She removed her hand from the gearshift and sighed. "As good as I'll ever be."

Tai watched her a moment before putting the car in gear. It took an extra fifteen minutes to get to the pop-up restaurant since he didn't go a single mile per hour above the speed limit. Ten minutes after that, they were seated at an intimate linen-covered table for two in the middle of a courtyard created by the dual shipping containers on either side, converted into a traveling venue for the chef's events.

"This place gives a new meaning to reuse, reduce, and recycle." Evangeline looked from the Edison bulbs hanging crisscrossed from the containers' roofs to the freestanding heaters glowing red to combat the nip in the early spring air. "I'd say it's very trendy, but I have a neighbor who has a bench made out of cinder blocks and railroad ties, so a restaurant from a few shipping containers seems right on point for this neck of the woods."

"We Tennesseans embraced farmhouse chic before the Gaineses made the style popular."

She let out a breathy laugh. "Something like that."

They both picked up their menus and perused the options. The server came along with tall glasses of ice water and took their order.

Tai settled his forearms against the edge of the table once the server left. "So, did you think over the questions I asked you?"

Evangeline pulled her gaze away from the hanging bulbs and settled her green eyes on him. "Oh, we've come to that part of the night already, have we?"

"Hoping I'd forget?"

"Maybe."

"Too bad for you, I have a great memory." He reached a foot out under the table and tapped her ankle.

Her head snapped up, and he grinned at her. "Want me to be a gentleman and go first?"

Her jaw seemed to unhinge in surprise, which made him smile even wider.

"What? You think I don't know how to be a gentleman?"

She quickly composed herself, sitting straighter in her chair and settling her hands in her lap like a debutante. "I've seen no evidence so far that would corroborate that statement, no."

He shrugged. "Maybe you haven't been looking. Or maybe your perception has been skewed."

"I highly doubt that's the reason. Maybe it could be you're a flirt who manipulated a situation to your benefit, obligating me into a date after I turned you down."

Tai dramatically rubbed his chin in mock contemplation. "No, that can't be it."

She huffed.

He laughed.

"Okay, Your Honor, I submit to the court evidence number one. I will answer the questions I posed to you in order to ease whatever discomfort you may feel by revealing these three simple things about yourself." Tai waited, but her expression didn't change. "If you recall, the questions were, What life lesson have you learned the hard way? Do you enjoy being yourself? And what would you do differently if you knew nobody would judge you? Lady's choice. Which question would you like me to answer first?"

She sat silently, seeming to consider and then reject every response that came to her mind. Finally, she reached forward and took hold of her water glass, bringing it to her lips and taking a sip. After she set the glass back down, she settled an assessing look on him. "What would you do differently if you knew nobody would judge you?"

Tai sat back so his shoulder blades rested against the cushion of his chair. "That's the easiest of the three." He paused and let the silence stretch between them, much like a fisherman lets a fish swim after taking the bait before he starts to reel it in. "I wouldn't do anything differently."

Her lashes fluttered as she blinked. "Nothing?"

"Not a thing." He leaned in conspiratorially and dropped his voice. "Want to know why?"

She dipped her chin in assent.

He kept the upper half of his body there, leaning across the table, and looked her squarely in the eyes. "Because I no longer make decisions and live my life based off what other people might think of me." He let his statement sink in, then slowly sat back to his previous relaxed position.

Her fingers danced along her collar bone like a nervous butterfly. "Everyone cares what people think of them."

Tai shrugged. "I concede it's safe to say most people have a base desire to be liked and accepted, but it's dangerous if we start living and making decisions that will only please the people around us and not make us happy."

She tilted her head, studying him. "Is that something you've learned from experience?"

"Ah, now we've moved on to *What life lesson have you learned the hard way?*" He fiddled with the tablecloth, then smoothed out the wrinkle he'd created. "To answer both those questions, yes. I learned that living to please others is confining instead of defining. Caring more about what they think instead of what I think is essentially stuffing myself in a box. Sometimes one that doesn't feel like it has any holes to let in oxygen."

He could feel her gaze take in the rose tattoo peeking out from above the collar of his shirt. "Trying to picture me before my care meter got busted?"

Her brows furrowed. "Yes, but I'm having a really hard time doing so." She lifted her eyes to his. "What was the catalyst for this epiphany, if I may ask?"

"I have asthma. It was pretty severe as a child. My mom worried about me a lot and became one of those super overprotective helicopter parents. She was so afraid that something would trigger an asthma attack that I wasn't allowed to do much of anything."

"That must have been tough."

Harder than he admitted, especially to his mom. "I tried to live up to her expectations for me, to stay safe and not do anything that would worry her or cause her to judge my actions, but . . ." He shook his head. "Anyway, now I do things I was never allowed to do as a child. Kayaking, hiking, and skiing are some of my favorite pastimes. And I'm a tattoo artist, which is an occupation that has caused a few judgy looks to come my way, especially when I came back to Little Creek and people jumped to the conclusion that I was still someone who was up to no good—although I'm sure you're surprised to hear that."

"I have absolutely no idea what you're talking about."

"Uh-huh." He smirked.

"Here we are, folks." The server stopped beside the table and lowered two steaming plates before them. "The chicken-fried chicken for the lady and the country-style steak for the gentleman. Can I get you folks anything else right now?"

"This looks delicious, thank you." Tai moved his napkin to his lap.

"I'm good as well, thanks." Evangeline eyed her plate with appreciation.

"All right. Just holler if you need anything."

Tai waited until they were alone again, then held out both hands across the table, palms up. "Mind if I say grace?"

For the second time that night, she gaped at him. "You do that?"

He pressed his smile down to keep it from fully forming. "Yes, I do. I'd ask if there was a reason you automatically assumed I wasn't a God-fearing man, but I'd rather eat this food while it's hot than wait while you list my apparent sins for me again. Not that you're the type to judge, of course."

Her cheeks pinkened, and he wiggled his fingers.

"Now, should I say a silent prayer or are we going to join hands? I promise you, nothing salacious is going to happen if you touch me." Because he knew it would irk her, he gave her a lopsided, playful grin.

Her mouth pinched as she shoved her hands into his.

His grin slid off his face the moment her fingers touched him. She hadn't placed her palm in his gently or delicately, but forcefully. And his pulse responded in kind—fierce and aggressive. A reaction so powerful it took him by the throat and made his life flash before his eyes. A life in which a matchmaking librarian played a central role. He shouldn't have opened his big mouth to make any promises that nothing would happen if she touched him. Because something had.

His entire world just split wide open.

17

Tai wasn't sure how he managed to get through saying grace without stammering or stuttering, but he silently thanked God for the miracle anyway. It was almost with relief when he muttered an amen and Evangeline removed her hands from his.

He needed a moment to think. To process.

It wasn't that he hadn't known he'd be affected by her touch, because he had suspected he would be. He was attracted to her, after all. No, what had surprised him was just how *much* he'd been affected.

It was kind of like someone wanting a tattoo and knowing that getting one would hurt, but it wasn't until they were in the seat and the needle was jamming into their skin repeatedly for hours did they realize just how much pain the process would be.

Prepared, but not.

Totally not *prepared.*

Tai folded his fingers into two fists and brought his hands down to his lap, as if by curling his fingers he could hold on to the moment forever. He wanted to shake his head and release his grip. Tell himself he was being ridiculous and making more out of things than what was really there. And maybe he was.

At least, he was making more of what was there *now*. But he had a feeling—a certainty, actually—that whatever this *thing* was between Evangeline and him was only going to grow and get stronger.

He glanced across the table to Evangeline. His Angel.

His Angel, who seemed to not be affected in the slightest.

His Angel, who was all but ignoring him, cutting a piece of meat with her fork and knife.

His Angel, who he'd had to coerce to even get her to give him the time of day.

His Angel, who had a telltale delicate blush to her cheeks that hadn't been there before.

His heart lightened. Oh yes. This was not one-sided. But a certain party was being particularly stubborn in ignoring the pull between them. She had her reasons, he was sure. Ones he hoped she'd eventually share with him. Although that wouldn't happen until she trusted him, and she wouldn't trust him unless she spent time with him and opened up to him. Two things he was currently working on.

He picked up his fork and stabbed a roasted potato on his plate. "So, now that I've demonstrated that I truly am a gentle-man, it's your turn."

She dabbed at her mouth with her napkin. "Pardon?"

"The three questions. Don't tell me you're still trying to get out of answering." She was, of course, but hopefully him teasing her would put her a little more at ease. "We'll do the easiest one first. Do you, Evangeline—wait, what's your middle name?"

"What's yours?" she countered, probably trying to buy herself some more time.

"Always going to make me answer first, are you?" He'd play along. "It's Albert."

She blanched.

"What? You don't like the name Albert? Take it up with my parents. Now, your turn."

She reached for her glass and took a long drink of water. Suddenly, she stood, her jerky movements almost disrupting the tray a passing server carried in her hand. She apologized profusely, then sprinted away, an excuse of needing the restroom following in her wake.

Tai watched her go. What had just happened? Newton's third law of motion—for every action there is an *equal* yet opposite reaction—had completely been thrown out the window. Retreat over revealing a middle name? Even if her parents had saddled her with something like Dorcus, running away while the blood drained from her face was an overreaction.

It was also a misstep on her part if she didn't want to spike his curiosity. Like a forbidden fruit, all he could think about now was her mysterious middle name. Did it rhyme? Evangeline Tangerine Kelly? Or perhaps it was embarrassing. Evangeline Bertha Kelly? Bequeathed because she was a Big Bertha of a baby? Or maybe she'd responded so strongly because they shared a middle name, or at least the feminine form of his. Evangeline Alberta Kelly?

Minutes ticked by, but she didn't return. He was about to flag down a female server and ask her to check on Evangeline when she finally appeared and retook her seat, smoothing out her dress as she did so.

"I'm sorry, that was terribly rude of me." She picked up her fork like nothing had happened and speared a morsel of food.

Tai cocked his head. "Are you okay?"

She pushed her lips into a false smile. "Of course. Why wouldn't I be?"

"Maybe because—"

"Your questions. Which one do you want me to answer first?"

Tai's brows rose. She was definitely flustered if she'd interrupt someone while they were speaking. No southern-bred woman would dare.

Yeah, he *had* to know what this secretive middle name was.

He folded his hands in front of him. "I've decided to offer you a three-for-one deal. We'll save the previous questions for another time. Just tell me your middle name."

The muscle in her jaw ticked as she set down her fork. "I may sound like a contestant on a TV game show for saying this, but no deal."

"Howie Mandel is devastated."

"I bet he is."

"I'm not going to let this go, Evangeline Tullalulah Kelly."

"Duly noted. And not even close."

Tai grinned. "Fine. Do you, Evangeline Clementine Kelly, enjoy being yourself?"

She didn't even bother trying to suppress her smile this time. It curved in a delicate bow, a soft and inviting slant that drew his attention. "You're colder than a penguin in the Antarctic with your guesses."

"Are you sure?" He couldn't look away from her mouth. "I'm feeling quite warm, actually."

Her smile froze, then dimmed. She looked away, but not before he saw a hint of sadness darken her irises.

Which made no sense. He could understand if his flirty comments embarrassed her or made her exasperated, but why would they make her sad?

"You shouldn't say things like that." Her voice was quiet, and she was again not meeting his eyes. Just like when he'd said she was beautiful.

"Why not?"

"Because you don't mean them."

His head jerked back. "Says who?"

She huffed out a breathy laugh that didn't even hold an ounce of humor within it. "Guys like you never mean the charming things they say."

"I'm glad you find me charming, but what do you mean by *guys like you*?"

She did a Vanna White impersonation and waved her hand in front of him. "The rakes, rogues, ladies' men, charmers, flirts, silver tongues. Whatever you want to call yourselves. You say things you don't mean. You love 'em and leave 'em."

Tai regarded her. She seemed to almost be itching for a fight, and he was conveniently located nearby. "Is that what happened to you? Someone you love left?"

She turned her face away, her jaw set in a stubborn line.

"I hate to break it to you, but contrary to popular belief—or *your* belief, rather—I'm none of those things you just listed. I may flirt with you, Evangeline Elly Mae Kelly—" Not even a flicker of response to his joke. She must be really upset. "But that doesn't mean I *am* a flirt or that my plans are to play with your heart."

She folded her hands in her lap. "We'll see about that."

"Yeah," he said softly. "I really hope you will."

18

It wasn't until they passed a near-empty Kroger parking lot on the drive back to Little Creek that Tai got the idea to teach Evangeline to drive a manual transmission.

"Why are we stopping here?" she asked as he pulled the car to a stop under a streetlamp in front of the deserted grocery store.

Besides the beat-up El Camino with a busted tire parked on the other side of the lot, the place was empty. Perfect for an impromptu driver's ed session.

Tai killed the engine. "You're going to drive the rest of the way home."

Her eyes went wide, the light shining down on her from the streetlamp making it look like she was the star of the night's stage.

"But I already told you I don't know how to drive a stick."

"I know." Tai could justify his wanting to teach Evangeline the mechanics of operating a vehicle with a manual transmission, but the truth of the matter was, most drivers in the United States no longer had the skill. Nor did they really need it since automatic cars were the majority on the road. Really, he just didn't want the night to end, and teaching Evangeline was the best excuse he could grab at when the opportunity presented itself

Tai opened the car door, a gust of a breeze wafting inside. His nose crinkled against the assault. Cool evening air mixed with the offensive odor of a blooming Bradford pear tree. How the pretty white blossoms could emit a smell that rivaled rotting fish, he'd never know. They were like the Trojan horses of trees, completely innocent and magnificent to look at but hiding something deadly you'd never expect.

"Those things are foul." Evangeline scrunched her face, pinching her nose against the onslaught of stench. "Tai, I can't drive. Take me home." Her voice had a clogged, nasally tone to it now, slightly muffled because of the hand in front of her mouth.

Tai pinched his own nose. "This is as far as I'm taking you. If you want to get home, you're going to have to drive yourself."

He couldn't believe she'd accused him of being a player. If he were experienced in the art of wooing the ladies for the fun of it, would he really have brought her to a place reeking like a wharf on a hot summer day, where they both had to plug their noses and talk like cartoon characters with bad sinus infections?

This was not suave. This was not charming.

This was probably not getting her to see him in a better light either.

Oh well.

Before she could offer another argument, Tai unclicked his seat belt and climbed out of the car. He left the door open, both as an invitation for her to take his place behind the wheel and also because the stench would work in his favor. The longer she sat there, the longer she'd have to endure the tree's odor. Sure enough, by the time he'd rounded the car and stood in front of her door, she'd pushed it open and was scowling at him.

"The sooner you get behind the wheel, the sooner we can shut the doors and we won't have to smell the blooms anymore."

"It's coating the inside of my mouth," she complained as she stalked around the front of the car, the headlights illuminating her shapely legs as she passed through the beams. "I can taste the smell."

She wasn't wrong, and Tai wished he'd chosen some other deserted parking lot. But they were there now. The only thing to do was make the best of it.

"Try this." He opened the glove box and retrieved a container of chewing gum. He offered her a piece and took one for himself.

"I'm not sure this is helping." She grimaced as she chewed. "Now it's like minty fish." Her body shivered in disgust, but she didn't spit the gum out.

"Okay, the first thing you need to do to start the car is—"

She held up her hand to stop him. "I may not know how to drive a stick, but I do know how to start a car." She reached forward to press the start button on the dash.

Nothing happened.

Her brows pulled together in confusion. She pressed the button again.

Still nothing happened.

Tai cleared his throat to combat the laughter bubbling in his chest. "As I was saying, the first thing you need to do to start the car is engage the clutch."

She flipped her hair over her shoulder and gave him a look out of the corner of her eye. "I knew that."

Tai swallowed his mirth. He watched as she correctly used her left foot to press the clutch pedal down to the floor, then tried the start button for the third time. The engine roared to life.

"Good. Now, press the brake pedal and release the parking brake."

She found the parking brake lever and pulled. A small pop sounded when the brake released.

"The car's in neutral. Do you know how to put it into first gear to move forward?" There weren't any cement parking blocks separating the spaces, and Tai figured she'd rather go forward than in reverse for her first attempt.

Evangeline licked her lips and stared at the gearshift.

"It won't bite."

She blinked wide eyes at him. "I know it won't bite. I'm just nervous."

"Don't be."

"I don't want to ruin your car."

"You won't hurt it, I promise," he said, infusing his tone with reassurance.

She swallowed, then gripped the shift, pulling it toward the left as far as it would go, then up into first gear.

"Perfect. Now all you have to do is give the car a little bit of gas while slowly letting off the clutch."

"That's all, huh?"

He grinned. "Yep. That's all."

She hesitated. "Okay. Here goes."

Except the only muscles that moved were those of her eyes. Her green irises flicked up and down between staring at her feet and peering out the windshield.

"You got this, Evangeline Jezebel Kelly."

The panicked look that had started to cloud her vision receded like sun burning off fog in the valley. The muscles in her shoulders lost some of their tension, and her grip on the gearshift loosened enough to allow color back into her white knuckles. "You're the worst guesser in the history of guessing."

The engine more moaned than revved as she slowly put pressure on the gas pedal. The car inched forward.

Evangeline's jaw unhinged in surprise but also delight. She pushed down with one foot while lifting up with the other. Tai opened his mouth to warn her to give it more gas, but before he could get the words out, the car lurched, throwing them against the seat belts, then stopped altogether.

"I'm so sorry." Her hands rose to cover her cheeks. "I'm so sorry."

Tai covered her hands with his own and lowered her palms from her face. He squeezed her fingers. "I told you, you're not going to hurt the car. Everyone stalls. Shoot, I still stall every now and again. It's not a big deal. And I promise, accelerating from stop is probably the hardest part of driving a stick. But once you get the hang of how much gas to give while you let off the clutch, it's a breeze. Now, try again."

She stalled a few more times, but each time she looked less horrified and more determined.

"That's it. Just ease off the clutch a little more . . . Just a little more gas . . . You're doing it! You're driving a stick!"

Evangeline beamed as she drove five miles per hour around the empty parking lot. Could a person on foot have passed her? Yes. But that didn't detract from her victory.

"Okay, give it some more gas. Listen to the engine. I'll tell you when to shift, but see if you can hear it yourself."

She gave the gas pedal more pressure, and the speedometer rose. The engine revved.

"Now. Shift to second."

A terrible grinding sound came from under the hood, and Tai couldn't help but wince.

"Oh my gosh. I just murdered your car." Evangeline's hands

fluttered, and the car jolted to a stop again. Once more, she covered her face with her hands. "I can't do this."

"Yes, you can. You're doing great."

Her palms lowered until just her eyes peeked out from above her fingertips. "Great? Your car sounded like I was torturing it to death."

It did. Honestly, grinding gears could damage certain parts of the car, but light grinding here and there wasn't going to kill it. "Just make sure the clutch is pushed down when you shift and don't release until the car is in gear."

It took a bit more encouraging before Tai could get her to try again. He walked her through every step, offering reassurance when needed and more encouragement. Finally, she was shifting between first, second, and third with confidence.

"Pretty soon you're going to be zipping around the raceway."

She laughed and shook her head. "Yeah, because going"— she flicked her gaze down to the speedometer—"twenty-five is going to give Chase Elliott a run for his money."

"An empty Kroger's parking lot today, the Daytona 500 tomorrow."

She snorted, but her shoulders relaxed. Tai had her practice in the parking lot for another twenty minutes. He hadn't really planned on making her drive the rest of the way home, but she'd learned fast and he didn't see why she shouldn't.

"Ready to take this baby on the road?"

She slammed on the brake, forgetting to engage the clutch, and the car stalled violently for the first time in a while.

"Sorry." She patted the steering wheel as if she were apologizing to the car. Wariness and uncertainty lined her brow. "Are you sure that's a good idea? A road with other cars is a totally different beast than an empty lot."

"You're ready. I believe in you. You just have to believe in yourself." Tai pointed out the window. "Plus, don't you want to get away from the Bradford pear's own special take on the fresh scent of spring?"

Her lips tilted in a soft smile. "To be honest, I don't even notice the stench anymore. I must have gone nose blind."

"Then quick, we need to leave before the damage becomes permanent."

She laughed as she restarted the engine.

Tai had stopped at the Kroger just outside of town, so it didn't take long for Evangeline to pull up to her house, even with her going under the speed limit to reduce the number of times she'd have to shift gears.

She didn't turn off the engine after she put the car in neutral and pulled the lever for the parking brake. "Don't think you have to walk me to the door since this isn't a real date."

Tai reached over and pushed the button to kill the engine. "Just because you keep saying that doesn't make it true. This *is* a real date." He opened the door and exited the car. He knew she wouldn't wait for him to get her door, and he was right. Her door shut a second after his did. He met her at the bottom of her porch steps.

"Thanks for coming out with me tonight." He shoved his hands into his pockets to keep from reaching out and touching her.

"You make it sound like I had a choice." There was a hint of amusement to her voice that lent to banter.

He shrugged and grinned. "You did. You chose to use my help with your matchmaking." He leaned his shoulder against the post of her front porch. "You know, you never did answer any of my three questions."

"Oh, look at the time." She glanced down at her wrist even though she wasn't wearing a watch. "I have to get up early so—" She spun on her heels and scurried away. "Good night!"

she called over her shoulder as she unlocked the front door and stepped inside.

Tai chuckled, pulling out his phone as he ambled back to his car. He opened his messaging app and clicked on Angel's name.

> You can run but you can't hide, Evangeline Puddin' Tame Kelly. Braves home opener is Sunday. I'll pick you up at ten.

19

'm once again at a table that's near the barista's counter of Cotton-Eyed Cup of Joe, a mug of tea in front of me more to blend in with the environment than because I make a habit of purchasing drinks I can make at home for a fraction of the price. Someone might get suspicious, though, if I sat here not drinking anything.

I feel like a thief casing the joint as I look around the room. I'm not here to steal anything, however. Arguably, I'm here to give back. To give love, more specifically. What greater gift can there be?

After more study and consideration, I've decided to attempt a coffee shop meet-cute after all. Because people are creatures of habit, I know that Kari Turner comes in every Friday morning at eight for her weekly splurge of a white chocolate mocha with two pumps of raspberry syrup. Meanwhile, Bo Fellowes swings by on his way to work five days a week for a simple black coffee at about the same time. Making the coffee shop the rendezvous point for their meet-cute was a no-brainer. The location is not only convenient, but I also don't have to contrive a reason to get them to the same place at the same time. I just have to get them to talk to each other.

I wasn't sure at first if I should match them together. Based off their reading preferences, their compatibility might be a bit of a stretch, but I'm going with the idea that opposites attract. It's a popular trope for a reason, although I'm not quite sure what that reason is. Wouldn't two people of opposing sides be more likely to fight than to fall in love? I mean, I get that in the field of magnetics it's the positive and negative sides that attract and cling to each other, but relationships aren't the same as science. If they were, then we'd have a nice little formula we could work with.

$A + B = C$.

Girl + Boy = Love.

But it isn't so cut-and-dried as that. There are too many variables. For instance, A can develop an autoimmune disease that causes physical changes, which in turn makes B no longer find A attractive, reducing the sum of C until it's one day gone completely.

Or B can say XYZ to multiple As, causing the coefficient to produce a negative instead of a positive integer. Or, in this case, B never has the potential to equal C, especially when added to A.

Not that A wants C with B anyway.

I shake my head and groan, checking the time. 7:55. I need Kari and Bo to get here. I need a distraction. If not, I'm going to do the thing I promised myself I wouldn't do. I'm going to think about *him*.

Yeah, because you weren't already.

I sigh, mentally giving up. Maybe if I let my mind process the night before for the next four minutes and fifty-two seconds then I can purge my thoughts and focus one hundred percent on the match between Kari and Bo without the essence of *his* memory trying to escape the corners of my mind I've been trying to shove him in.

Of course, for this to work, I'm probably going to have to step out of the nice little comfy retreat of denial I've made for myself. I whimper a bit at the thought. Good-bye, fluffy throw pillows that cushioned my head and helped me stuff my ears and hide my face from possible truths right in front of me. I'll miss you, mantras of inner rebuttal and justification that made me feel better, even if they were delusions.

I wince as I mentally step outside that comfy corner and brace myself for what I've known but haven't wanted to accept. Despite my defensive responses and futile attempts at vilifying him, Tai Davis has managed to breach the protective layer I've tried to erect around my heart. Leather-wearing, fast car–driving, tattooed, Granny-would-have-a-heart-attack-if-she-knew Tai Davis.

Do I even have a chance when he refuses to stop pointing his devil-may-care grin in my direction? It's only natural that I feel a jolt behind my ribs when his eyes crinkle with a little sunburst when he smiles at me. Or that the joy that seems to come from a well deep inside him, bubbling up like a spring and then overflowing, draws me in every time and dares me to smile back.

Our similar statures cause my gaze to snag and tangle with his more than it ever has with any other man. A delicious type of shiver runs along my limbs when I catch him looking at me. I want to blame it on the fact that it's been so long since I've been the recipient of an appreciative male gaze, and that may be partially true, but I can't help but think a bigger part is due to the man himself. Before, I might have said I was like most women and attracted to a taller man, but Tai has proven that untrue.

I find myself mesmerized by his form, by the lines and curves inked into his skin, and by the fact that many of his tattoos are a mystery, covered by the length of his sleeves. It's the curiosity of the pictures and what they depict that draws and beckons my attention so often. The appeal of the unknown, the dangerous, the forbidden.

I hate how much I secretly enjoy when he flirts and teases, my starving soul and wounded pride soaking up the attention. I have to remind myself that I can't take what he says—how he calls me beautiful—too much to heart. His words are like a hot-air balloon, something that will drift away in a strong breeze. I'm ashamed when I find myself clinging to the strings attached, wishing that it wouldn't deflate. That it would last even though I know it won't.

I've let Tai's attention worm its way past my defenses, but that physical pull he incites in me isn't enough. It doesn't change the fact that if he saw me stripped of any of the fake accessories I don, the spark of desire I see in his eyes now would likely be snuffed out.

The front door of the coffee shop opens and a behemoth of a man in steel-toed boots walks in. Bo Fellowes, everyone. He has a tan Carhartt jacket draped over his broad shoulders, and a plaid flannel shirt peeks out from under the collar. His jeans are faded and work-worn, ready for another day on a jobsite.

I sit up straight, shooing my thoughts of Tai back to their corner. Now I can concentrate and focus on two people who actually have a shot at real romance.

Bo strides to the counter and orders his usual. I peer around the dining room. There are a couple of people sipping drinks and nibbling baked goods, but not the person I'm looking for. Where is Kari? Of all the days for her to be late or not show up, today isn't one of them.

Bo tucks his receipt in his back pocket then heads to the opposite end of the café and disappears behind the door of the men's restroom.

The front entrance opens again, and I sigh with relief. Kari walks in, a flush to her cheeks as she hurries to the counter to give the barista her drink order. I take a moment to study her. She's petite in stature. If I had to guess, I'd say the top of her head would graze the bottom of my nose. Which means she'd have to stand on her tiptoes if she even hoped of making it to Bo's chest. But opposites, right? If the trope proves true, then these two will have an instant connection the moment their eyes land on each other.

Kari moves away from the counter to wait for her drink. Time to put my plan into action.

"Hey, you can sit down here if you'd like." I indicate the other chair at my table and give her my most friendly smile.

"Oh. Thanks," she says as she moves her purse to her lap and sits. "I've been going nonstop already this morning, and it's only eight o'clock. I can't imagine how the rest of my day will be."

"Good thing you're about to have a caffeine pick-me-up," I say. "Sounds like you're going to need it."

"You're telling me." Kari's phone pings in her purse. "Sorry. I don't want to be rude, but I'm kind of dealing with a situation at the moment so I really need to answer that."

"No problem."

Looking over the top of Kari's bent head, I watch Bo exit the bathroom. Right on time. Now if only—

"Black coffee for Bo."

Perfect! Giddy expectation percolates in my diaphragm. I can see the next few moments play out in my mind like a scene of a well-crafted book.

I'm going to tell Kari, who is distracted by the text message, that the barista said her name to pick up her coffee. Kari will thank me, at which point I'll mentally respond that she has no idea just how much she'll be thanking me later, as she stands up and approaches the counter. Of course, Bo will also be there because it's really his coffee that's ready. They'll both reach for the coffee.

At this point, fate can take over because my work is done. Fate can decide if it wants their hands to bump, making them look at each other and then be hooked by that instant magnetism science is assuring me will happen with these opposites.

Or maybe fate would rather Kari get to the counter first and pick up the coffee cup, at which time Bo will say, *Excuse me, but I think that's my coffee*. They'll laugh over the mistake then linger, bantering back and forth, magnetism again doing its job and pulling the two together.

I can barely keep the excited anticipation off my face as I clear my throat. "I think they just called your name."

Kari looks up from her phone. "Really? That was fast. Thanks." She stands and walks the couple of steps to the counter.

I lean back in my chair, not the least bit embarrassed to be eavesdropping. In fact, the swell in my chest feels more like pride than humility. Besides, there's no way I'm missing out on the romance unfolding before my eyes. Or ears, rather, as I'm facing in the opposite direction and it would be too obvious if I turned around now just to watch.

"I think that's mine," a male voice says behind me.

"Oh, sorry about that. My mistake."

I grin. Here it comes. The magical moment. The instant connection. The meet-cute.

I strain to hear the next words sure to come from Bo. A compliment. A witty response. A fumbling, awkward comment that Kari will find endearing even if it makes everyone else listening in the vicinity cringe.

But nothing comes. The only sounds filling the space are the constant stream coming from the old-fashioned coffee machine and the clacking of a keyboard as the patron in the corner types away on their laptop.

"Raspberry white chocolate mocha for Kari."

The front door opens, and I turn my head and watch Bo walk out of the shop. A few seconds later, Kari follows. They both get into their separate vehicles and drive away.

Disappointment sinks in my gut, and my shoulders slump as if the two are tethered together. What went wrong? Where

were the sparks? That defies-all-reason fascination with someone not like oneself?

I sigh and stand, tucking a couple of dollar bills under my
empty mug as a tip.

Matchmaking might be a *little* harder than I thought it
would be—especially when the love interests aren't cooperating as they should—but I'm not giving up. Romance merits
the effort, and it will be worth it in the end.

20

"Turn green," I plead as I stare at the red light taunting me. I've been sitting here half of forever waiting for the light to change. My car is the only vehicle on the road, but I know as soon as I give up on waiting and press the gas to go anyway, Sheriff Jacobs will come out from behind his hiding place around the corner with his lights flashing.

This is his favorite spot to meet his traffic violation quota each month. I swear this one traffic light has single-handedly funded the city's improvements for the last few years, including the commission of the chainsaw sculpture Dalton's working on now.

The red on the light dims, and the green brightens.

"Finally." Even though I drive an automatic, I find myself pressing an imaginary clutch with my left foot and reaching for a gearshift that isn't there. As the speedometer needle moves on my dashboard, I mentally shift gears like I had in Tai's car.

Brett had tried to teach me how to drive a stick shift once. To say the experience hadn't gone over well would be an understatement. He wasn't nearly as patient or encouraging as Tai was. And I get it. Repairs to transmissions are beyond pricey. When the gear had slipped out of second and a terrible thud sounded from under Brett's hood, I'd thought the transmission had fallen out onto the road and I'd ruined his car for good. Or at least did a couple thousand dollars' worth of damage.

To Brett's credit, he hadn't yelled or cursed at me. He'd merely pursed his thin lips together and clenched his jaw so hard he'd been in danger of chipping a tooth. Then, in a voice that would raise the hair on even Alfred Hitchcock's arms, he'd said the lesson was over.

I figured I was a lost cause. Turns out, I just needed a different teacher.

Who would've thought Tai fit that bill so well? There's not much of his hard-edged exterior that gives a person a hint to the patient, even-keeled man under the surface. I'd been waiting with bated breath the entire lesson for his lid to pop, especially after the sickening sound of the gears grinding for the third time. But he'd appeared unbothered and just encouraged me to try again.

The whole evening left me confused, but nothing more so than that confounded driving lesson that had come out of the blue. Like an actor tired of playing pigeonholed roles, he'd stepped out of the part he normally played—the charmer promising a good time—and into a part that fit him surprisingly and convincingly well.

Admitting I'm physically attracted to Tai comes with little risk. To paraphrase Forrest Gump, "Pretty is as pretty does." Like Tai's tattoos, I'd tried to convince myself that his particular brand of pretty only went skin deep.

But if that's the case, then he wouldn't have treated me with such kindness and long-suffering. He wouldn't have gone the extra mile to make me feel at ease and boost my confidence to attempt something I was more than reluctant to try. Not when there was absolutely nothing in it for him but the possibility of an astronomical mechanic bill.

But none of that really matters, does it? My attraction to

him. Whether he's hiding a deep soul worth getting to know beneath his wolfish façade. The fact that I enjoyed myself an alarming amount.

None of it matters because I know exactly how things will play out if I allow myself to walk down that road at this time in my life. I can't do it. Not yet. I'm not strong enough to watch the desire dim from a man's eyes again when he looks at me after he realizes I've been stripped of basic physical features we take for granted. I'm not sure if I'll ever be strong enough to risk that again.

I pull into the library's back lot and park in the space farthest from the building, leaving the closer spaces for our patrons. There's a cloth tote full of books in the back seat that I need to return, so I grab those and make my way to the rear entrance, key in hand. Both Hayley and Martha's cars are sitting in the upper lot. Looks like my little detour to Cotton-Eyed Cup of Joe has made me a bit later than I expected. And all for nothing.

I sigh and slip the key into the deadbolt, unlock the door, then step into the dimly lit building. I lock the door behind me. There's still five minutes until we officially open.

"What have you been up to this morning?" Hayley's voice comes out of nowhere.

I give an unladylike squeal, pressing a palm against my knocking pulse. "Sheesh. You about gave me a heart attack."

Her smile is unrepentant. "Sorry."

"Sure you are. I swear you're the master of jump scares. You should hire yourself out to haunted houses around Halloween. You'd make a pretty penny."

She falls into step next to me, her grin wide. "I never beat you to work. Hot date keep you out late last night?"

A jumble of sounds clog my throat. Like Scrabble tiles being shaken in a Yahtzee cup then spilled onto a table, the letters are there to form a response, but they aren't in any intelligible order to form coherent words.

I hadn't thought about this aspect of my arrangement with Tai. Of course people are going to see us spending time together and form their own conclusions. Unless our not-a-real-date outings are beyond the city limits. Is that a stipulation I should make?

Or maybe I should let people, and Hayley especially, think we're dating. Maybe that will get her to stop dropping hints about my lack of a love life. She's been subtle so far, but I know my stance on staying single is driving her curiosity to crazy-monkey heights. Pretty soon she'll no longer be appeased by my vague answers and throw down the friendship card to try to get me to spill.

I plan to tell her about my alopecia. One day. It's not like I think she'll see me any differently, it's just . . . well . . . yeah, she might see me differently. I'm not ready to give up my anonymity and normalcy yet.

Saying I'm dating her cousin will throw her off my scent, if only for a little bit. We'll have to concoct some plan about our mutually ending the relationship once I've successfully made a few love connections and gotten to know my fellow townspeople enough not to need Tai's help anymore. I'm sure I can think of something convincing that won't paint either of us in a bad light.

"Actually—"

"What am I saying?" Hayley shakes her head. "Evangeline Kelly doesn't date." She peeks in my tote and retrieves the top book. "Your tardiness must've been caused by—" She reads the title, then looks back at me with a smirk. "Got a thing for elves and hobbits, huh? No wonder no mortal man can do it for you."

"Yes, you've found me out," I say dryly. "It's the heroes of Middle Earth for me or none at all."

She laughs as she hip-checks me. "My cousin never stood a chance."

An image of Tai in battle armor fills my imagination. He may be on the shorter side, but the definition of his muscles and the broadness of his shoulders make me think he could fill out a suit of armor nicely.

Time to think of something else.

"Did you reread the series for the book club discussion today?" Hayley asks. "I can't imagine this is the first time you've made it through Tolkien's classic."

"Third time, and yes."

Hayley returns *The Fellowship of the Ring* to my tote. "Will I lose librarian street cred if I admit that I've never read the series?"

I stop and stare at her. How could she make it through her academic career without cracking the spines of *Lord of the Rings*? Even more baffling, how could she have never read the books for sheer pleasure?

"If I had the power to fire you, I'd do so here and now." I start walking again. "I feel like I don't know you."

"I've never read a single Brontë novel either."

She's like the Luftwaffe, dropping bombs left and right.

I shake my head. "And you call yourself a librarian."

She giggles and pulls on my arm. "What were the names of those children who got lost in a wardrobe?"

I dig in my heels, my lack of movement and her grip on my arm swinging her around to face me. "The Pevensies? You've never read *The Chronicles of Narnia* either? Have you ever read *any* book?"

She looks at me, then bursts out laughing. "Oh, Evangeline, you should see your face." She hooks her arm more fully through mine. "I'm so glad you moved here. I knew the moment we met that we would be bosom friends."

"At least you've read *Anne of Green Gables*," I grumble. Honestly, I can't tell if Hayley is pulling my leg or is serious about her lack of reading.

169

"Have I? Or have I just seen the movie adaptation with Megan Follows?"

"We're open!" Martha hollers from the front of the library.

I step behind the front desk and return my books into the system, placing them on the return cart to reshelve later.

A man walks in through the glass doors and strides toward the desk as if he's on a mission. His hair is cut in a military style, his bearing one of command. Who knows, maybe a mission is exactly what he's on.

Hayley takes one look at him, squeaks like a mouse, then scurries away.

My painted-on brows jump to my artificial hairline as I watch her retreating back.

What in the world? I've never once seen Hayley run from anyone, impending general or not. If anything, I would have expected her to turn on the charm that must be a family trait and walk away with a date for the evening.

"Can I help you, sir?" I ask when he stops in front of me.

"Yes, ma'am. I'm looking for a book." His eyes dart around the shelves as if waiting for enemy combatants to jump out at any minute. "It's, uh, blue, I think?"

I offer him my most polite smile. "Do you know any other information about the book? The title or author, perhaps?"

He seems as if he's trying to recall some top-secret redacted files before shaking his head. "Sorry. I think it was military related somehow. Maybe written about or by a sergeant? My sister asked me to pick it up for my nephew, if that helps."

"So, a children's book, then?"

He nods once. "Yes, ma'am."

"Our children's section is over here." I tap my chin as I walk around the desk to direct him toward the part of the library most likely to shelf the book he's looking for. "Let's see, a children's book about a sergeant. Oh! Could you be looking for a book about Sergeant Stubby? He was a stray who became a national icon and famous war dog of World War I."

The man shakes his head. "That doesn't sound right. Do you have a book written by a sergeant? My sister mentioned a name, but I can't recall it at the moment. A Sergeant Skivvies, maybe?"

I stop walking and think. I've never heard of an author named Sergeant Skivvies. What a funny name too. Skivvies. Isn't that the military term for underwear?

Dawning comes on a wave of laughter that I manage to choke down. "Could Sergeant Skivvies be Captain Underpants?" Wouldn't Dav Pilkey, the author, get a kick out of this one.

I lead him to a book with a blue background, just as he'd said, with a comic-style grown man wearing nothing but a pair of tighty-whities and a red cape around his neck. The nearly naked cartoon on the cover is the principal of two kids who accidentally hypnotize him into becoming Captain Underpants. I pick the book up and hand it to him.

A myriad of emotions march in formation across his face as he examines the book in his hands, shock leading the charge. He glances back at me, a hint of red to his cheeks that wasn't there a moment ago. "Thank you, ma'am."

"You're welcome." I turn before the chuckle I've been suppressing makes it past my defenses. Sergeant Skivvies. Martha is going to lose it with this one when I tell her.

"Is he gone?" Hayley whisper-shouts from her hiding place behind a shelf of books about communicable diseases. I should give her a feather duster while she's back there. No one ever checks out those books. Not that I can blame them.

I peek over my shoulder. The man finishes at the self-check kiosk, then heads to the door. "He's leaving now."

Hayley visibly relaxes. "Good."

My attention snags on two spines with Dewey decimal

numbers out of order. I reach for the books to reshelve them correctly. "Care to explain what that was about?"

"Not without a pint of chocolate chip cookie dough ice cream, no."

I chuff out a laugh. "Fair enough." It would take more than ice cream for me to want to discuss Brett, so I get it.

She adjusts the hem of her shirt. "This month's book club attendees have started to arrive, by the way."

I glance at the clock on the wall. "Already? But it's not supposed to start for another twenty minutes. I haven't even set the room up yet."

Hayley shrugs and walks past me. "I'm pretty sure he won't mind helping."

The nonchalance in her voice sounds false, and my suspicion-detecting-antennae instantly rises. "He?"

"Oh, didn't I tell you? Tai loves Tolkien too."

21

Of course Tai loves Tolkien. Why wouldn't he? Everyone loves Tolkien.

Except Hayley, the possible Tolkien virgin who I can't persuade into taking over this discussion because she claims she has no idea who Legolas or Aragorn are, much less Frodo or Samwise Gamgee. Not that I want her to take over, necessarily, because I have a plan—or *had* a plan may be more apt. Not sure if I should still go through with it, as I hadn't expected an audience who was privy to what I was up to.

My immediate reaction on hearing Tai would be in attendance was a flush of pleasure and swell of anticipation. Which is a very dangerous response for my heart to have, and one I cannot under any circumstances allow myself to entertain. Because of that, I shove my unwanted delight down to the ground like a school bus bully and invite the secondary emotion simmering beneath the surface to take its spot.

Annoyance.

I resist the urge to stomp across the carpeted entry of the library toward the side room we use for community events like the monthly book club meeting. Tai Davis is becoming a thorn in my side. A fly in my coffee. A pain in my . . . well, you know where. I need to forget about his grin that momentarily makes my head spin, causing all logic to spill out of my ear. At the moment, I need every single ounce of good sense I can hold on to. It's the only thing keeping me safe from a soul-crushing repeat of humiliation from tangoing with love.

I square my shoulders, resolved to do a better job of resisting his attention. He can keep his wolfish smiles. I'm not going to become a victim like Little Red Riding Hood. There will be no eating me up.

I can't demand he leave, as this is a public community event. And loving Tolkien or not, there's no way I think he's here because he wants to debate whether Galadriel and Gandalf were ever romantically involved or whether Tolkien wrote *The Lord of the Rings* trilogy as an allegory. In the six months that I've worked here, he's never once come to a single community event the library has hosted. In fact, I'd not seen him step foot in the library before Hayley's dare. I'd been nothing but a joke to pass the time then, and it would be good for me to remember that his motives are likely the same now—I'm but a game for him to play.

As if sensing my presence in the doorway behind him, Tai pivots and faces me, his eyes lighting when he sees me.

I plant my feet and set my chin. I will not be sweet-talked into lowering my defenses again. Although maybe that's my problem. I'm always the one playing defense when it comes to Tai. Maybe I should try offense for once.

I sweep into the room as if I couldn't care less that Tai is here. As if his presence hasn't knocked me off-kilter or made me reconsider my primary objective for today's book club. I'm not going to change my plans. I'm going to double down. Two for one.

Once I'd gotten over the disappointment of this morning's meet-cute not working out like I'd hoped it would, I'd realized the day didn't have to be a total matchmaking loss. The perfect opportunity for seeds of love to be planted had already been prearranged for me.

I can picture it clearly. Two kindred spirits bonding over their love of Middle Earth. The obsession of a ring will bring them together in this room, and a ring on each of their fingers as they say "I do" will keep them together for eternity.

Which leads to another interesting possibility. I don't know why I'd never thought to matchmake Tai before, but I'm definitely thinking it now.

I steel myself against the ache of loss that shoots from my belly and radiates down my limbs. It isn't the idea of losing Tai's attention and watching him turn his flirtations on someone else that has me reacting so intensely, although I fully admit that having his intense gaze rest on me as a man interested in a woman has been a bit of a balm to my soul.

But it's not real. It's not based on truth. And neither is the empty feeling currently residing in the pit of my stomach. It's merely the aftershocks of grief. Of once again losing the idea of the possibility of love itself. Tai's waning interest is bound to happen eventually anyway. Might as well happen on my terms and on my timetable.

Might as well happen today. Here. Now.

"I didn't expect to see you at book club," I say as cordially as possible. I've never been very good at keeping my feelings off my face and developing the neutral expression Granny insists genteel Southern ladies should possess. Whatever thin façade I'm able to project, I don't doubt he can see right through it.

Tai faces me, a thick book in his hands. A smirk hovers over his lips, but he doesn't allow it to settle. The spark of amusement in his eyes, however, he's less successful in hiding.

"Why not? I hope you aren't making assumptions about me again, Miss Marion?"

Every time he calls me Miss Marion, the song "Ya Got

Trouble" from *The Music Man* pops into my head. I've got trouble with a capital *T*, and that stands for Tai Davis.

I cross my arms over my chest before I remind myself I'm no longer on the defense and drop them to my sides. "I wouldn't dream to."

He chuckles under his breath. "No, of course not." After setting the book on the waist-high counter along the wall, he opens his hands and makes a sweeping gesture around the room. "Can I help you set up?"

We spend the next few minutes unfolding chairs and placing them in a circle. I'm not sure how many people are going to attend, but we usually have about six or seven who like to get together to discuss the book of the month.

As soon as I set out the last chair, patrons begin to arrive.

"Welcome, I'm so glad you could make it." I greet each person with a warm smile. I'm not naturally an outgoing person and often have difficulty with small talk, but if the subject is books, then I'm like an imbiber who's had one too many drinks, and it's often hard to get me to shut up. "There's tea and coffee over there, so help yourselves. We'll begin in just a little bit."

I wait a few minutes after the designated start time to make sure everyone who'd wanted to participate has arrived. From my perch near the door, I watch the interactions of the others. Three people hover near the Keurig, selecting teas and talking about the weather. I recognize Ken from last month's book club when we discussed *Beneath a Scarlet Sky* by Mark T. Sullivan. He said he'd be back, and I'm glad to see it's true.

The other man I haven't seen before, but the woman looks vaguely familiar. I don't think she's ever previously participated in book club, but I've more than likely seen her around the library. Ken and the other man are probably old enough to be my father, and the woman could pass as my older sister. Could a match be made among the trio? Perhaps a May/December age gap romance? I'll have to get a look at their ring fingers to make sure there aren't any wedding bands.

Besides them, Carla is here. She's in her scrubs, which means she just got off a shift at the hospital in the next town over. She's sitting by herself, as always, a thatch of dark hair falling out of the bun at the nape of her neck and tickling her cheek as she looks down at the open book on her lap. She doesn't usually get to finish reading the books before club discussions since she works such long hours, but she's never missed a meeting.

Tai takes up residence along the opposite wall. His feet are braced shoulder-width apart, and he has his hands shoved into the front pockets of his faded jeans, his head turned to the side, giving me a perfect view of the rose on his neck.

Trouble with a capital *T* all right.

I tear my gaze away and swallow the thickness that has suddenly lodged in my throat.

Number one on my matchmaking checklist for Tai: Find a girl who is mesmerized by tattoos. Shouldn't be too hard, as his body art has a hypnotic quality to it.

"Sorry I'm late!" A woman in her late twenties with long brown hair breezes past me, leaving a trail of caramelized apple scent in her wake.

I remember Bella Johnson for two main reasons. One, her personality is as effervescent as an Alka-Seltzer tablet. It just bubbles and bubbles. Two, the cascade of thick waves that fall to the small of her back make my insides twist with unchristian-like envy.

She's the epitome of a classic fictional heroine, the well in which romance authors plunge for inspiration. She has the bright smile that lights up a room and hair the hero can't wait to run his fingers through.

I glance between her and Tai. The bad boy and the good girl. A pairing romance readers go gaga over.

Bella dumps an oversized purse on the floor by one of the chairs, then shrugs out of her jacket. It's as if a spotlight is bathing her in an aura of light. She's the star; we, her spectators.

"Did I miss anything?"

"No, we haven't started yet," I assure her.

She gives me a bright smile. "Perfect. Do you mind waiting a couple more minutes? My brother is on his way."

"No problem. Help yourself to some tea or coffee."

She spins back around and glances toward the trio loitering near the hot beverage supplies. Her quick look is like a defibrillator on their conversation, starting it back up. Instead of getting herself a cup of tea, she leans over and riffles through her large purse, straightening with a copy of *The Fellowship of the Ring* in her hand. She places it on her seat, looks up, and seems to notice Tai for the first time. She's in profile, but that doesn't eclipse the brilliance of the smile that just lit up her face.

With the confidence of a leading lady, she struts over to Tai and offers him her hand. "Hi, I'm Bella. I don't think we've met before."

It's like the cells in my body collectively shush one another. My whole body strains to hear the exchange about to happen. It's one of those defining moments. Whatever happens in the next few minutes between Tai and Bella is going to affect more than just a simple conversation.

"Tai." He shakes her hand but doesn't linger.

Why doesn't he linger? All the men in books linger more than propriety dictates when offered an opportunity to touch the heroine. Helping her alight from a carriage, assisting her off a horse, steering her in the right direction. Instead, Tai drops her fingers as soon as possible and shoves his hand back inside his pocket.

Bella pulls her thick, luscious hair over one shoulder. "Wait, are you the guy who owns the tattoo shop on the other side of town?"

"Guilty."

"I've been meaning to stop by. I've always wanted to get a tattoo right here on my shoulder." She turns slightly to present him the slope of her shoulder, then tugs on the sleeve of her shirt, exposing a column of creamy skin. She looks at him through her eyelashes in a way that has bewitched men since the beginning of time.

Tai might as well be made of stone. He doesn't so much as twitch a muscle. "Call the shop to set up an appointment and we'll see what we can work out."

What in the world is going on right now? Bella looks as confused as I feel as she lets the collar of her shirt slip back over her clavicle.

Tai isn't being rude, but he's also not being . . . well, Tai. Where are the weighty, suggestive looks? The flirty turn of phrases? The rogue-like behavior? Bella isn't exactly being subtle in showing her interest, but instead of lapping up her feminine wiles, he looks . . . bored.

He glances over her shoulder as if searching for something. When our gazes collide, the intensity in his grips me like it has fingers to hold me in place. It wasn't a *what* but a *who* he was looking for. He has the personification of femininity and every man's dreams standing in front of him, and he looked around her to find . . .

Me?

22

All I'm saying is, Tolkien could've written a few more lead female characters instead of restricting the women in the book to the margins. A female dwarf or elf as a member of the fellowship would have been nice. Or think about how the quest would've been different if either Frodo or Samwise were women." Bella waved her graceful fingers as if casting a spell on the group.

Murmurs rippled around the room.

Tai waited to see if anyone would disagree. Not that he did, per se. The three main female characters—Arwen, Eowyn, and Galadriel—each had their moments of splendor, but not well balanced with their weaker moments, and no one could argue the books weren't definitely male dominated. But . . .

"Not to play devil's advocate here—"

Evangeline muttered something under her breath, and he could only imagine it had to do with the phrase that made it sound like he was on the devil's side. She was bound and determined to cloak herself with a low opinion of him even though he was trying to prove to her he didn't deserve it. It almost made him want to live up (or down, rather) to her expectations.

There were plenty of things she'd consider bad behavior

that he could do. Things like finding a dark, empty corner of this library, pressing her against a bookshelf, and kissing her senseless. He may have let his thoughts drift there (he was no saint) and imagined how good her sassy mouth captured by his would feel, but he'd never actually do such a thing. Some might argue he was already forcing himself on Evangeline, but coming to an agreement in which she had to spend time with him was different than stealing a kiss without consent.

He speared her a pointed look, raising one of his brows. "What was that, Angel?"

"Sorry, tickle in my throat." She touched the base of her neck, feigning innocence. "Please, continue."

Bella's brother, Aiden, stood, then walked behind the circle of chairs. His hand landed on Evangeline's shoulder, and he leaned down and whispered in her ear. She gave him a small smile and mouthed *thank you* before he strode to the beverage counter and poured her a glass of water.

"As I was saying . . ." Tai pulled his thoughts away from the exchange and back to the book discussion, although he kept his focus on Aiden and Evangeline. "It makes sense that the series would be more male driven given the time period in which they were written—the 1950s—as well as the fact that Tolkien drew on his own experiences during World War One and the male bonds and camaraderie he was a part of during that difficult time."

Aiden walked back and touched Evangeline's shoulder again as he handed her the water. The man was obviously interested in her. Ever since the book club meeting had started, he'd done nothing but compliment her, steering the conversation in ways to drop clues that he found her beautiful and intelligent, essentially hitting on her in the most literary fashion. Now he was conjuring up ways to give her small touches and secret moments even though they were in the middle of a group event.

The interesting part, however, was Evangeline's response to Aiden. She'd turned Tai down point-blank when he'd asked her out. But if Tai was a dark figure in Evangeline's eyes, then Aiden should be noon on a summer's day. While Tai's tattoos and black leather apparel made him appear edgy, Aiden's whole vibe was as wholesome as a Sunday afternoon PBS special.

But she wasn't encouraging Aiden's attention any more than she had Tai's. Even though she was single. Even though she was clearly obsessed with the idea of love and romance and marriage considering the lengths she was willing to go to in order to continue her matchmaking shenanigans. Even though on the outside Aiden and Tai were opposites and therefore Aiden should be her type since she professed Tai wasn't.

Evangeline Kelly, lover of love, didn't seem to be interested in the experience for herself.

Why was that?

"That's an interesting point." Bella brushed her pink fingertips across Tai's forearm. "I hadn't considered such a thing before."

Tai shifted in his seat, the movement enough to make Bella retract her hand, but not before he noticed Evangeline's intense stare burning a hole on the spot of their connection. Emotions warred with one another on the battleground of her face. Longing with a hint of jealousy, although that last one may have been more his wishful thinking than reality. Before he could analyze further, however, her mouth firmed into a thin line of determination and she ripped her gaze away, focusing on the participants on the other side of the circle.

"Ken, Samantha, did anything else stand out to either of you as you read the books that you'd like to discuss?"

This wasn't the first time Evangeline had put Ken and Samantha in the spotlight. Never separate, though. Always together. Tai dipped his chin to hide a grin against his shoulder. She was trying her darndest to spark a flame among the library patrons. Too bad her efforts worked about as well as igniting a fire with wet wood and no matches. Ken and Samantha might've been giving each other curious eyes over by the coffee maker before the discussion began, but after arguing about the lack of diversity in the books—Samantha saying more representation was needed while Ken defended the nearly all-white cast—they'd been giving each other cool glares.

"I think I've said enough for today," Ken responded curtly.

Samantha mumbled, "More than enough."

Evangeline looked around the room with a painted smile on her face. "Well." She looked to Bella, then to Tai, then back to Bella, a calculated gleam in her eye to go along with the determined set of her shoulders.

A weight of foreboding pulled at Tai's stomach. He felt a bit like a rabbit about to be caught in a hunter's snare. Ken and Samantha weren't cooperating, so it seemed Little Miss Matchmaker was going to pour her efforts onto him.

Too bad for her, he didn't plan to be any more accommodating.

"There's always a lot of discussion about who the hero of the story is, although there's arguably more than one heroic figure within the pages." Evangeline turned her deceptive smile on Bella. "Which character would you say bears the title of true hero?"

Bella tipped her head to the side in thought. "Well, the most obvious answers would be either Frodo or Samwise. Frodo because he bore the burden of the One Ring and was willing to sacrifice himself for the good of the world. Samwise because of his loyalty and because without his help Frodo would have failed in his quest. Even Tolkien himself called Samwise the chief hero."

"That's true," Aiden added with a confirming nod.

"However." Bella flicked her gaze toward Tai. "Neither Frodo nor Samwise are the heroes I'd personally pick."

"What do you mean?" Carla asked. "Who would you choose if not one of the hobbits?"

"I know Tolkien didn't write the books as a romance, but I can't help but look for love within the pages." She shrugged her dainty shoulder. "I guess I'm a romantic at heart. So, for my book boyfriend, I'd choose—" She drew out the word to add a touch of suspense. "Gimli."

"The dwarf?" Aiden asked incredulously.

Bella notched her chin, then looked openly at Tai. "He may've been short in stature, but his presence was larger than a giant. Besides, I like that he was a little rough around the edges. Explosive, even. A man like that is exciting. Imagine what he could do with a woman."

Heat climbed up Tai's neck, and he cleared his throat before the feeling strangled him. Tai was flattered by Bella's attentions, but his interest lay elsewhere. The sooner Bella—and Aiden, for that matter—realized that, the better.

He turned his head and stared straight into Evangeline's eyes. "What do you think, Angel? Do you prefer a layered antihero who may be misunderstood and wrongly judged by the world around him or a more patent, cliched hero who's not only boring but also may be too good to be true?"

Evangeline's throat worked as she swallowed hard. She was an intelligent woman. She knew exactly what he was saying. "Oh, look at that. We're out of time." Her voice held a nervous, breathless quality as she shot to her feet. "Next month we'll be discussing *A Man Called Ove* by Fredrik Backman. There are copies at the front desk that you can check out." She turned and marched to the refreshment counter, her movements jerky as she began cleaning up. "I'll see you next month," she called over her shoulder.

Samantha was the first to gather her things and storm out

of the room—in a hurry to get away from Ken and his mildly racist comments, no doubt. Hopefully the man ruminated on the discourse and the things Samantha had said about diversity and representation in fiction and how it weighed in the world they lived in. Tai didn't think Ken even realized how his comments had sounded or that he'd acted as a microaggressor. Tai just hoped the man learned from the experience and did better in the future.

Carla took a little while longer to gather her belongings, hiding a yawn behind her hand as she exited the room, followed by Ken and his friend. That left the siblings. Bella and Aiden seemed to be in some sort of heated argument, though they kept their voices so low that Tai couldn't hear what they were saying. Finally, Aiden shook his head and sighed, turning his chin so he could look at Tai. Tai met his gaze head-on. Aiden shook his head again, but this time a smile cracked his lips.

Aiden leaned forward, resting his elbows on his knees. "Settle an argument for us. You and the librarian." He jutted his chin toward Evangeline. "Are you two together?"

When Tai didn't immediately answer, Bella swatted her brother on the arm. "See?"

Aiden held Tai's gaze a second longer. "All right, then. I'm going to throw my hat in the ring."

Tai's jaw clenched as he watched Aiden stand and saunter toward Evangeline. He wanted to bolt from his chair and block the other man's path. Tell him to back off and keep away from her. He'd never had a possessive bone in his body before, but watching the golden boy approach his Angel had his instincts spiraling toward a primitive nature. Every knock of his heart against his ribs seemed to be saying *mine, mine, mine.*

He gripped the edge of his chair to keep himself seated. He would not act the Neanderthal.

"She's a lucky woman."

Bella's voice barely made its way through the thick haze clouding his mind. With great effort, he pulled his attention away from Aiden as he leaned against the counter, chatting Evangeline up.

"Excuse me?"

"I said, she's a lucky woman. She may not realize it yet, but she is."

Tai's nostrils flared. "Because your brother is such a great guy, she should feel lucky he'd ask her out?"

Bella's lips quirked. "She's not going to go out with him."

"How do you know?"

She rolled her eyes. "Because, you handsome idiot, she's obviously already interested in someone else."

Tai just stared at her.

"You!" She flung her arm in Evangeline's direction. "She's interested in you. Gosh, men are dumb."

Tai couldn't move.

"What are you doing still sitting there? Go interrupt them. Don't let another guy hedge in on your woman."

Tai didn't need to be told twice.

23

It turned out that an interruption wasn't necessary. Even before Tai got close enough to physically separate the two by making himself a third wheel, Evangeline had already shut Aiden down. The man didn't look too dejected, however. He reached out and gently squeezed her arm, then turned to walk away.

He paused when he approached Tai. "No hard feelings, man. I had to try."

Tai couldn't blame him. Only an idiot wouldn't make a move on a woman like Angel. She was everything a man could ever want. Unpredictable enough to keep him on his toes. Sweet and sassy at the same time. She had a way about her that enchanted him. Mysteries that he wanted to explore.

Aiden clapped him on the back. "Good luck."

Evangeline glanced at Tai over her shoulder. "You still here?"

"As you can see." He leaned against the laminate countertop and folded his arms over his chest. The sleeve of his black tee rose to the top of his bicep. He opened his mouth but then shut it when he noticed her go still. Her eyes trailed the length of his arm, her cheeks flushing.

Well, well, well. Wasn't this an interesting development. He'd noticed her curiosity over his tattoos before. Each time her gaze raked over one of the artistic pieces on his body, it felt like sweet torture. A caress without being touched.

He flexed his muscles and was inordinately pleased when her throat bobbed and her breath hitched. She was not as unaffected by him as she would like him to believe. On the contrary, she seemed to be just as drawn to him as he was to her. The only difference was, she was fighting the attraction.

"See something you like, Evangeline Aphrodite Kelly?" he asked in a low, husky voice.

She licked her lips, blinked, then tore her gaze away. "I don't know what you're talking about."

He chuckled. "Sure you don't, sweetheart." He leaned closer to her and whispered, "Ask nicely and maybe I'll let you see more."

She pushed her shoulders back and gave him one of her prim Southern belle looks. "I'm not your sweetheart, and my middle name isn't Aphrodite."

"Seems to me your parents missed an opportunity."

"Why do you say that?"

He reached out and traced a finger down her jaw in a featherlight touch. "You definitely should've been named after the goddess of love and beauty."

She flushed and pulled away. "Save your flirting for a woman who will fall for such malarky."

He only heard her with half his brain. The other half was processing the feel of Evangeline's skin. He'd never felt anything so soft and smooth. Almost as if . . .

He tracked the contours of her face. The soft swell of her cheekbones down to the outline of her jaw. Every inch of skin was sleek and silky.

Tai worked on bodies every day. He knew the shape of people, the feel. The touch of coarse hair and of fine and the fact that the human form, even women's, grew the slightest amount of fuzz on their faces.

Not Evangeline.

Without thinking, Tai reached out and gently cupped her upper arm, letting his hand trail down her elegant limb until he gripped her fingertips.

"What do you think you're doing?" Her voice was thick and breathless.

Smooth as butter, every inch of her.

But now wasn't the time to puzzle out this new piece of information about his Angel. Not when she was staring at him with wide eyes, equal parts accusation and poorly concealed longing.

"Tell me your middle name."

He wasn't sure why he was so hung up on knowing her full name. There wasn't any rational reason, although there wasn't any rational reason why she'd keep it a secret from him either. Which was maybe why it was so important? Her middle name seemed to be more than just a name between them now. It signified a wall. When she finally told him, it would mean that she finally trusted him.

She took a step back in answer, and he sighed. He pushed off the counter and pivoted to stand square with her. "Just so you know, you're wasting your time trying to match me with someone else."

Her mouth opened and closed a few times before firming into a thin line. "Fine." She picked up an unused mug and replaced it on the shelf in one of the cabinets. "But if you had showed Bella even an ounce of interest, maybe turned on the charm that you so love to shower on me, then you would've had her eating out of your hand." Her hair bounced along her shoulders as she slightly shook her head. "I'm not sure why you didn't," she muttered under her breath.

"I've told you why."

Her brows furrowed, the pinched edges drawing Tai's attention.

The shape of them was lovely, but the texture . . .

He could've kicked himself for not noticing before. How had he missed it? His tattoo license should be revoked for his lack of observation. Evangeline's eyebrows were tattoos. Temporary ones, at that.

She stared at him, confusion written on her face. For goodness' sake, he needed to stop letting these revelations about her derail him so much. She was going to think he'd missed the plot completely.

He lowered his gaze to delve into the depths of her green eyes, the jeweled tone so rich an emerald would be jealous. "Despite what you think, I'm not a flirtatious man by nature. I only act this way with you. You bring out whatever charm you see in me."

He let his words sink in, hoping that she heard him this time.

"What about you?" he finally asked.

She tilted her head. "What about me?"

"Aiden seems like a *nice* guy." Maybe it was petty to emphasize the word *nice*. Draw attention to the fact that she didn't think Tai could claim the character trait. "Why don't you take your own advice? Why don't you turn your matchmaking energy on yourself?"

The same look of longing he'd noticed in her expression earlier returned, dampened, however, by a veil of hurt and fear. Tai recognized the look. He recognized it because it was one he'd worn himself once upon a time. When he'd first considered defying his mother's wishes. When he'd contemplated living in the moment instead of by the fears of what could happen. He'd yearned for the freedom and independence to try new things and gain new experiences while simultaneously being held back by years of ingrained anxiety. But he'd had to let that fear go. He'd had to take a leap into the living instead of watching from the safety of the sideline.

"I already told you. I don't date." She said it with such finality, as if slamming the door not only on the conversation but on her love life. Forever.

But Tai wasn't ready to let the topic drop. "Why?"

"That's none of your business."

"I disagree. I think it is very much my business."

"You presume too much."

"I'm sorry to have to disagree again, but from my perspective, I presume just the right amount. No matter how much you play that you don't understand what I mean, I know you do. Because you are one of the smartest, cleverest people I've ever met."

Tai stepped in front of her, blocking any escape. He could see it in her eyes, the desire to flee. From him. From the conversation. From the truth right in front of her face.

She took a step back, but her retreat was halted by the counter. Their bodies lined up in perfect symmetry only inches apart. Enough space to keep things professional in her place of work but close enough that he could feel the heat coming off her. The exhale of her breath across the sensitive skin of his lips. When she moved her hand to press it against her stomach, the back of her fingers grazed his own middle, causing his abdominal muscles to tighten in response. Thickness built in his throat, but he wasn't done saying what he needed to say.

"So," he finally continued once he got himself under control. "You know it's my business why you choose to date or not because you know that's what I want. A relationship. With *you*. But you say I'm bad and, heaven help me, maybe I am. Maybe I am bad because I'd do anything to be with you, to spend time with you."

He had more to say. More in his heart that he was willing to split open and lay bare for her. But her lips parted, and the small movement scattered his thoughts with the force of a tornado. He could focus on nothing but the plump fullness in front of him. The swell and curve of her mouth. His heart was knocking that familiar rhythm again, chanting *mine, mine, mine.*

A sharp knock sounded, causing Evangeline to squeak and dash around him.

"Evangeline? You in here?" an unfamiliar female voice said from the direction of the door.

"Penelope? What are you doing in Little Creek?"

Tai ran his fingers through his hair, tugging at the ends. He took a few deep breaths before he turned around. He felt he'd been thrown in a wood chipper, and he needed a few quiet moments to put himself back in order.

A woman who resembled Evangeline in the shape of her face and the slope of her nose stood in the threshold, her eyes wide as she flicked her gaze between Evangeline and Tai.

"I'm sorry, I didn't mean to interrupt," her mouth said while her look with Evangeline communicated so much more.

Evangeline flushed. "You didn't interrupt anything."

Tai vehemently disagreed, but he stayed silent.

"This is Tai, by the way." She waggled her fingers in his general direction.

Taking his cue, Tai stepped forward and held out his hand. "Tai Davis."

"Penelope." She placed her hand in his. "Evangeline's sister."

"It's nice to meet you."

She took his measure in a single glance as if she were accustomed to weighing and sorting men within seconds of their introduction. As always, he knew the conclusions people jumped to when they first laid eyes on him, heavily inked with a preference for dark clothing. He expected Penelope to follow along the same line of thought her sister had, so when she responded by saying, "It's very nice to meet you as well, Tai," and then gave her sister a knowing and approving grin, Tai was stunned.

"You know I always love seeing you, sis, but I didn't expect you here today."

"I can see that." Penelope waggled her brows not so subtly in his direction.

He held in a snort of laughter. Looked like he had an unexpected ally on his side.

Evangeline squirmed a little where she stood, obviously uncomfortable with the implications her sister was hinting at. Taking pity on her, Penelope opened the large purse slung over her shoulder and pulled out a gallon-sized Ziploc bag filled with what appeared to be old letters.

Evangeline sucked in a breath. "Are those Grampie and Granny's love letters?"

Penelope handed over the storage bag, and Evangeline cradled the aged envelopes with the care a newborn baby would receive.

Penelope pulled out a folded sheet of paper and handed that over as well. "And this is the guest list. I thought I'd bring them both by and drop them off so you can get started on the invitations and decorations." She turned to Tai. "We're planning a big party to celebrate our grandparents' fiftieth wedding anniversary."

Evangeline looked up from the list of names. "You didn't have to drive out here. I was planning on coming to visit this weekend."

Penelope shifted her weight. "I was going to be in the area anyway."

"Really? You? In Little Creek?"

Tai got why Evangeline was incredulous. Her sister had on a pair of expensive-looking stilettos, a pantsuit that was probably tailor-made for her, and the oversized purse hanging from her shoulder was definitely designer. The residents of Little Creek usually shopped for their clothes at the nearest Walmart.

"I have an appointment later today, if you must know. And before you ask, no, I'm not going to tell you where. I don't want a preemptive lecture."

"You aren't going to one of your and Grampie's murder sites, are you?

Tai choked on his spit. Murder? He looked at Penelope again, trying to picture her with some sort of weapon in her hands.

"No, and you're scaring your friend," Penelope chided her sister.

"Good." Evangeline grinned unrepentantly.

Penelope rolled her eyes and turned to Tai. "Don't worry, neither my grandfather nor I are hardened criminals. We just have an unusual hobby."

Evangeline snorted as she pulled out her phone, unlocked it, then opened her camera app and scrolled. She tapped the screen, then turned the device so Tai could look at a picture. "They re-create real crime scenes in miniature."

So many thoughts crowded Tai's mind, but what he managed to squeak out was "Impressive."

"Thank you." Penelope clasped her hands in front of her. "I'm not going to tell you where the appointment is beforehand, Evangeline, but I am going to ask you to go with me. I might need some support while I'm there."

"Way to make me die of curiosity."

"Sorry." Penelope smiled before rotating on her heels to face Tai. "It was nice to meet you. Maybe we'll run into each other again sometime."

"Maybe we will."

24

Tai wasn't one to consult Dr. Google about health conditions or treatments. Probably because his mother had spent years sending him articles from various medical sites. Some reputable while others . . . well, not so much.

His cell phone vibrated in his hands, a text coming in. He looked at the top of the screen to the drop-down notification and grunted. Case in point.

Mom

Read this article on ASHMI, an anti-asthma herbal medicine intervention. It's an herbal combination from Chinese medicine to help improve asthma.

If he scrolled up, he would see similar links from her touting the effectiveness of acupuncture, essential oils, anti-inflammatory diets, and a whole host of other remedies she thought he should try. It wasn't that he was against alternative medicine, but there did seem to be a problem when the average Joe who hadn't even graduated high school thought he knew more than a licensed pulmonologist who had studied, specialized, and devoted their entire professional life to lung health.

He swiped out of the messenger app without clicking on the link, opening instead the previous webpage he'd been looking at.

Alopecia, he read. An autoimmune disorder in which the immune system attacked hair follicles. Some people experienced balding in spots. Others, a total loss of hair on their scalp. And for some, he read on, a complete loss of hair across the entirety of their bodies. Alopecia universalis was a rare condition, and less than ten percent of people who experienced the disorder ever had their hair grow back.

Tai glanced up from his phone as a few of the questions he'd pondered about Angel fell into place. The reason she wore a wig. Why her skin was smoother and softer than a newborn babe's, not a hair in sight.

She had an autoimmune disease.

He read on, wanting to know if alopecia caused any other symptoms autoimmune disorders were known for. Did she experience pain, fatigue, or recurring fevers?

He clicked on another article and read some more. The band across his chest lightened. Beyond the loss of hair, it didn't seem that alopecia came with a host of other symptoms.

There also wasn't currently a cure.

"Doesn't matter," Tai said out loud even though there wasn't another soul with him at the shop. He stopped himself from uttering the words *it's just hair* because he realized it wasn't *just* hair. So much more was affected by the loss. Self-esteem, confidence, belonging, image, and probably a lot more that he couldn't even begin to think of.

He put his phone down and picked up a sketchpad and set of charcoal pencils. His fingers had been itching to draw ever since he'd left the library, his mind going over and over every detail of Evangeline's face. The curve of her brow and how it would look without the temporary tattoo's painted lines. The radiance of her eyes and the details of the different shades of green in her irises that would shine even without the frame of lashes. The contours and elegant lines of her head and neck if she were to go without her wig. He could see it in his mind's eye, and he had an insatiable need to get the stunning image onto paper.

His phone vibrated again, this time his calendar alerting him that there was ten minutes before his appointment arrived. He needed to make sure his equipment was ready to go.

The front door opened, a familiar voice drifting to the back of the shop. "I can't believe you're getting a tattoo, Penelope."

Just hearing the lilt with which Evangeline spoke caused a reaction in his bloodstream. Equal parts thrill for the adventure before him and a sense of settling in. It was like running a river in his kayak for the first time. He never really knew what lay around the next bend, but he also never felt more alive or that he was where he belonged.

"Oh, don't get judgmental on me, Evangeline. And don't pretend you don't like tattoos. I saw the way you salivated at Tai's ink back at the library."

"Shh. He might hear you."

"So what? I saw the way he looked at you too. What's the problem?"

"You know what the problem is."

"Evangeline—"

"Let's not get into it now. Tai could come out from the back somewhere at any moment."

Now he'd need to wait a few minutes so the ladies wouldn't suspect he'd overheard their conversation.

"Oh, wow. Look at these drawings. Do you think Tai's the artist?"

He pictured them in front of the wall where he'd hung

framed pieces he'd done of local history. A Cherokee chief. A war-battered Confederate soldier. An eighteenth-century Scots-Irish immigrant. He'd practiced art in multiple mediums and a variety of styles, but he particularly loved the details and emotions evoked in the human face.

"I've never seen any of his work, but I imagine so."

"You've never seen his work? Evangeline, you need to look up his social media account. That man is super talented. It's why I chose to get my tattoo here instead of from one of the artists in Chattanooga. His realism will take your breath away."

Tai figured it was as good a time as any to make his presence known. He slipped his hands inside his pants pockets and stepped around the wall separating the reception area from his workstation.

"Evening, ladies."

Evangeline spun around first, a splash of pink highlighting her cheeks.

"I'm not sure why I didn't put two and two together earlier," he said to Penelope.

"I was thinking the same thing. Although, in my defense, your social media accounts are under the shop name and the only photos are of your work. Not a selfie among the lot."

Tai hooked a thumb over his shoulder. "You want to come on back and we can get started?"

The women trailed him as he did an about-face and made his way back to his workstation. He patted the adjustable black leather chair that he'd set up to lie flat. Penelope had said she'd wanted her tattoo on her hip, so she'd need to lie on her back for the session. "Climb on up."

While Penelope got situated, Tai dragged a rolling chair from across the room and set it on the opposite side from where he'd be working. "Go ahead and have a seat, Angel."

"Angel?" Penelope asked, her voice curious and a little shocked.

"A nickname," Tai supplied.

"I figured as much. Also, very interesting."

"Not that interesting," Evangeline argued. She looked around the shop, eyes wide. There was a pretty good chance this was the first time she'd stepped foot in a tattoo parlor. She probably had some preconceived notions of what the interior would look like, but by the look on her face, Inked by Design was nothing like she'd expected.

Tai hid his chuckle under his breath and reached for the printout of the design he'd drawn for Penelope's tattoo. He handed it to her. "Are you still good with the design? Any tweaks you want me to make before we put it on your skin?"

Penelope studied the picture he'd drawn using the design software on his tablet. Liquid pooled in her eyes, and she blinked the emotion away. "It's perfect."

"Can I see?" Evangeline held out her hand, curiosity tilting her lips.

Penelope sniffed and handed the paper over.

Evangeline blinked, her features softening. She reached out and squeezed her sister's hand. "It's beautiful. Mama would've loved it."

Penelope dabbed at the corner of her eye. "Our mother loved butterflies. All butterflies, really, but she had a particular fondness for the blue morpho. They're rare—endangered, actually—and can only be seen in Central and South America. One day, she was feeling desperately alone—I don't remember why exactly, but that was never the important part of the story. Anyway, she was feeling alone and invisible and unloved. Then she looked up and there it was. A blue morpho butterfly sitting pretty as you please on the cone of a black-eyed Susan. She said it was like God had spoken to her through that butterfly. He was telling her that He saw her, that she was never alone, and that she was deeply loved."

"That's beautiful," Tai whispered. He walked quietly away

to prepare the stencil as the sisters gripped each other's hands. He came back a few minutes later, stencil ready. "Still want it above your right hip bone?"

Penelope lay down on her back. She raised the hem of her shirt, exposing a couple of inches of her midriff. The band of her pants was elastic, and she tugged it down until the ridge of her hip bone was uncovered. "Right here." She pointed to where her skin sloped from her hip toward her bikini line.

Tai prepped the area, then applied the stencil. The ink he'd need was already arranged on his workstation. He pulled on a pair of black medical-grade disposable gloves and picked up his tattoo gun. When he switched the machine on, a buzz filled the air. "Ready?"

Penelope let out a deep breath. "Ready."

Tai dipped the tops of the needles into the container of black ink. He'd work on the outline and shading before adding color. Pulling Penelope's skin taut, he began the work of inserting ink into her body.

People reacted differently the first time they felt a line being pulled across their skin. Some screamed a stream of curse words. Some cried. Some shook uncontrollably. Penelope did none of those things. She set her jaw and lay as still as a statue.

"You're doing great," Tai encouraged.

"Like the queen you are." Evangeline beamed at her sister.

Penelope grinned back at Evangeline. "Takes one to know one." She rolled her head to look at Tai. "Sorry. You probably have no idea what we're talking about."

Evangeline blanched. "Penelope, I don't think—"

"Our father said his daughters would grow up to be queens, so he gave us middle names after great British female monarchs. Mine is Elizabeth, and Evangeline's is Victoria."

Tai lifted the tattoo gun, then pinned a look on his Angel. "Evangeline Victoria Kelly." His grin grew. This was better than any of the names he'd guessed. No wonder she hadn't wanted to tell him. "Wasn't Victoria the one madly in love with Prince Albert?"

"You know she was." Evangeline crossed her arms over her chest and huffed.

Penelope looked between them. "Now I feel like I'm the one out of the loop."

Tai dipped the machine to gather more ink. "After your sister learned my middle name, she refused to tell me hers."

"Why wouldn't you tell him?" Penelope asked. She sucked in a hiss as Tai put the needle back to her skin.

"Does it hurt?" Evangeline stared intently, looking both worried and spellbound.

Penelope threw her a disgruntled look. "It feels like I'm getting stabbed over and over again. Not exactly a day at the spa." She exhaled through her nose. "But back to the topic at hand. Why wouldn't you tell him your middle name?"

Evangeline sealed her lips. She turned her head so she was looking at the opposite wall. Finally, her mouth moved, but just barely, and she couldn't be heard over the vibrations of the tattoo machine.

"What was that?"

She flung her arms out wide in frustration. "I said, he'd read too much into it."

"My middle name is Albert," Tai supplied helpfully—and maybe a bit smugly.

Penelope's mouth formed an O. "You're Albert." She pointed at Tai. "And you're Victoria." She pointed at her sister.

"No," Evangeline ground out. "I'm Evangeline, and he's Tai. They're just names. They don't mean *anything*."

"She's playing hard to get," Tai said to Penelope.

Penelope nodded. "She does that. Especially since—" She cut herself off.

Tai wanted to ask *since what*, but he knew he wouldn't get

an answer out of either of the sisters. He chose instead to pretend he didn't hear the beginning of the sentence.

"I'm sure she just didn't want to encourage me. Although there's nothing she could do to *dis*courage me."

Penelope seemed to study him for several long minutes. "Good," she finally said. "My sister isn't easily won, but she's worth the effort."

Tai pierced Evangeline with his gaze. "I'd go so far as to say that she's worth *everything*."

25

hy are you punishing yourself? If you ask me, Brett did a fine job of that all on his own. You didn't deserve it then from his hand, and you certainly don't deserve it now from your own."

"I'm not punishing myself." *I'm protecting myself.*

But Penelope doesn't get it. She thinks I'm being stubborn. She doesn't understand that I'm hanging on by a thread, the last string of my self-preservation.

The truth is, I'm not as strong as she is. If our roles were reversed, if she'd been the one to develop alopecia and lose her hair and the man who was supposed to promise to love her in sickness and in health, she wouldn't have let the knocks keep her down. She would've found a way to rock her baldness—in a sophisticated, ladylike way, of course.

But I'm weak. I'm weak, and as Tai has pointed out, I care what other people think of me. I don't want to be whispered about behind my back. I don't want to be pitied or treated differently. I don't want people's opinions to change when they see me without a wig.

I don't want Tai to look at me differently.

I'm weak because I crave the way his eyes darken with desire when they capture my own. I've sworn off love for myself because I can't go through the pain of watching that flare of interest in a man's eyes dim again. Yet every secret smile, every flirtatious remark, no matter how disingenuous I might tell myself it is, has been slowly filling a corner of my empty heart.

I'm weak because I don't want to go back to when that corner of my soul was a dried-up well. I'm weak, and I'm stuck. I don't want to go back, but I can't allow myself to move forward. Either direction would be like pulling a plug and watching everything that has been filling me up drain away once more.

"Give me one good reason. One good reason that doesn't include Brett in any sort of way."

"If you're so obsessed with the man then why don't you date him?"

"He's not my type."

"But he's mine?"

"The reason he's not my type but he's yours is the same. The man has eyes only for you, Evangeline. Listen to me. Any man who looks at you the way Tai does is your type."

Pressure has been building in my chest ever since this conversation started. Now I feel as if my lungs are going to explode if Penelope doesn't change the topic. I grasp at anything that might make her stop acting like a hound dog on a hot trail.

"He's blackmailing me." The words explode from my mouth.

Penelope's face darkens as she goes completely still. "What did you say?" Thunderclouds roll behind her eyes.

I wince. I really shouldn't have opened my big, fat mouth. "Well, it's more like we struck up a bargain than blackmail in its strictest sense. But don't worry about it. Just . . . maybe now you can stop singing his praises and trying to get me to throw myself at him."

"Oh, I'm going to do a lot more than worry about it," she seethes.

Gosh she's scary when she gets like this. I'm almost afraid to ask. . . . "What are you going to do?"

Her nostrils flare. "I don't know yet, but I'm not going to just sit here. I should've protected you from Brett. This is my chance for a do-over."

I set my hand on her arm. "Don't."

She eyes my hand holding her back. "Why not? What aren't you telling me?"

I have no choice. Unless I tackle Penelope to the ground and physically keep her from marching out the door in a crusade for my honor, I have to tell her the whole story.

So, I do. I start with Mrs. Goldmann and how her love story had given me the idea to do a little matchmaking of my own. How Tai had discovered what I'd been up to, the mess I'd made of my first attempt as a marriage broker, and the deal we'd struck. By the time I'm done, Penelope is clutching her middle, simultaneously laughing and groaning.

"Oh man, laughing is hurting the tattoo." She peaks down to where her new tattoo is wrapped in a protective layer of clear plastic. Her mirth recedes, her eyes shining for another reason.

My own heart swells when I look at the blue morpho butterfly permanently inked into her skin. If I didn't know any better, I'd think the winged insect merely rested on Penelope's hip. That at any moment its vibrant indigo wings will beat and it'll take flight.

"This actually makes me like him even better."

"Not big on consent without a little arm-twisting first, are you." I scoff because that's the reaction I need to maintain. The unaffected front.

She makes a derisive raspberry sound with her lips. "Please. That's not even close to what this is."

I fold my arms protectively across my chest. "Oh really? Then what is this exactly?"

She places both of her hands on my shoulders and looks deep into my eyes. "This is a chance. For you to see beyond yourself. Beyond the mirror and your reflection."

"Are we having a *Mulan* moment here?" I attempt to joke, but it falls flat.

"I'm being serious. The way I see it, he's given you the gift of time. Something you wouldn't allow yourself to have on your own."

I don't answer because, honestly, I don't know what to say to that.

"Tell me truthfully. Have you hated every minute you've been forced to be in his company, or have you been making excuses to keep your walls up?"

She doesn't understand. I need those walls. If they come down, they're going to come down on my head and crush me.

"You don't have to say anything. I already know the answer." She drops her hands and reaches for her purse. "Thanks for coming with me tonight."

"Of course," I say, but it comes out weak, like I'd just run a marathon. An emotional marathon, to be more precise.

Penelope stops with her hand on the knob of my front door. She looks back at me over the top of her shoulder. "You should bring him to Grampie and Granny's party. I think they'd like him, although the real prize would be the look on Brett's face at seeing you two together."

"I'll think about it," I say because I know that's what she wants to hear.

"Love you, sis."

"I love you too."

She walks out, and I shut the door behind her, leaning back on the wood as my body sags.

How have I gotten myself here? How have I let my plan—my life—get so muddled? I was supposed to stay along the edges, not get caught in the fray. I was supposed to be ordinary, unremarkable, invisible.

What am I supposed to do? No way forward. No way back.

Kitty Purry scrambles out from under the couch. She always hides when people come over. Except she hadn't when Tai had arrived. Huh. Strange, that.

She comes over and butts her head against my shin. I reach down and pick her up, snuggling her soft fur against my cheek. She starts to purr, the sound and vibration comforting.

I resettle us on the couch, and she curls in a ball on my lap. With one hand, I stroke the top of her head and with the other I reach up and hook my fingers under my wig, pulling the hairpiece off my scalp. I set it on the couch beside me, making sure the strands are lying correctly and won't get tangled.

I'm feeling vulnerable and fragile so I know I shouldn't but I also can't help myself. I pull out my phone and open the camera app, then switch the lens to selfie mode. My face is framed in the screen, staring back at me. I've studied my reflection before. Mostly from the way Brett must have seen me.

At first, my hair had come out in patches. Big clumps pulled away from my scalp in fistfuls in the shower, clogging the drain. Half dollar–sized perfect circles of smooth skin surrounded by long tresses. In the beginning, I could hide the bald spots by how I arranged my hair. With a strategically placed bobby pin and some hairspray, no one was the wiser.

But the hair kept falling out, the bald spots multiplying. The strands of hair still clinging to my head appeared thin and scraggly. With tears streaming down my face, I'd eventually taken a razor to the last thin wisps.

When I'd first developed the condition, Brett had looked at me with concern. He'd held my hand as the doctor inserted multiple injections of steroids into my head with a sharp needle. But my hair didn't grow back. We tried other treatments. I got balder. Brett's concerned looks turned to antipathy, then distaste and finally revulsion. There came a point when he couldn't even bring himself to look at me at all. When he'd called off the wedding and asked for his ring back, he'd done so while staring down at his hands.

I take a deep breath and try to push those memories and the feelings they stir up back down. I realize how I see myself is so tainted and wrapped up with how Brett saw me. It's hard to trace the slope of the naked dome of my head without the same sick-to-my-stomach feeling that I felt the last time Brett let his gaze touch me, his mouth pulled down in disappointment and eyes darting away as fast as they could in aversion.

I thrust up my chin and stare into my eyes. My eyes are unchanged. They're still the color of an Irish meadow after a spring rain. At least that's how Grampie describes them. My lips, they're the same too. Although maybe a little sadder. A little more reserved and not as free to laugh as easily as they once were. My cheekbones, my nose, my chin. I recognize each feature. With a bracing breath, I force my gaze higher and wider. I take in the whole picture of my face instead of each of its individual attributes.

I know what Brett saw, but for the first time I ask myself, *What do* you *see, Evangeline?*

I wait, silent, hoping for an epiphany. For some lightning strike of brilliance and self-realization.

But nothing comes. Inside, I still feel . . . blank.

What would Tai see?

The thought comes unbidden, and I hate that it crosses my mind. Not wanting to give it a second of consideration, I exit the camera app and take a deep, cleansing breath.

Kitty Purry stretches out a paw, her claws extending and retracting as she sets her tiny pads on my thigh and begins to knead.

I switch over to a social media app to search for Inked by Design. The photo Tai had snapped of Penelope's butterfly is the first picture in his feed. I have to agree with my sister that the man is insanely talented.

Instead of browsing his newest posts first, I flick my thumb over my screen, causing the tiles of pictures to roll like the *Price Is Right* wheel. Finally, the scrolling slows and stops. I click on the last picture so it will enlarge and fill my whole screen. Then, I scroll much more slowly, studying each tattoo he's posted like it's a priceless work of art hanging in a museum.

There are pictures of animal tattoos like the one he'd done on Penelope. Details so intricate I almost convince myself I am looking at the real thing. The flowers he's created on people's skin make me think of something you'd see in a botanical garden. I can almost smell the sweet, floral fragrance from one woman's peony tattoo.

My breath hitches as the familiar outlines of a particular full sleeve tattoo unfold before my eyes. Penelope had been wrong. Tai did have a picture of himself on his social media feed—or at least a picture of his fully inked arm.

I'd only been able to get glimpses here and there. Little pieces when he'd shed his jacket and had a T-shirt on underneath. But I'd never been able to see the whole piece to its full effect before. Along the outside of his forearm is the negative space of a cross, rays of sunburst light shooting ethereally out from behind the center of the crossbeams. Almost resting on top of the cross is a dove with its wings stretched out in flight. The ink wraps his arm in clouds and wisps. On his upper arm is a majestic lion with a full mane in black and white. The only color are the cerulean blue eyes that appear kind and inviting. I can almost hear him telling me, as Aslan did to Lucy in *The Chronicles of Narnia*, "Courage, dear heart." Nestled off to the side is a baby lamb curled serenely in slumber.

Tai Davis, the town's reputable bad boy, has the redemption story memorialized on his body for the world to see.

Conviction sits uncomfortably on my chest, and I squeeze

my eyes shut. In order to protect myself, I've tried to judge Tai's story by his cover.

And that's only conviction number one.

I'm sorry, God, I pray as I let my chin fall to my chest. I've been so hurt. I've wallowed. I've blamed even God.

All my life I've called Him Father, myself His daughter. Learned in church that as a father, He delights in giving good gifts to His children. But what good gift did He give me but disfigurement and heartbreak?

I didn't consciously turn my back on Him, but I see now that's what I've done all the same.

I'm sorry.

Kitty Purry hops down from my lap, then stretches, her front paws in two straight lines in front of her, her bum sticking high in the air as she yawns.

"I'll get your dinner in just a second," I assure her. I scroll through Tai's feed a bit more before pausing on a picture that causes my heart to stutter in my chest. It's a collage, the same woman in each photo but taken from different angles.

She's bald. And she's *beautiful*.

26

I don't know how many times I've looked at the photo of the bald woman with the henna tattoo on her head on Tai's social media page, but every time I do, a surge of strength pulses through me. The caption under the photo says it all: *Beautiful. Brave. A warrior off to battle.* Tai had given this woman armor as she'd marched off to fight cancer.

You can be just as brave. You can be just as beautiful, a small voice whispers to me whenever I look at her radiant, smiling face daring the world to contradict her.

I don't believe the voice yet. There are still doubts. Weeds left too long that have grown roots too deep to dig out in a day.

But it's a start, I think. A small hope that even though I'm stuck now, maybe I won't be stuck forever. Maybe one day when I look at my reflection, I won't see myself through Brett's eyes.

Anticipation hums through my veins. I temper the feeling but don't quash it completely like I would've even a day ago. Tai will be here in a few minutes to take me to the baseball game, and I've accepted the truth that I've known all along but didn't want to admit—he's one-hundred-percent hero material. Maybe slightly morally gray with the whole I'll-help-you-but-only-if-you-go-out-with-me thing, and I'm sticking to my guns about him being a rake, although maybe a less philandering one since he swears he flirts only with me. But that just means he's layered. Three-dimensional and full-bodied. Like the best heroes are.

My character status, however . . .

Well, it's still a little less certain. I'm still not a heroine. But that quiet voice inside my head whispers back, *yet*. I'm not a heroine *yet*. But the possibility is there when I've not seen it since losing my hair and Brett leaving me.

I've decided I'm going to approach today as a heroine practice day. Kind of like trying on a pair of shoes and seeing how they fit. What will allowing myself to step into center stage of my own life feel like? Tailor-made or forever the wrong size?

The doorbell rings just as I finish dabbing on a little lip gloss. Kitty Purry lifts her head from where she's curled up on my pillow, blinks at me, then goes back to her nap.

I've forgone my usual pencil skirt in favor of a pair of skinny jeans but have donned my usual bookish tee. This one sports Louisa May Alcott's famous quote, *She is too fond of books, and it has turned her brain.*

I grab my purse, which has a loaded Kindle in it because I don't leave the house without reading material and I can't see myself paying attention to the game for nine straight innings, then I open the door. Tai stands there in a pair of dark jeans that hug his hips and an Atlanta Braves jersey that makes him look like he should be the newest draft to the team. A baseball cap with the franchise's signature tomahawk is settled on his head. He flicks the flat brim up and sweeps a glance down my body.

I flush, warmth filling every pore as he scans the length of me.

"This won't do at all," he says softly as he takes a step forward, invading my space.

It's disconcerting how close our faces are, how our bodies

line up perfectly. How each of my muscles immediately goes taut simply because of his proximity. Awareness tingles down my spine like old friends recently reunited.

I should take a step back. Or maybe not? Heroines stand their ground, don't they?

Slowly and without breaking eye contact, Tai lifts his hand and removes his hat. His inky hair shines in the morning sunlight. Despite how much I hate reading the phrase in books, I really do want to run my fingers through his hair right now. I'm not sure of his intent until I feel the band of his cap touch the top of my wig.

All thoughts of how his hair would feel between my fingers vanish. Panic pulses in surging waves. My eyes widen. My heart pounds. My breathing labors. Any second the hat or his hand is going to knock my wig askew or pull it off completely. When that happens, it'll be like I'm standing naked in front of him.

I can't let him see me like that.

I can't.

The palm of his other hand gently slides against the side of my neck and anchors me to the spot, cutting off my escape. His eyes still haven't left mine. It's as if they're saying *It's okay. Trust me.*

I don't have time to make a decision because a second later the hat is settled on my head. My wig didn't so much as shift. My secret is still safe. Tears of relief stab at the back of my eyes, but I blink them back.

Tai smiles softly, releasing his hold on me and taking a step back. "There. Have to show team spirit in the stands."

"Th-thank you," I stammer, still trying to get ahold of myself. This heroine practice day is off to a seriously rocky start.

"It looks good on you."

I smile my thanks and follow him to his car, where he opens the door for me.

Once we turn out of my driveway, I think I've pulled myself together enough to talk without stuttering.

"Are you a big baseball fan?" There. That came out in a perfectly normal pitch.

"My childhood dream was to play professionally."

I remember watching him at the game I'd attended to get intel on Dalton. He'd been the best player out on the field. "What happened?"

"An asthma attack between second and third base," he says casually, the same way he'd state that he'd simply changed his mind.

For the next 110 miles we talk about baseball. How he never fell out of love with the sport and how he'd felt the first time he'd picked up a bat as an adult and overcome a decade of being denied the opportunity to play. I tell him the story of how my parents met at a professional game and were victims of the kiss cam. I love the story, but I can't help the sadness that creeps in. I can't help but wonder what my mom would say to me if she were here now.

"Are you okay?" Tai asks, observant to my change in mood.

"I just miss them. Which is silly because they died when I was so young that I don't even have any memories of them. Just the stories my grandparents have told me."

"That's not silly."

He doesn't ask me how they died, but I find myself wanting to tell him anyway. "My father always had an interest in aviation and was taking flying lessons at a small municipal airport so he could get his pilot's license. My mom went with him and his teacher on one of his training flights. Something went wrong with the plane and, well, it crashed. The three of them lost their lives that day."

Tai reaches over the center console and squeezes my hand. "I'm so sorry."

After a moment, he returns his grip to the steering wheel,

leaving me to wrestle with the unexpected disappointment that follows being bereft of his touch.

The drive should have felt long and tedious, but before I know it, Tai is pulling his car into a parking garage near Truist Park. People are making their way to the entrance, and we join the melee. The attendant scans the QR code on Tai's phone for our tickets, and we push our way through the turnstile and into the stadium proper.

"Should we hit the concession stand now before the game starts or sometime between one of the innings?" Tai eyes a large box of Cracker Jack that one of the other spectators is holding.

Tai's tough guy shell is hiding a five-year-old little boy at its center. It might as well be Christmas morning for the excitement buzzing off of him.

"I think the correct answer to that question is yes, both, and all of the above."

He beams when he looks at me. "A woman after my own heart."

He's joking. I know he doesn't mean anything by the words. It's just a saying. I shouldn't let myself read into it, but I'm overly sensitive today. Reflection and soul-searching will do that to a person. And now that I've started, it doesn't seem that I can stop. Do I *want* to be a woman set after Tai Davis's heart?

I blink and notice Tai is ten feet in front of me, beelining for a vendor. I hurry to catch up and arrive at his side at the same time he exchanges a crisp bill for two boxes of Cracker Jack.

Tai turns and holds out a box to me. "Take me out to the ball game, take me out with the crowd," he sings with a grin.

I roll my eyes as I grab the box, but he doesn't let go. Instead, he raises his brows expectantly.

"Isn't this song saved for the seventh-inning stretch?" I do *not* want to sing. Granny says I sound like a frog that's just been stepped on any time I try to carry a tune.

Tai shakes the box and grins wider. He still has that five-year-old little boy look about him, and I find that I can't disappoint a younger Tai.

"Buy me some peanuts and Cracker Jack, I don't care if I never get back."

If I thought he'd been beaming at me before, then I don't know what the look he's directing at me now is. It radiates over me, casting me in a warm glow.

It's joy, I finally settle on. And delight. Tai Davis delights in . . . me.

He tugs me along, and we find our seats behind home plate. I try to get comfy in the pull-down plastic chair and count my blessings that at least they aren't metal bleachers. The players from each team come onto the field and line up in front of their dugouts, hats over their hearts as a local musician sings the national anthem. "Play ball!" is shouted, and the crowd cheers.

I've never been much of a baseball fan, but I have to admit that seeing a game in person is a lot different than watching one on TV. There's an energy to the crowd that's hard to ignore, and I find myself cupping my hand over my mouth and yelling in protest along with other fans when a runner is called out when he was clearly safe. Well, it was clear to everyone who wanted him to get the run, anyway.

Tai grins at my enthusiasm. He pops a handful of caramel-coated popcorn and peanuts into his mouth. It's the start of the fifth inning, and the Braves are jogging to take their places on the field.

"So, how's the matchmaking been going? Anyone fall in love yet?" He smirks in my direction. Probably because he somehow knows no one has been cooperating with my plans.

I shake out some popcorn into a cupped hand. "Not yet, but I'm still working on it."

"Not one to give up, huh?"

"No."

"You and I have that in common then." His attention is fixed on me, and I can't pretend to not grasp his meaning—that he also is not going to give up on the idea of us together.

"I'm not heroine material," I blurt out of seemingly nowhere. My hand shoots to my mouth, scattering popcorn everywhere, but the damage is done. I can't unsay the words.

Tai's taken aback but recovers quickly. "Pardon?"

I lower my hand and clear my throat. "In answer to your question of what life lesson I have learned the hard way. That's the lesson I've learned. I'm not heroine material."

He blinks and visibly collects himself. "I thought you'd either forgotten the questions or had decided to ignore them entirely." He shifts his body in his seat and squares off with me, his hands rising to hold the sides of my face and force me to look him in the eyes.

"Now you listen to me and you listen to me well, Evangeline Victoria Kelly. Whoever told you you're not a heroine is a liar. A heroine is determined. Compassionate. She loves unconditionally, and she doesn't need a man to rescue her. She may be flawed, but she never stops learning and growing or making the world a better place for the people around her. You *are* a heroine, Angel. Don't let anyone tell you or make you feel differently, do you hear me?"

My heart swells in my chest, and it's hard to keep the tears at bay. The dry and parched places of my soul are soaking up the words and reflection of myself that Tai's offering me.

"Dude, you guys are on the Jumbotron."

The man sitting behind us reminds me that Tai and I are not alone. And, apparently, we now have an audience of thousands. I look to center field, and, sure enough, Tai and I are being displayed in high def, the words *Kiss Cam* written on a banner at the bottom of the screen.

Tai's hands are still cupping my face, and now his thumb is

caressing my cheek, pulling my attention back to him. When I meet his gaze, I realize he'd never even looked away. He'd kept his eyes on me the entire time.

There's a question in them as they sweep over my face, settle for a moment on my lips, then rise again to my eyes.

"Kiss, kiss, kiss," the crowd chants around us.

I search for the cautionary voice in my head. The one that warns against giving in to the moment. That reminds me that Tai doesn't know the whole truth about me. That he hasn't seen me how I truly am, and that if I lean into him now, I could lose my balance and fall completely and irrevocably, with only pain to follow.

But that's not the voice I hear. Instead, I hear Tai's low timbre claiming I'm a true heroine, not just a side character in my own story. That I'm worthy of moments just like this one. Besides, hadn't I already decided I was going to use the day to see if I fit, even a little bit, into that role?

I close my eyes and hear Tai say, "You're so beautiful," and whether it's the Tai in my mind or the one right in front of me, I don't know. I just know I've needed to hear—and listen—to those words for way too long, and the sound of them in my ear pushes me forward until my lips are met with Tai's welcoming kiss.

27

The chant of the crowd immediately hushes the second Tai's lips gently sweep over mine. My focus narrows to one spot—Tai's warm mouth covering my own—as everything else is drowned out. Where other parts of him are hard lines—the cut of his jaw, the slope of his broad shoulders, the occasional slash of his brows—his lips are soft and light, almost as if promising to always be a safe place to land if I find myself needing one.

Sensations are just registering in my brain when Tai begins to pull away. It takes every ounce of my willpower not to chase after his mouth. I'm not ready to leave the cocoon of this moment. Not nearly ready to let go of this feeling welling up from my center. I want to soak in it. Revel. Explore. I want to grow strong and bold and feast on this feeling.

As soon as the kiss ends, the noise of the crowd comes roaring back. The whistles, the cheers. I can feel the heat of the afternoon sun and smell a hot dog someone is eating a few seats away. But these are peripheral sensory inputs. Tai's lips are no longer pressed sweetly against mine in a chaste kiss appropriate for a family event, but he hasn't withdrawn much either. Our faces are still only inches apart, and he's looking at me, his dark eyes probing, a familiar expression on his face, and I realize what it really is that he's doing. He's not merely looking at me; he's *seeing* me. He's seeing me in a way that I don't think Brett ever did, even when I still had my hair.

I want to be known, I realize. *Really* known. I want this thing between Tai and me, this attraction or interest or . . . possibility—whatever undefinable thing this is—I want it to be real. And it can't be real unless *I* am real.

Fear weighs heavy in my chest. Once Tai sees me without my wig, there's no turning back. I could possibly find myself right where I was with Brett—staring at the face of a man who no longer wants anything to do with me. Who would never again say I'm beautiful. I could lose the parts of myself again that I just now realize Tai has been giving back to me piece by piece. The shattered remnants of my self-esteem.

I want it to be real. Need, really. I *need* it to be real. With Tai, I think that it maybe, possibly, could be. I just have to be strong and vulnerable. Like a real heroine.

"Tai." His name comes out raspy, my throat thick with emotions.

His thumb moves to outline my bottom lip. "I can do better."

My mind must be more addled than I thought because I can't have heard right. "What?"

"Kiss you. I can kiss you better, the way you deserve. With abandon. With ardor. With devotion. I want to show you everything that's bursting to be let out of here, Angel." Tai places the palm of my hand over his heart. "Everything I see, everything I know in my heart when I look at you. Please tell me you'll give me another chance to kiss you right. That I didn't blow my one opportunity because of the cameras."

His head tilts forward, and he rests his forehead against

mine. "I need to kiss you again more than I need oxygen," he whispers in a strangled voice.

I lick my lips, imagining what a second kiss from Tai would be like. The first had felt like heaven on earth, yet he claims he can do even better. I doubt any kiss can rival the first, but I'm more than willing to let him prove me wrong.

I nod jerkily. "Okay."

His head lifts off mine. "Okay?" he asks in a way that sounds like hope is a tangible thing he's gripping in his fingers.

"Okay."

His smile lights up his entire face. My hand is suddenly engulfed in his and he's tugging me toward the stairs that lead to the exit.

"What are you doing?" I ask with a laugh.

He's completely serious as he regards me. "You just said I could kiss you again. Do you really think I want to sit around and wait until after a baseball game so I can get you alone?"

Even with the game only half over, we aren't the only ones trickling out of the stadium. Tai looks more serious than I've ever seen him. His usual smiling, teasing demeanor is no-where in sight. He moves his gaze to me, but his expression doesn't soften. If anything, he gets even more intense than before.

"I would do anything for a few minutes of privacy right now." His voice is rough, almost battle-worn, like he's barely keeping himself in check.

And it acts like a battering ram to the last of my defenses, my resolve to stay on the outskirts of romance snapped. Over Tai's shoulder, I see a hidden alcove behind the large concrete walls. No one walking by would be able to see us.

I'm on cruise control, every part of my body hijacked by this one moment, and now I'm the one tugging Tai behind me.

"Where are we going?"

I don't answer, my heart hammering as I beeline for the concealed recess. As soon as we turn the corner, I pivot and face Tai. "No audience. There's no one here but you and me."

Tai's chest is rising and falling in sync with my own. I don't think I've ever been this bold in my life. It feels powerful. Freeing.

"I'm ready for you to prove that you can kiss me better."

One second Tai is a foot in front of me and the next he's on me—his lips, his hands. The concrete wall at my back holds me up against the onslaught of Tai's mouth. His lips move over mine in feverish insistence, demanding and crushing in their need.

Tai isn't kissing me in gentle caresses. He's not treating me with fragile delicacy or even with an ounce of tenderness. He's kissing me like he can no longer hold himself back. Like I've driven him wild and need of me has overtaken his senses.

He's kissing me exactly how I didn't know I needed to be kissed. Every heated stroke of his lips is a balm to my wounded heart.

Brett, society, the world—they told me I wasn't desirable.

Tai kisses me as if I'm the sole object of his desire.

They said no one would want me.

Tai kisses me as if he's never wanted anyone else before and will never want anyone else ever again.

A warm tear escapes the corner of my closed eyes and tracks over the swell of my cheek, pooling on the pad of Tai's thumb that cradles my face. I know when he feels it because his kiss changes. He slows himself down, gentles himself, sweetens the contact. His lips move from my mouth to my cheek, and he kisses the salty liquid.

"I-I'm sorry if I came on too strong." He sounds pained, and I know it's because he feels guilty, worried he might've hurt me.

I place a fingertip on his lips to stop any further apology. "You were right."

"I was?" His brows draw together in confusion.

"You *can* kiss better."

28

I wake up the next morning a little more in love with love than I ever have been. The missing ingredient—hope. I don't know for sure how Tai is going to respond to my revelation, but for the first time in a long time I have hope that a man—that Tai—will still see me as a woman he wants to be with whether I have a full head of hair or my scalp is as shiny and smooth as a cue ball.

Don't get me wrong, I'm still quaking-in-my-boots scared. I admit that my heart is on the line here. The thought of rejection . . . well, it's enough to chase me to the toilet to toss my cookies. But there's also anticipation. Fear and hope, battling it out like two WWE wrestlers using my stomach as their ring.

Unfortunately, I have to wait until tomorrow until I can see Tai again. I'm headed to Granny and Grampie's today, and Tai has a client that's going to keep him busy all evening. But tomorrow we have plans to picnic at Chilhowee, a nice spot overlooking the Ocoee River. That's where I'll tell him about the alopecia and let him see me without my wig.

In the meantime, I'm not giving up on matchmaking. Poor Stacey at Cotton-Eyed Cup of Joe is probably wondering what happened to her secret admirer since I haven't written her any other letters, not since the dumpster fire results of the first one. Time for that to change. After reading Grampie's letters to Granny for inspiration, I'm ready to try again.

An hour later, with two letter-stuffed envelopes in hand and the addresses of Caleb and Stacey that I pilfered from the library's system loaded into my GPS, I depart on my morning's love mission. Stacey lives downtown in an apartment above the hardware store, and I slip the envelope with her name on it through the mail slot. Caleb is fixing up an old Victorian-style house on the outskirts of town. Much easier to leave his letter in his mailbox instead of hiking to the middle of nowhere, like I had to with Dalton's workshop.

I have a good feeling about these two. This time my matchmaking scheme is going to work out the way the others were supposed to. In fifty years, they're going to be telling people how they met and fell in love, just like Mrs. Goldmann does.

I point my car south down the 411 toward my grandparents' house. As usual, once I hit I-75, I strip off my wig and set it gently on the passenger seat next to me. I haven't cued up the audiobook I'm in the middle of, opting instead to bebop to an oldies station. Aretha Franklin and I are demanding a little r-e-s-p-e-c-t when a deer teleports itself right into the middle of the road. I scream, slamming on the brakes and holding the steering wheel in a death grip. I squeeze my eyes shut tight, bracing myself for impact, the crunch of bones and metal, and the torment of knowing I killed Bambi's mom.

But the impact never comes. My car stops, the smell of burned rubber singeing my nostrils, and I finally allow my eyes to slit open. The deer stands there, looking at me like she doesn't have a care in the world. Like I didn't almost mow her over with my Toyota or that I'm now recovering from a mini heart attack. The doe picks her way across the rest of the road and then disappears into the woods.

My pulse is still pounding, and I think the fright has shaved at least a few years off my lifespan, but that seems to be the only lasting damage done. I wiggle my fingers and toes, mentally cataloging my limbs and torso. Yep, intact. I look around the inside of the car. Everything seems—

I suck in a sharp breath through my teeth. There, on the floor, is my wig. My wig that is changing color right before my eyes as it soaks in the tea that apparently got knocked out of the cupholder and onto the floor. I groan but leave it. There's nothing I can do about it now. Hopefully the wig isn't completely ruined and a good washing with a special shampoo and conditioner for synthetic hair, along with some time to air dry, will make it as good as new.

Finally, I ease my foot off the brake and on to the gas pedal. I drive ten miles per hour under the speed limit and scan the surroundings on either side of the road like my gaze is a metal detector and any animals that might jump out are made of alloy instead of flesh and bones.

Five minutes from my grandparents' house, my cell rings with an incoming call, Granny's name showing on the screen. I accept the call with the car's Bluetooth and practically yell to make sure she hears me. "Hey, Granny."

"Sweetie, you there? I need you to go to the store for me. I'm making potato salad, and we're out of mayonnaise. Make sure you get the good stuff. Duke's mayonnaise, Evangeline. Can you hear me?"

"I can hear you, Granny. A jar of Hellmann's. Got it." I shouldn't tease her, but it's too easy and too fun.

"Duuuuuke's." She draws the syllable out long and loud, then sputters, "Hellmann's. Don't even know a good mayonnaise. Where did I go wrong with this girl."

I laugh, the last of my nerves sliding back into their rightful places. "I'll pick up the mayo, Granny."

"Duke's," she clarifies.

"Duke's," I agree.

The call disconnects, and I steer my car to the neighborhood Kroger. Once I kill the engine, I sit back and worry my lip, looking at my hopefully-only-temporarily ruined wig. I have two choices. I can put on the wet, stained, stinky hairpiece and look like I have a dead drowned rat on my head, or I can walk into the grocery store naked as a jaybird from the chin up. Either way people are going to stare.

You shouldn't care so much what people think. It just holds you back. Tai would say something like that if he were here and could read my mind. He'd encourage me to live my life more uninhibited.

I flip down the windshield visor and stare at my reflection in the small mirror. The top of my head is a pale, ghostly white. As soon as I step out of the car, the astronauts aboard the International Space Station will probably be blinded by the reflection of the sun off my scalp. From now on, I'm going to at least sit outside in my backyard without my wig so my head can match the same palette as the rest of my face.

Staring at myself isn't helping and Granny is waiting and this situation isn't changing, so I flip the visor back up, step out of the car, and march into the grocery store like I'm heading to the front lines.

If I'm lucky, I won't run into anyone I know. It'll just be strangers picking up groceries during a midmorning lull. No one will recognize me, and I won't have to smile politely and answer questions like *How have you been lately?* that sound innocuous but are really code for *oh, you poor jilted girl. There's no way you can be doing all right because you no longer have a man, and by the looks of you, you won't be snagging one any time soon.* If I'm lucky, I won't—

But I'm not lucky. I'm the unluckiest woman on the planet. Brett turns the corner to enter the condiments aisle. And he's not alone.

"Evangeline." Brett's voice is familiar in a way I wish it wasn't. Like leftovers in a Country Crock container forgotten for who-knows-how-long. Once something delicious that could make you groan with pleasure but now a rancid, rotting mess that makes your stomach turn at the mere sight.

I'm crouching down because the Duke's is on the bottom shelf. There's no quick escape from this position. Instead, I slowly rise, bringing the jar of mayo in front as if it can shield me from what's happening.

The woman beside Brett has her arm threaded through his the way couples do. She's tall and slender, wearing a cute summer dress and a cropped denim jacket that shows off her figure. Her hair—

My throat thickens, and I try to swallow past the lump that's formed.

Her blond hair is long and flowy, naturally wavy with a healthy shine. She has beautiful hair. The kind that makes you want to reach out and touch it to see how soft it is. The kind that hypnotizes you with the way it bounces and moves when she walks. The kind that chips away at the small fragments of my self-esteem—the same ones where the glue has barely dried at holding them back together.

"Hello, Brett," I finally manage to say.

He's looking at me the way I'd been studying the woman with him. I can only imagine what's going through his mind. None of it flattering.

I lift my chin. But then my gaze snags on something shiny encircled around one of the woman's fingers. An engagement ring. *My* engagement ring.

Brett must notice where my attention is because the next words out of his mouth are, "It's good to see you, Evangeline, but we're in a hurry. Maybe we can catch up some other time?" He whispers something in his fiancée's ear, then pushes the cart around my comatose body before I can kick my brain back into functional mode again.

I pay for the mayonnaise, climb back in my car, and drive the rest of the way to my grandparents' house on autopilot. There are too many thoughts taking up space in my head, and I want to shout at them to GET OUT, but of course I can't because that's not how thoughts work. I have to get ahold of them somehow, though. Organize them into groups instead of letting them have free reign in the space between my ears.

In one corner I push thoughts of Brett. I saw him again. I didn't instantly want to murder him or imagine him a victim in one of Grampie and Penelope's miniature crime scenes. He still looked at me with a mixture of pity and revulsion.

That look brings up the doubts, which I shove into another corner. Will everyone who sees me without a wig for the first time have the same reaction? Will people ever be able to look past the baldness? Will Tai?

I need a practice round. A neutral person I can reveal myself to. Someone I care about and who cares about me but doesn't have the same emotional risks involved as with Tai.

I put the car into park and reach for my cell.

> Hey Hayley. Can you come over after your shift? I want to show you something.

Hayley
What is it? If it's weird Chuck Norris fanfic, I'll pass.

Hayley
No, wait. I take it back. I'm sorry Chuck Norris! Don't roundhouse kick me into another galaxy!

Hayley

You know why there aren't any streets named after Chuck Norris, don't you? Because no one crosses Chuck Norris.

It has nothing to do with Chuck Norris.

Hayley

I'm oddly disappointed.

Can you swing by or not?

Hayley

See you around 7:15

29

've tried not to imagine a thousand scenarios of how this will go, of how Hayley will respond. I might as well write every emotion on Powerballs and put them in one of those lottery spinner thingies. The chances of predicting the seventeen-million-dollar numbers and the outcome of this right now are roughly the same.

I'm not sure what I'm going to say or how I'm going to do this. Shouting *ta-da!* and whipping my wig off without any preamble might be too much of a shock to her system. I've taken CPR classes and theoretically should be able to resuscitate someone, but giving mouth-to-mouth is kind of like changing a tire. Just because I understand the mechanics doesn't mean I have any desire for practical application.

I settle a spare wig on my head and check my reflection in the mirror. It's as good as it's going to get, which is a good thing because the doorbell rings. I take a deep breath, get out of Kitty Purry's direct path as she dashes under the bed, and make my way to the front door.

Hayley's showing her teeth on the other side, and at first I think she's smiling but then realize it's more of a grimace. She bounces on her toes in some kind of dance, then pushes past me in a hurry.

"I had a Big Gulp from the 7-Eleven on my way over here, and if I don't pee right this second, it's going to be an improv of a not-housebroken puppy on your floor." A door slams behind me, followed a moment later by a loud, relieved sigh.

I laugh despite how nervous I was five seconds ago. The sink runs in the bathroom, then the door opens and Hayley steps out.

"I feel so much better." She walks into the living room and plops down on my couch. "What did you want to show me? I'm feeling marginally safe that it isn't a hickey from my cousin since you don't seem like the kind to kiss and tell, but then again, you swore up and down that you don't date and we both know that's no longer true. Which, for the record, I'm one-hundred percent on board with and happy about." She grabs my *One More Chapter* throw pillow and snuggles up with it. "The two of you have gone to the top of my list with a huge check mark beside your names. I'm quite proud of myself, actually."

"What list?"

She blanches. "Uhh . . . Wait, didn't you have something you wanted to show me?"

She's trying to change the subject and not being even remotely subtle about it. But I don't mind. I don't have the bandwidth to chase whatever this list is or why Hayley's being secretive about it. If I don't reveal my own secret soon, I'm going to lose my nerve.

"Yes, I do." I wrack my brain. I should've checked out a book from the library to do this. An intro to alopecia with pictures and diagrams. Most people haven't even heard of the disorder.

Oh, wait. That might not be true anymore. "The slap heard around the world," I blurt out.

Hayley gives me a quizzical look. "You wanted me to come over so you can show me a clip of Will Smith slapping Chris Rock at the Oscars?"

"No, I—" I'm already muddling this up. "Do you know why Will Smith slapped Chris Rock?"

She frowns. "Didn't he tell an insensitive joke about his wife or something?"

"Yes. Jada Pinkett Smith has alopecia. And so do I." I reach up, slip my fingers under my false hairline, and bring the wig down to my lap, watching Hayley's face and reminding myself to breathe.

Not until that moment did I know how I needed Hayley to react. Or *not* react would be a better way to put it. I needed her eyes to never stray from mine. To not widen in surprise or shock. To not glisten a second later. I needed her lips to not part. To not mutter, "Oh, Evangeline" in pity. I needed her to not hug the pillow in her lap tighter. To not use it as a shield. I needed her to not be affected in any way whatsoever. To see me exactly the same way as she had before. Like nothing had changed.

I realized what I needed because Hayley does the exact opposite, and my barely mended heart shatters all over again.

30

I can't go on this picnic with Tai. I can't get Hayley's reaction to seeing me bald out of my head, and I can't go on this picnic with Tai. I can't stop crying for more than ten minutes, and I can't go on this picnic with Tai. I can't think of an excuse to cancel, but I can't go on this picnic with Tai.

Anyone sensing a theme to the mantra repeating in my head right now?

Saying I have to work is futile because the library is closed today, so Tai will know right away that I'm lying. Telling him I'm not feeling well would only backfire and he'd probably want to come over to take care of me. I could make up an elaborate story of an opossum getting into the house and attacking Kitty Purry and now I need to rush her to the animal hospital, but he'd probably want to come along with me to that too.

But how can I be with him right now? How can I see him and not imagine his soft, adoring eyes changing to resemble the disgust in Brett's or the pity in Hayley's? How can I bear being near him when his presence is only going to remind me of what I almost had and was once again viciously snatched from my grasp?

I can't. And I can't talk to him about any of this because

234

I'd have to reveal my secret and we know how well that went over last night.

The only thing left to do is to go back to how things were before. Before I ever entertained the idea that maybe I could be a heroine. Before the baseball game and the kiss that ruined me for life. Go back to pretending that Tai doesn't make my stomach flip with his charming grin. That the way he focuses his attention on me doesn't make me feel like I'm the only woman in the world who could make him happy. Go back to trying to convince myself of his insincerity. That none of this means anything.

The doorbell rings, and I take in a deep shaky breath, dabbing my eyes to make sure the moisture from my past tears has dried. I can't let him know anything is wrong. I can't have him worming his way farther into my heart. I can't let him kiss me.

I open the door and force a bright smile on my face. "Right on time."

His gaze sweeps over me appreciatively, the way it always does when he sees me again after any time apart. I should've expected it. I should've prepared myself. Instead, the gleam of desire in his eyes as they track my body is a jagged edge slicing away at my barely there composure.

He leans in to give me a kiss, but I turn my head and his lips land on my cheek. He pulls back and studies me, concerned. "Are you okay? Is something wrong?"

I breeze past him, my fake smile in place. "Why would something be wrong?"

"I don't know. That's why I asked." He opens the passenger door for me, and I slide in.

After he shuts the door, everything in me wilts. I don't know if I have the energy to keep up this false cheeriness for long.

Tai settles behind the wheel and turns the car on. "How was your visit with your grandparents yesterday?" he asks as he pulls out of my driveway.

I can feel his eyes on me every so often before focusing back on the road again. I keep my own attention fixedly out the windshield. "Fine."

"Just fine?"

"Yep."

He studies me for as long as he safely can while driving. "Are you sure you're okay?"

"I'm fine."

"Fine again, huh?"

"Yep." I'm still not looking at him. Add that to my can'ts list.

He sighs and rakes a hand through his hair, frustration coming off him in waves. He tries a few more times to start a conversation, but I can only muster one-word responses. By the time he pulls the car over at the Chilhowee overlook, I'm exhausted from faking it and he looks like he wants to shake me until I crack.

He puts the car in neutral and engages the emergency brake, turning to look at me head-on now that he doesn't have to focus on driving. I keep staring out the windshield.

"Angel, please talk to me."

"I am talking to you. See my lips moving? Hear the words coming out of my mouth? Talking." I'm trying to be funny, to lighten the mood, but it's falling flat, even to my ears.

He exhales another long, slow sigh. He's losing his patience, and I can't really blame him. "Will you please at least look at me?"

The muscle in my jaw ticks as I brace and force myself to do what he asks.

"Why are you doing this?" he whispers.

"Doing what?" If I play dumb, maybe he'll let me off the hook. I can't take much more. Already my eyes are burning with the threat of more tears. My chest feels like an elephant is sitting on it, and if I don't get out of this car soon, I'm going to lose what little control I have.

"This." His voice is earnest. "Acting like nothing happened between us. I woke up this morning, and the first thing I thought about was seeing you again. I thought we were finally on the same page. What happened between yesterday and today?"

My throat is thick with emotions, making it hard to swallow. I don't want to hurt Tai, but I don't know how else to get him to stop making my heart bleed. "I'm holding up my end of the bargain. What more do you want from me?"

"Forget our deal," he explodes, patience completely gone from his voice. "*We* have never been about that stupid agreement and you know it."

"I made my position quite clear from the beginning. You're the one who manipulated the situation. If you don't like the terms now, you can always just take me home."

He considers what I say for about a tenth of a second. "No. You don't want to fight for us, that's fine. I'll fight hard enough for the both of us."

"There is no us, Tai." It hurts so much to say that. To let go of that tiny sliver of a hope that maybe I'd been wrong before. That maybe I could have a love of my own and that this man in front of me would be that love. But if Hayley can't even bear to look at me without my wig the same way that she did with it, then there's little chance of things going differently with Tai.

"That's where you're wrong. There was an us the moment you spied on me between the bookshelves, and there will be an us until we're both old and gray." He reaches over and grabs my cold hand. "I'm not giving up. Not until you finally let me love you the way you deserve."

The muscles in my throat push past the lump as I swallow. My eyes lower, catching on my pale hand in Tai's tanned one. Some of the tightness around my eyes loosens. I want his words to be true so badly, but they're destined to be a fantasy never realized.

We get out of the car, and Tai retrieves the blanket and picnic basket from his trunk. There's a grassy spot away from the road but not too close to the edge of the mountain where he unfolds the blanket and lays it on the ground.

I lower myself onto a corner of the quilt and tuck my legs under me. Speaking is dangerous, but I need to say something to put us on an easier path and defuse this tinderbox between us.

"It's so beautiful," I finally manage as I look out over the vista. The Ocoee River winds below, the crystalline blue water glistening among the lush green of the Cherokee Forest. A hilled peak rises above the rest, standing sentinel, its imposing presence forcing the river to bow to it. "You can see for miles. It's breathtaking, really."

The weight of his gaze settles on my profile, daring me to turn and catch him staring. I don't, but my cheeks bypass the memo to ignore his attempts of telling intent and infuse with heat instead.

I duck my head to try and hide my blush. "So, what's on the menu?"

Tai pulls out two paper-wrapped sub sandwiches and a bag of Doritos. He points a slow-forming lopsided grin my way. "Be impressed by my culinary prowess."

Tension releases in my chest at his endeavor to return to his usual teasing manner. "Well, I've heard sandwich-making is an art form."

"And I won't be the one to depose you of that belief since it serves me well today."

My lips curve into a real, albeit small, smile, and I unwrap my sandwich.

"How's the party planning going for your grandparents' anniversary?" Tai pops a chip into his mouth.

"You remember that?"

"Of course. I've been meaning to ask if you need any help."

"Really?" I should turn his offer down. Spending more time with him would only be torturing myself.

Then I remember the length of my to-do list. Help wouldn't be the worst thing. And I doubt Tai will respect my need for distance. Maybe if I at least have him busy doing something useful, his attention will be diverted and I can have a sliver of breathing room when he's around.

"I've got excellent penmanship if you need invitations addressed," he offers.

I chew on my lip, considering. "Okay, that would be helpful. Thank you."

Without warning, a strong wind blows from the valley below, gusting over the top of the mountain and sending our napkins cartwheeling out of reach. Tai makes a dive for the paper products, and I move to help him. The wind blows even harder, a sharp updraft that whips around our bodies, flinging my wig from my head before I can even suspect a thing.

A scream of horror mixed with deep emotional pain rips from my throat as I throw my arms up and attempt to cover my head and hide my shame. I can't believe this is happening. Even without wig tape or glue, my cap has always fit as snug as a beanie. How could it have just blown off like that?

I curl into a ball, trying to make myself small, invisible. I wish I could disappear altogether. Anything to not let Tai see me right now. Double chins gather at my neck as I press my face as tightly to my chest as I can. Tears stream down my cheeks, and my eyes are wet and already getting puffy. My nose is running, and my breath is hot and stuffy in the little cave I've made. My shoulders shake as I cry, and I dig my hands into the base of my skull to help my arms hide my baldness.

"What is it? What happened?" Tai's voice is thick with alertness, breaking through the sound barrier of my shoulders pinned over my ears.

"Don't look at me!" My voice cracks as I repeat myself on a broken sob.

Grass rustles under boots behind me and I flinch, folding myself even tighter.

"Angel," Tai murmurs. He settles himself behind me, his thighs on either side of my hips, and draws me back to his chest, gathering me in his arms even as I resist. "You're beautiful, sweetheart. So beautiful."

He repeats this mantra over and over as he gently rocks me back and forth as I cry, hiccupping and pleading with him not to look at me, my arms a citadel over my head.

I feel a little like Katniss Everdeen must have after she learned she had to go back to the arena for the Quarter Quell. She somehow managed to make it out of the first Hunger Games alive; she knew she'd never survive a second time.

How can I survive another rejection? How can I go through that again?

"Angel, darling, you have to stop crying," Tai finally says after my energy is completely spent. He gently circles his fingers around my wrists, and I allow my arms to fall to my sides without much of a fight. What's the point? There's no way to hide my hair loss from him any longer.

Breath warms the crown of my head before soft lips press a kiss to my scalp. I freeze in Tai's arms.

Is my mind playing tricks on me? My heart so desperate that it's imagining a kiss to my naked crown?

"You've never been more lovely to me than you are right now." His arms tighten around me, the tip of his nose nuzzling the shell of my ear.

I have to be hearing things. First my body betrays me by shedding all my hair, and now it's turned on me again by making me have audible hallucinations. "No one wants me like this," I manage to croak.

Tai cups my cheek and leans forward, tilting my head so I

have to meet his eyes. They're deep pools of earnestness and adoration. "I want you like this, Angel," he says fiercely. "I've *always* wanted you."

He can't mean that. I'm unnatural, unwomanly. No one could be attracted to me this way. What movie or book or piece of art shows the leading man falling in love with a bald woman? Beauty has standards, and I fall way below them. Tai's trying to be nice. To make me feel better. There's no way he'd want me the way that I am, and there's no way he's always wanted me because he didn't know about my hair loss before now.

It's easier to believe the multitude of voices I've heard on repeat since my diagnosis than it is to accept what Tai's saying.

"Angel, I've known. About your alopecia. I've known, sweetheart. Before our kiss, I knew. I knew you were sporting a beautiful bald head under your wig."

"It's impossible." I shake my head. "You're just saying that to make me feel better, but you couldn't have known. Couldn't. If you had, you wouldn't . . ."

"Wouldn't what? Find myself daydreaming, distracted by the torture of wanting to be near you when you kept pushing me away? Imagining finding some secluded corner of that library of yours and kissing you until you realized what I've known all along—that you drive me crazy in the best way possible? That I wouldn't resort to any means necessary to spend time with you? Because that's what I did, Angel. That's what I did, and I knew."

That can't be possible . . . can it?

"I can prove it." He shifts his weight and pulls his cell from his back pocket. After opening the phone, he taps on the screen a few times until he finds the picture he's looking for and then angles the screen so I can see. It's a snapshot of a sketch he'd drawn. Me, without a stitch of hair anywhere on my face or head.

I suck in a breath, tears filling my eyes once again. I blink them back so I can study the drawing. How had he known? How had he known and still wanted to be with me? To touch me and kiss me and call me lovely?

"There was something about you I couldn't put my finger on. Something incongruous that I couldn't place. Then I did a head tattoo for a woman, and the thing I'd been obsessing over clicked into place. It was your hair, I realized. You wore a wig. Then I looked closer—which was no hardship because you really are beautiful, Angel—and I noticed your brows and eyelashes."

"You really already knew?" I ask, still wrapping my mind around this revelation. "And you still wanted me?"

Tai's gaze dips to my lips. "Want, Angel. Present tense. I want you more than I've wanted anything in my entire life."

He leans forward slowly, as if giving me time to pull away if that's what my heart is telling me to do.

"I want you too, Tai," I murmur right before our lips meet.

Where our last kiss had been driven by passion and need, this one is soft and tender. Tai seems to take his time to savor the feel of my mouth on his. He reaches up and cups the back of my bare head, swallowing my sound of surprise and protest, telling me over and over again how lovely I am to him with every caress, every touch.

Chee chee chee!

A high-pitched chittering sound not unlike an angry, scolding rodent screams at us from the tree line.

"Why is there always an audience when we kiss?" Tai grins against my lips.

I turn my head toward where the sound came from, freeze, then groan.

On a low branch of a nearby elm tree stands a bushy-tailed squirrel carrying what looks to be . . .

"Is that a squirrel with your—"

"Wig. Yep." What is it with me and forest animals? "First the raccoon, then the deer, and now a squirrel. Woodland creatures seem to have it out for me for some reason."

"What?" Tai asks on a laugh.

"Nothing. Just that I'm the antithesis of a Disney princess, apparently. Instead of singing and helping me with my household chores, the woodland creatures in my life like to wreak havoc instead."

Tai's smile widens. "Should I try and get your wig back?"

I clasp my hands to my chest and bat my fake lashes at him. "You'd be my hero."

He gives me an exaggerated salute, then marches off.

31

It had taken almost a half hour, a bit of cajoling, and the bribery of half of Tai's sandwich to get Evangeline's wig back from the squirrel.

"Yes! Finally!" Tai held up the wig in victory, panting slightly from his efforts.

The squirrel chittered from his branch, looked at the processed meat and bread in its tiny hands, then back at the wig.

"Oh no," Tai said, backing up. "We made a trade. No take backs."

Evangeline laughed from where she sat on the picnic blanket.

Tai glanced at her, relieved to see her happy and relaxed. He'd gladly make himself dizzy chasing the blasted squirrel around the trunk of a thousand trees just to glimpse the look on her face right then. Her guard was down, and she'd lost the self-consciousness and embarrassment that had blanketed her when the wind had ripped the wig from her head. If he could make it so she always felt this way, he would.

He shook out the strands of synthetic hair, hoping to untangle some of the knots that had formed from the squirrel's treatment. "Here. I think that creature is either related to Pepé

Le Pew or Scrat from *Ice Age*. When he sees something he wants, he becomes obsessed. You decide if you'd rather think he saw the wig as a girlfriend or . . ."

Evangeline set the wig on her fist, picking at the strands and looking it over. Her lips twitched. "The poor thing does look rather defiled now, doesn't it?"

"I hear bedhead is all the rage."

She snorted, letting her grin unfurl.

The squirrel threw down the hunk of sandwich and descended the trunk of the tree, chittering as he went. He scurried toward the blanket, stopping feet away, then standing on his hind legs, his front paws clasped in front of him as if pleading with them.

"I think he's begging you to not keep them apart. He's ruined her reputation with his dalliance and now he wants to do the right and noble thing."

She barked out a quick laugh. "But can he provide for her and make her happy? Give her the life she's used to?"

Their eyes met over the horribly disarrayed crown of the wig and both lost the last of their control over their amusement, laughing hysterically.

Tai recovered his ability to speak first. "Is it salvageable?" He nodded toward the wig.

Evangeline shrugged, still chuckling. "I honestly don't know." She turned to the begging squirrel. "Do you promise to love and cherish her as long as you live?"

The squirrel got down on all fours and hurried forward to the edge of the blanket, stopping there to resume his pleas of undying love.

"I think that's a yes."

"Then I now pronounce you—" She shook her head wryly. "What am I even doing right now?"

"Performing a squirrel and wig wedding," Tai said in a voice full of forced seriousness. He looked at her, and their eyes locked.

"That has to be the most ridiculous thing to ever pass your lips."

"Says the person officiating."

Impatient, the squirrel ran forward, snatched the wig, then retreated as fast as he could to the safety of the trees.

"I hope he treats her right."

"That wig is never going to be the same again." Tai winked at her, which set her into another fit of giggles.

He could watch and listen to her laugh all day. Her cheeks were pink, her eyes bright. Although that wasn't the only part of her with color.

"I'll be right back," he said as he walked to the car. He opened the trunk and went to a side compartment where he kept a few outdoor supplies. Grabbing a bottle of sunscreen, he shut the trunk and walked back to the blanket.

"The top of your head isn't used to seeing this much sun, and I don't want you to get burned." He wiggled the lotion in his hand. "May I?"

"I can do it."

"So can I, and I want to."

She pressed her teeth into her bottom lip. She didn't appear convinced that anyone would want to touch her bald head.

"Angel, you're beautiful," he reassured. "Please, let me."

Finally, she nodded, though still looking hesitant and unsure. Tai sat behind her and squirted sunblock into the palm of his hand. Evangeline's shoulders were stiff, her whole body rigid in front of him.

He leaned forward, his mouth by her ear. "Relax," he whispered. He placed a kiss along the curve of her neck, lingering and breathing in her scent, nuzzling her with his nose until she drifted back toward him. He applied the sunscreen evenly over her skin, then firmed his hands, massaging her head.

"That feels so good," she nearly moaned.

Tai swallowed the flood of moisture in his mouth at the sound. He almost changed his mind in broaching the question that had been plaguing him but pressed on.

"Angel," he said as he applied pressure with his thumbs at the base of her skull. "Why have you been so set on this matchmaking thing of yours?"

"What?" she asked dreamily, as if he were waking her from another place.

"Why have you been working so hard and investing so much of yourself in other peoples' love lives? I understand you're a romantic and want to see people happy, but then with yourself you . . ."

How could he say in a gentle way that she'd shut out the possibility of love for herself?

She reached up and gripped his wrist, pulling his hands away. Slowly she turned so they were facing each other.

"I stay on the sidelines. The only place I thought was safely left for me. If I wanted love and romance in my life, I thought I could get it secondhand by helping other people find their happily-ever-afters." Her lips tipped, but it was a smile painted with sadness and shadowed by acceptance that should never have been allowed.

Tai leaned forward and rested his forehead against hers. He reached around her until his hands splayed across her back, then he tugged her closer, nestling her onto his lap. He couldn't protect her from past hurts, but he could hold her while she hopefully healed from them.

"Why do I feel like there's a guy whose butt I need to kick?"

More tension seeped from her body as her lashes lifted and she looked into his eyes. Her smile grew warm. "Probably because there was a guy, but you don't need to kick his butt."

Tai squeezed her tight. "If he hurt you, Angel, I'm not sure I'll be able to stop myself."

She tilted her chin up and pressed her lips against his, comforting him and assuring him the way he was supposed to be doing for her.

Tai angled his head and deepened the kiss, her words that she only belonged on the sidelines ringing in his mind. In the game of love, Evangeline was the most valuable player—she should've never been benched, never have been made to feel as if she didn't belong in the game. He wanted to erase every doubt that had ever entered her mind, every negative voice she'd ever heard. He wanted her to see herself how he saw her. But more importantly . . .

He gentled the kiss, then eased away, resettling his forehead against hers. He licked his lips, getting one last taste of her before he pressed on.

"Angel, whoever the guy was, whatever he said or did to make you feel no one would love you or want you—it was a lie. You've always been loved and wanted, sweetheart."

Her brow furrowed beneath his.

He placed his hands on her shoulders, adding physical weight to the weight of his words. "God is the lover of your soul, Evangeline. He woos you every single day of your life, wanting you to fall in love with Him over and over again the way He loves you. He calls you beautiful, beloved, and lavishes you with more tenderness and affection than a groom does a bride on their wedding day. And nothing can change that. Not an autoimmune disorder or physical changes in appearance. Certainly not hair loss. He loved you from the beginning, and He'll love you for all time."

A tear escaped the corner of her eye. It physically pained Tai to watch it roll over her cheek and collect on her chin before falling to her lap. He pressed a kiss against its track, tasting the salt on his lips.

"If you let me, Angel, I'll love you too. No more watching from the sideline." His mouth hovered in front of hers. "Please join the game with me."

He felt more than saw her head nod once before her lips crashed against his.

32

Evangeline shook out her wrist. "How's your hand not cramping?" she asked as she pressed a thumb into the heel of her right palm. She and Tai had been sitting at her dining room table for the last hour, filling out party invitations and addressing envelopes.

"You forget what I do for a living, sweetheart. The muscles in my hand won't start to protest for another few hours, and even then, they'll still be thankful it's only a pen I'm holding instead of the tattoo gun. No vibrations." Tai finished writing the last number of a zip code and added the envelope to the pile.

Evangeline plucked the finished product from atop the others. Her face scrunched as she inspected his work. "Yours look so much better than mine."

Tai chuckled. "Should I apologize?"

She tossed the envelope at him. "Yes, you should. You're making me look bad."

"Not possible. You could never look bad."

She blushed as she slid a blank envelope out of the box between them.

Tai never let an opportunity pass to tell Evangeline how attractive she was. With someone else, he may worry about feeding an ego that would lead to vanity, but Evangeline had listened to voices that had distorted her view of herself for so long that Tai wanted to be intentional about helping her repair her self-image.

The doorbell rang, and Evangeline lifted her head, setting down her pen. "I wonder who that could be." She stood, re-adjusting her backup wig by tugging at the cap behind her ears. "I'll be right back."

Tai waved her away as she walked toward the front door. He was seated in a position with a direct view of the front of her little cabin and looked up from the invitation in front of him when Evangeline opened the door.

"Hayley, what are you doing here? And what happened to your hair?"

"Evangeline, I'm so sorry. I feel just awful. You shared something private and obviously difficult for you, and I'm afraid I didn't react the best way. I was shocked was all, but then you made up that excuse so I had to leave and I never got to say anything."

"It's okay, Hayley."

"It most certainly is not. Bald is beautiful. If you don't believe me, just look at ZaraLena Jackson and Ayanna Pressley. Those women can rock the no locks, and so can you."

"Thank you."

"I'm serious. Wig or no wig, you turn heads. My cousin is an excellent example. He can't keep his eyes off you."

"I always have admired a nice view," Tai chimed in from his chair.

Hayley froze, her face going white. "Evangeline, I'm so sorry. I didn't know anyone was here. You told me something in confidence, and I just went and blabbed. Tai, you didn't hear anything!"

"It's okay. He knows."

"You told him?"

Evangeline nodded.

Hayley peeked over Evangeline's shoulder, visibly relieved. "Hi, cuz."

Tai waved. Evangeline opened the door wider so Hayley could come inside.

"It's sweet of you to say those things, but you don't—"

Hayley held up a hand, cutting Evangeline off. "I do. But I also came to bring you something." She let the strap of her bag slide down her upper arm and stop at the crook of her elbow. Reaching inside, she scrounged around, then pulled out a Ziploc bag with three sectioned strawberry-blond ponytails nestled inside.

"We're friends. I don't ever want you to think you have to hide part of yourself from me because you're afraid I'll see you any differently. Friends support each other, and that's what I want to do. What I should have done without any hesitation from shock the moment you confided in me."

"Hayley." Emotion clogged Evangeline's voice.

"I had Connie down at the salon cut off twelve inches. I'm going to donate the hair in your honor." Hayley moved the plastic bag to her other hand and reached back in the bag. "I brought you a few more things as well." When she pulled her hand back out, she held packages for three new inexpensive cosplay wigs—one black, one red, and one blond. "Meet Roxanne, Natasha, and Astrid."

Tai grinned and pushed back his chair. He walked toward the foyer, then leaned against the wall with his hands in his pockets as he watched the emotions march across Evangeline's face.

Hayley set down her purse so she could separate the black wig from the others. "This is Roxanne. She's a no-nonsense woman who likes to be in charge and doesn't take any grief from anyone."

"Oh dear," Evangeline murmured.

Tai nudged her playfully with his elbow and winked. "You should try it on. A little roleplaying could be fun."

She blushed even as she tipped her chin in challenge. "You think you could handle a woman like Roxanne?"

Tai's tongue thickened in his mouth. The way Evangeline was looking at him—bold, head-on, no hiding or relegating herself to the sidelines—made the blood heat in his veins. No words formed. Evangeline flirting back with him seemed to have a misfiring effect on his brain, so he put his mouth to better use. Gripping her chin, he brought her face toward his and seared her lips with a kiss.

Hayley cleared her throat. Loudly.

Tai groaned but pulled away, pinning a glare on his cousin. "Don't you have somewhere else you have to be?"

She smiled brightly. "Nope." She reached out and pulled on Evangeline's hand. "Come on. I want to see how they look." Evangeline let herself get dragged toward her bedroom, throwing a smile over her shoulder toward Tai.

Tai smiled back unconsciously, a reflex when it came to his Angel. Whenever she was around, he just . . . reacted. She created responses in him that he hadn't even known were possible. Made him feel things he'd never felt before.

He took a deep breath and tried to slow his erratic heartbeat. It wouldn't do to get too far ahead of himself. Too far ahead of Evangeline, even though he knew he was already there. But he'd been steps ahead of her ever since they'd met, feeling before she felt and now knowing before she knew.

He loved her. Loved her when she believed no one ever could. He was in the deep end of these feelings while she was still just dipping her toes in and testing the waters.

But he'd wait. He'd wait, and he'd be there beside her and coax her into the deep end with him.

"Fashion show!" Hayley shouted with glee from behind the closed bedroom door. Tai grinned as he took a seat in the living room. This was not his first Hayley Holt fashion show. She'd often put on performances like this when they were growing up. At least this time he was just a spectator instead of one of her models.

All of a sudden, Evangeline's cat streaked out from under the couch and pounced on his shoelaces, batting them between her paws.

"Well, hello there." Tai reached down and picked up Kitty Purry. "Seems like there's going to be some runway models on the catwalk in a minute. Want to watch?"

The cat sniffed, then bounded out of his arms. She walked away from him, swinging her hips and swishing her tail. About halfway across the room, she stopped and turned back as if striking a pose. She sauntered toward him, jumped on the couch, then lifted a paw and licked it daintily.

Evangeline's bedroom door opened a crack. "Tai, I left my phone in my car. Be a good sport and put on some runway music," Hayley instructed.

Tai pulled out his phone. "What exactly is runway music?"

"I don't know. Do I look like I've been to Paris or Milan?"

"Sorry I asked," he mumbled. He clicked on the search engine app, typed in *fashion show music*, then tapped on the first video option that came up. Percussion beat out of the handheld device's speakers.

"That works!" Hayley shouted her approval. "Okay, here we come."

Tai sat beside Kitty Purry, who continued her grooming.

"First down the runway is Hayley Holt wearing an Evangeline Kelly original." Hayley strutted out the door, lips in an exaggerated pout and hands on hips that were in danger of needing to be put back in their sockets if she swung them any wider.

Hayley was wearing one of Evangeline's pencil skirts and graphic tees. An Evangeline Kelly original indeed. She flipped brown hair over her shoulder, and Tai realized she was also wearing Evangeline's wig, the one she'd had on before the two had jolted off to her room.

"What do you think? Do I look like Evangeline?" Hayley struck a pose.

"Thankfully not even a little."

She stuck out her tongue, then pivoted and walked back to the bedroom.

"Next up is Astrid, uh, Johanson. She's traveled from Sweden to be with us today."

The door opened again and Evangeline stumbled out, no doubt helped by a shove from Hayley. Cheeks pink, she adjusted a flowy summer dress that put Tai in mind of a Scandinavian meadow. Unlike his cousin's flamboyant movements, Evangeline tiptoed forward, keeping her eyes down.

"Oh, is Astrid Johanson a shy country girl leaving her village for the first time? Maybe a handsome man can sweep in and show her a bit of the wonderful wide world?" Was he putting it on a bit thick? Absolutely. But the smile that topped her lips and the look of suppressed laughter in her eyes was worth it.

"*Askersund beckvam alang ektorp.*" She fluttered her eyelashes at him.

Tai couldn't help the laughter that spilled out of his mouth. "Did you just speak IKEA to me, sweet Astrid?"

At the end of the catwalk, Evangeline popped her hip. "Maybe." The bangs of the blond wig brushed the top of her eyelashes. She reached up and swiped them to the side.

"How do you like the blond?" Tai asked quietly so his voice wouldn't travel to Hayley.

She shrugged, unsure. "I feel like I'm pretending."

"Is that bad?"

She seemed to think for a moment, and then her eyes sparkled before she gave a twirl. "Actually, it's kind of fun at the moment."

She retreated back to the bedroom and came out a few minutes later wearing the red wig. The synthetic hair ran down her back, stopping at the curve of her waist.

"And who do we have here?" Tai leaned forward, resting his elbows on his knees.

This time she slinked toward him like a femme fatale, reeling him in with each step she took in his direction.

"I am Natasha Petrov, KGB agent," she said in a butchered accent.

His brows rose. "KGB? Didn't they cease operations in 1991?"

Her step faltered, but then her shoulders squared. "Zat is vhat we vanted you to think." She *tsk*ed. "Americans."

Tai sat back with a grin. "So, Natasha, are you going to interrogate me?"

"I vill uncover your secrets."

Tai spread out his arms. "I'm an open book. No secrets here."

She narrowed her eyes. "Hmm. Ve shall see." She walked back to the room with her posture perfectly straight.

Hayley came out a second later, back in her original clothes and with her newly shorn hair pulled into the shortest ponytail Tai had ever seen. "Roxanne will be out momentarily."

Tai stood and pulled his cousin into a hug. "Thank you."

"For what?" Her voice was muffled by her face in his neck.

He loosened his grip and stepped back. "You helped her to find the fun in a situation where she couldn't see it before." *Just like you helped me when we were kids.*

Hayley studied him. "You really like her, don't you?"

She meant *love* and . . . "Yeah, I do."

She squeezed his shoulder. "I'm really happy for both of you." She grabbed her bag. "And now I'm going to get out of here and give you two lovebirds your privacy back. Don't do anything I wouldn't do."

Tai laughed. "There's not much you wouldn't do."

"Exactly." She winked.

As the front door closed, the bedroom door opened. Evangeline must have grabbed his leather jacket earlier without him noticing because it draped over her narrow shoulders and hit the curve of her hips. The raven wig made her pale skin seem even more porcelain, and she planted her hands at the curve of her waist as she stopped in front of him. He stared into her eyes, and she stared back.

"Nice jacket."

A hint of a smile played at her mouth. "I've always thought so."

"Is that right? What other thoughts have you been keeping to yourself?"

Her gaze dipped to his mouth, then farther south, halting at his throat. Or, rather, the side of his neck. It intensified as her eyes tracked over the lines of his rose tattoo. He could feel her look like a physical touch and then it was, her fingers rising and ever so softly brushing against the lines.

"It's as soft as I imagined. Like the petals of a real rose."

Her breath feathered across his lips. It took all his self-control to sit still. To not pull her flush against him and claim her parted lips like the rogue she'd claimed him to be.

Her eyes lifted to his. He swallowed.

"I wonder," she murmured. Her gaze lowered again to his tattoo, but this time, her mouth followed. Her warm breath fanned across his skin a moment before her lips settled in a kiss over the strumming of his pulse.

She pulled back slightly, only long enough to whisper a surprised "Oh" before her mouth was on him again, another hot press of her lips on the flower's center.

Tai groaned, his arms snaking out to band around her back. Her knee bumped the side of his and pitched him backward. He rotated her in his arms so Evangeline landed on his lap.

She giggled and looked at him with wide, fake-innocent eyes. "Hi."

He smirked at her. "Hello, Minx."

She giggled again. "I take it you like Roxanne." She said it as a statement, but he still heard a hint of a question there.

He leaned over and nuzzled her nose. "I do. I like Roxanne and Natasha and Astrid."

She clasped her hands behind his neck. "Which did you like the most?"

He leaned even farther forward and caught the lobe of her ear between his teeth, tugging gently. He let go and whispered, "I like them all, because they are all you."

Pulling back, he looked at her. Slowly, he lifted his hand and removed her wig. He brushed his fingers over the shell of her ear as if tucking away errant strands of hair. "Evangeline *Victoria* Kelly"—he winked, caressing the curve of her jaw with his thumb—"will always be my favorite."

33

id I miss the memo about a library employee salon trip or something?" Martha asks as she approaches the front desk. She dabs at her temple with the back of her hand, a feminine sparkle about her (because women don't sweat, according to Granny; they either glow or sparkle). A newly erected six-foot cardboard cutout of the Cat in the Hat now stands near the entrance of the children's wing, Martha showing every sign of her stubbornness and fight to put it up by herself.

Hayley shoots me a look out of the corner of her eye. I can read her expression like an open book. She's not sure what to say because she doesn't want to betray my confidence, but with her dramatically shorter hair and the fact that I'm wearing a wig that's a slightly different shade and style than my usual one—well, there's obviously some explanation needed here.

Martha pats her own curls that rebel with the humidity, creating a wild riot of a halo around her head. She laughs a bit sadly, and I realize she probably feels left out.

"I doubt even a salon could tame this bird's nest. But you, Hayley, that bob frames your face beautifully and really highlights your cheekbones." She turns to me. "And, Evangeline, the new layers really give your hair volume and the lighter shade of chestnut is perfect for summer."

Her smile doesn't reach her eyes as she pivots and retreats to her corner of the library.

Honestly, I don't know Martha well. Hayley kind of kidnapped me as a friend as soon as I arrived in town while Martha has kept more to herself and the shelves of the children's books that line the west corner of the library. All that I really know about her is that she's a hard worker, dedicated, knows everything there is to know about children's literature, and often jots things down in a Moleskine notebook that she keeps on her at all times. She's quiet, except during story time when she gives each character of the book she's reading aloud their own voice, almost acting like a one-woman theater production for her captive audience of little ones.

It's time, I think to myself. I'm not ready to march down Main Street with my head bare, but I am ready to take a step forward out of the shadows.

"Martha, wait."

She stops beside the giant Dr. Seuss icon and turns on her heel. "Yes?"

I walk over to her, Hayley right behind me. The oversized cat in the red-and-white striped hat has mischief written on his face. I'm almost expecting him to let a Thing One and Thing Two out of a box, indoor kite-flying with disastrous results immediately to ensue.

I look at Martha. "First off, your hair is beautiful. I would give anything to have hair like yours."

"This frizz?" She smooths her hand over her curls, but they pop back up a second later. "Trust me, you wouldn't."

"Trust *me*, yes, I would." I take a deep breath. The library is relatively deserted right now, but anyone could walk through the front doors at any moment.

It's time, I say to myself again.

"Hayley did go to the salon, but I didn't. I haven't gone to a hairdresser in . . . well . . ." I lift my hand and pull the wig off my head. "Not since I lost my hair."

Martha's eyes track over the dome of my head without a flick of outward reaction. "Just like Sparkle Moore."

Out of all the things I expected her to say, that wasn't even on the radar. Especially since I have no idea who Sparkle Moore is. I put my wig back on, hoping it's straight since I don't have a mirror to check. "Excuse me?"

"Sparkle Moore. Hold on. I'll show you." She walks over to where the middle-grade fiction books are shelved. As if she has the placement of each title memorized, she quickly plucks a chapter book off the shelf and walks back to me, holding it out.

Sparkle by Lakita Wilson. The cover has a green background with an illustrated preteen in profile. Instead of a head of hair, she has sparkly stick-on jewels attached to her scalp in a colorful flower pattern. My breath catches.

A book with a heroine who has alopecia. The main character. Not a sidekick or supporting cast.

My eyes warm right before my vision starts to swim.

"It's about a twelve-year-old girl who begins to lose her hair in middle school. She tries to hide her diagnosis from her friends at school while also trying to help her family financially by becoming a superstar. She has to deal with itchy wigs that she's not used to, as well as new and strange medications, on top of navigating family and friends. Not to mention the hit that her self-esteem takes because of her diagnosis."

I look at Martha, not sure what to say.

"The publisher may have marked the book for ages eight to twelve, but if you ask me, children's literature can touch the hearts and lives of readers of every age."

I hug the hardcover to my chest. "Thank you." She has no idea the gift she's just given me.

"Of course."

261

The sound of the automatic doors opening pulls our attention toward the entrance.

Tai walks in wearing his signature dark-wash jeans and fitted black T-shirt. The temperatures have begun to climb along with the humidity, canceling the need for his leather jacket. I can't say that I mind, as the sleeve of his tattoo is now on full display. The lion and lamb and dove. The cross and rays of light through the clouds. Even the rose. All physical and permanent reminders of the deep roots of Tai's faith and convictions.

I can't believe I ever considered him anything but hero material. Quite possibly my very own book boyfriend in the flesh.

I step around the protruding gloved hand of Dr. Suess's anthropomorphic feline so I don't knock myself out and approach a grinning Tai as I would any other patron. "Hello, sir. Can I help you find something specific, or are you just looking today?"

His dark eyes spark as he makes a show of checking me out from head to toe. "Oh, I'm definitely looking."

My cheeks flush. I'm not sure I'll ever get used to his bold flirting. I'm also not sure I ever want him to stop.

The pencil skirt I'm wearing today came with a skinny belt. Tai hooks his fingers through the belt loops set just below my rib cage and tugs me to him. "But I've also found what I'm looking for," he says with his lips a breath away from my own.

"At least take the make-out sesh to the academic periodicals section." Hayley breezes past us. "Hardly anyone frequents that aisle."

"I really don't—" I protest at the same time that Tai grips my hand and starts dragging me in that direction, a quick "Thanks for the tip, cuz," thrown over his shoulder.

As soon as Tai stops, a rack of medical journals behind him, my hand shoots up. "We are not reenacting the *Friends* episode with Ross's book at the university library."

"That wasn't my plan, but thanks for giving me the idea." He winks.

I shake my head at him, but the smile curving my lips counteracts any disapproving librarian matron vibes I was trying to project.

"I'm here on an errand for my mother."

"Oh? Did she want you to get a book for her?"

"Not exactly." Tai squeezes my fingers. "The small-town rumor mill has been busy."

"Oh." Realization dawns. Honestly, I'm kind of surprised it's taken this long for word of our relationship to get back to his family.

"My parents want to meet you."

Meeting the parents. I never thought I'd be here. With Brett, our families had known one another since the beginning of time. His mom and dad still remember when I'd take off my diaper and streak around the house butt naked. I've never met the parents of a guy I've dated before. And *after* Brett . . . well, I just didn't think I'd ever be here, you know?

"In case you were wondering," Tai says when I don't immediately respond. Or respond at all, now that I think about it. I've kind of been in a daze. "I want my parents to meet you."

"With or without a wig?"

Tai cups my face in his hands and looks deep into my eyes. He's willing me to see the truth. To focus on him and nothing else.

"Whatever makes you the most comfortable, Angel. Wig or no wig, you're beautiful and my parents are going to love you either way simply because I—"

He cuts himself off and doesn't finish the sentence.

Because you what, Tai? I want to scream. I'm hanging by a thread that's about to snap, a dark unknown waiting to swallow me whole if I plummet into its abyss.

I know how I want him to finish his sentence. It's as clear

as a mountain stream and as scary as a raging river. He's given me every indication what the next two words out of his mouth would've been. While I may have tried to convince myself of a different narrative about his intentions from the very beginning, he's made me a liar at every turn.

So why am I so afraid to hope? Why am I more willing to believe Brett's lies than Tai's truths?

I swallow hard and cling to the thread rooting me to the spot. Ground myself to Tai's dark eyes, to the way he sees me . . . No one has ever looked at me the way Tai does. His look gives me strength, emboldens me.

"Because you what?" I breathe out the question.

The movement is infinitesimal, but Tai shakes his head. His lips thin, as if he's biting back what he wants to say.

I lift my hand and set my palm above his beating heart. "Because you what, Tai?"

It's unfair of me to ask. Especially considering I'm unsure whether I'm ready to say the words to him. But my need to hear them has made me selfish. Desperate. I *need* to know that it's possible for someone to have these feelings for me. For *Tai* to have these feelings for me.

His face softens. "Are you sure you're ready to believe it, my Angel?"

It's my turn to shake my head. "No. I'm pretty unsure about everything right now." My fingers fan over his pectoral muscles. "But tell me anyway," I whisper.

Tai's gaze brands my soul. "My parents will love you, Evangeline." His voice, his touch, the look in his eyes—all are an invitation to accept what he's offering to me. "Because *I* love you."

I'd hoped he'd say it. I'd known, hadn't I, that those would be the next words to come out of his mouth. *I love you*. I should have been prepared.

But nothing would have made me ready for the overwhelming surge of emotions that hearing those three little words would bring forth from the core of my being. *I love you* might as well have been a sledgehammer to the protective shell around my heart, cracking it open and releasing every hurt feeling, every doubt, every suppressed longing and quashed hope. Each bubble to the surface comes in suffocating waves, forcing me to feel all the things all at once that I refused to acknowledge until now.

I gasp as a deep, silent sob sticks in my throat, my shoulders shuddering and my eyes welling. There's no blinking back these tears. They're marching forward with reinforcements right behind them, an onslaught against my defenses.

Tai's own eyes widen in alarm. "Angel?"

What must the poor man think? He tells me he loves me and instead of answering with a sane response of *I love you too*—what he was probably hoping for and what I'm pretty sure is somewhere within this whirlpool of feelings currently creating a vortex in my chest cavity—he gets a blubbering mess of a woman who can't even squeak out a coherent word past the choking sobs caught in her throat.

I've done nothing but push Tai away. What if he thinks my reaction—my snotty nose and leaking eyes and uncontrollable crying—is another rejection?

My hands shoot out, and I grab fistfuls of his shirt in a death grip. He'll have to pry the cotton out of each of my fingers if he wants to get away. Once I can catch my breath, I'll tell him . . . tell him . . .

"Ah, sweetheart." His voice nearly breaks. He gathers me to his chest and hugs me tight. "Shh. It's okay. You are loved. Let it out. I'm here. I'm not going anywhere."

It hurts. To face the image of myself I've let develop in my mind. My insecurities and vulnerabilities. To grieve what I thought I'd lost. It hurts, but the tears are cleansing. The sharp, stabbing pain lessens to a dull ache. I'm able to shudder in deeper breaths. With each exhale, the voices in my head—Brett's, society's—grow fainter. Now that they aren't shouting at me, drowning everything else out, I hear something else. Faint but familiar. A steady beat like my own heart.

You are loved. You are loved.

Tai said the same thing, but this is different. Deeper. Ancient. Not a romantic love, but a never-ending, never fading, eternal, supernatural type of love.

"God has never stopped wooing you, Evangeline. He is the lover and romancer of your soul."

Tears course down my cheeks. Not in grief or sadness but in healing. The weight that has crushed me for so long has lifted, and I'm floating. I'm like a phoenix rising from the ashes of my past pain, ready to fly again with hope and renewed strength.

And I know just where to start my flight.

I pull away from Tai's chest, his arms loosening their hold to allow my movement. A wet patch darkens his shirt where the material absorbed my tears. I'll apologize for that later. Right now, there are more important things to say.

Tai's brows are drawn down in concern.

"Tai." Emotion still clogs my throat, but I croak past it.

As soon as I say his name, his eyes jump and lock onto mine.

Words seem like an inadequate conveyance for my feelings, but they're all I have. Hopefully they'll be enough. "Thank you for seeing me clearly when I couldn't see myself. For speaking truth to me when I could only hear the lies. For never giving up on me and showing me what it means for my heart to be intentionally pursued. You've given me your strength when I've been weak and hope when I'd all but given up. Tai Albert Davis—"

Tai's face lights up at my use of his middle name. I've never let my tongue curl around the syllables before, while he never misses an opportunity to remind me of mine—of *ours*, really.

My palms run up his chest, my fingers interlocking behind his neck. "I'm in love with you too."

He smirks, his expression toeing the line just this side of gloating. "Albert and Victoria. I told you it was meant to be."

I huff out a laugh as I bring my hands forward to frame his face. "Shut up and kiss me."

"Your wish is my command, Madam Librarian."

I roll my eyes, but as soon as Tai's lips touch mine, my lids slide shut. Everything else fades away; the freestanding shelves of periodicals surrounding us, the low-pile square-patterned carpet under out feet. I'm transported to a place that transcends time and space. There's just me and Tai and this kiss that romance writers wish they could capture on the page. It's heat and heart. Passion and devotion. A culmination, while at the same time just a beginning.

A throat clears behind us, and I jump away guiltily. I am, after all, on the clock, and this is a public library.

"Looks like the matchmaking librarian has finally met her own match."

34

I wince and turn slowly. My day of reckoning has arrived. Stacey stands in the center of the aisle, her hands planted firmly on her hips. A few envelopes peek out between her fingers, her name addressed across the top in my familiar script.

Her expression gives nothing away. The jig is up, but is she mad that I've been meddling? And how did she figure out the secret admirer letters have been coming from my pen?

"Hello, Stacey." My smile wobbles.

"Evangeline." Her gaze flicks to Tai.

So does mine. *Help!* I try to silently communicate.

He gives me an encouraging smile and nods his head slightly toward Stacey.

I sigh. Looks like this is the day for facing the hard things.

He presses a kiss to my cheek. "I'll text you my parents' address and what time dinner will be. Nice to see you, Stacey."

"You too, Tai."

Tai hooks his thumbs through his belt loops and strides toward the front of the library and the exit. When he disappears past a bookshelf, he takes my excuse of not facing Stacey with him.

Knowing it's time, I turn to her, but I can't bring myself to look higher than her nonskid work shoes. "Are you mad?"

"I think I've earned the right to be the one asking the questions here."

The words bite, but the tone . . . I still can't decipher her feelings. "That's fair."

"Why Caleb Chapman? You're writing letters to me pretending they're from him while also sending him notes that are supposed to be from me. I got that right, didn't I?"

I hang my head even farther. "Yes."

"Okay. So, why Caleb? Why'd you think we'd make a good couple? You and I don't really know each other that well, and I'm assuming you probably don't know him any better. Am I wrong?"

"You're not wrong."

"Were you bored? Are our love lives nothing but a game to you?"

My chin shoots up, and I finally meet her eyes. They aren't throwing daggers at me like I deserve, but neither does she appear on the threshold of thanking me for my interference. If I played poker, I'd never want to sit across the table from Stacey. Her expression gives nothing away.

I, however, do nothing to hide my contrition. "It may seem like I was moving the two of you like pawns, but I assure you, I wasn't playing a game."

"What were you doing then?"

"On the surface, just what it looks like. Matchmaking. I studied the library patrons' check-out histories and attempted to set people up based off their reading preferences."

"Based off—" Stacey shakes her head, eyes widening in disbelief. "Wow." She snorts. "And to think it actually worked." She says this last part under her breath.

I blink, not sure I heard right. "It worked?"

Her expression softens. "Probably not like you were expecting, although I'm not quite sure what you were thinking would happen." She points to a worktable in the corner and we sit.

"Caleb came into Cotton-Eyed Cup of Joe with one of your letters in his hand. I recognized the handwriting at once and showed him my own letters. We started talking and put two and two together. I was impressed with his reaction. Instead of getting upset, he cracked jokes." She smiles, remembering. "I've always appreciated a man with a good sense of humor."

I can't help but smile as well. It *worked*. I made a real match.

Stacey sees my grin and frowns, a stern slant marking her mouth. "Just because it's going well for the two of us doesn't mean people—Caleb, myself, whoever else's lives you meddled with—couldn't have gotten hurt by what you did."

I bank my happiness and lift my palms. "You're absolutely right. I shouldn't have tried to play matchmaker without consent. I promise I won't do it again."

She gives me an uncomfortable amount of eye contact before saying, "Good. Even though I'm sure there's more to the story, that's what I came down here to say." She stands. "And now that you have a love life of your own, I'm even more assured you'll stop messing with everyone else's."

"That's it? I'm really off the hook so easily?"

The corner of her mouth twitches as if she's holding back a smile. "Caleb is taking me to Knoxville to a surprise date destination so I'm having a hard time holding on to my outrage with all this giddy anticipation inside me." She leans forward, her palms planted on the table and her face mere inches from mine. I can smell the peppermint gum she's tucked into her cheek as she stares me down. "If, however, Caleb breaks my heart, I'm blaming you and we're picking up this conversation right where we're leaving it off."

"Fair," I squeak out.

She straightens and smiles again. "Well, I'm off to get ready for my date. Sounds like you'll be doing the same here shortly as well. See you around, Evangeline."

I wave weakly, both happy for a successful match and Stacey and Caleb's budding romance but also a tiny bit frightened that they won't work out and Stacey will come back to finish the conversation.

"What was that about?" Hayley says from behind a bookshelf, startling the living daylights out of me and causing my heart to knock against my ribs in an erratic rhythm.

I jump-turn in my seat, my hand pressed against my chest. "For goodness' sake, Hayley, you have got to stop sneaking up on people like that."

She grins unrepentantly as she steps into view. "What did Stacey want?"

"Oh, uh, nothing really." I haven't filled Hayley in on my side endeavor, and I sure as shootin' am not going to change that now. But by the way she's staring at me expectantly, she isn't going to just leave it be without some sort of crumb to nibble on.

And of course, because my brain likes to snowball, *crumb* reminds me of *dinner*, which reminds me of Tai's parents, which creates a tiny knot of dread in the pit of my stomach.

I chew on my bottom lip. "Hayley, you know Tai's parents."

"I faintly recall my own aunt and uncle, yes."

"Funny."

She smirks. "I thought so."

"What are they like?" I chew on my lip some more.

Hayley's eyes brighten. "Tai's bringing you to meet them."

I nod.

Hayley takes the seat that Stacey had vacated, then reaches over and squeezes my hand. "You have nothing to worry about. Aunt Missy and Uncle Walter are really very sweet. I mean, she's a little overbearing and protective of Tai, but that's more with his health than anything else."

"What do you think their reaction would be to—" I wave weakly at the direction of my head.

Hayley tilts her chin as she considers me. "Are you thinking wig or no wig?"

"I don't know. I haven't decided yet, I guess."

"Okay, let me ask you another question. Are you serious about my cousin?"

My face heats, a neon sign declaring just how much I feel for Tai.

"Oh, it's like that, is it?" Hayley says knowingly, her grin as wide as the Mississippi is long.

I clear my throat. "It might be a little like that, yes," I say as primly as possible.

Hayley laughs. "If that's the case, you'll probably be seeing Aunt Missy and Uncle Walter quite a bit. A conversation about your hair is more a matter of when and not if, right? You control the timeline, Evangeline. No one else."

There's a whole town who knows me as a brunette with shoulder-length beach waves and curtain bangs. Once I start leaving my house without my wig on, I'll have to have countless conversations explaining the change. It might be nice, for once, to start an introduction without the need of an explanation down the road hanging out in the background.

"What if they don't like me?"

Hayley rolls her eyes. "Your self-worth is not tied to your hair follicles' ability to function. And, news flash, everyone obsesses at least a little about their significant other's friends and family liking them, so I hate to break it to you, but you're nothing special there." She pauses. "You've got nothing to worry about. Except, perhaps, Aunt Missy sending you a bunch of internet articles on alopecia that you won't want to read. But that's her way of loving people, so remind yourself of that fact when the twenty-seventh link comes in on some new theory about how fifteen minutes of meditation a day can make your hair grow back."

She studies me a moment, then taps the edge of the table in a decisive move. "What you need is a little boost of confidence, and I have the perfect thing that will give you just that."

35

Stick-on craft gems?" I eye the sheet of stickers warily.

"What girl doesn't need a little bling in her life?" Hayley shimmies her shoulders in a way that makes me think she's been watching too many Lady Gaga music videos.

I turn to Martha and raise my brows at her in a silent plea for help. Surely she'll be the sound of reason.

"Don't look at me like that." Martha pulls out two more sheets of sparkly jewels in different colors. "I agree with Hayley on this one."

I groan but let Hayley push me down into one of the extra kid-sized chairs we have in the storage area, plastic bins holding puppets and craft supplies lining the wall opposite me. There's barely room enough for the three of us in here, and there's a little voice in the back of my head reminding me that we're librarians *at work* and we should be, you know, working. Thankfully our supervisor, who mostly works remotely from another branch, isn't scheduled to come in today and won't catch us shirking our duties.

But as Hayley peels off a turquoise gem and I remove my wig, I can't make myself care about the responsibilities on the other side of the open door, just glad that for now the library is deserted and if someone stops by, then Hayley has volunteered to go out and help them. I should be too old and mature for a makeover montage à la every teen movie, but, surprisingly, I find I'm not.

"This is the day Evangeline gets her groove back." Hayley snaps her fingers four times in a *Z* pattern, her head bobbing back and forth with each snap.

Martha and I stare at her, then bust out laughing.

"Please never do that again," Martha begs between chuckles.

Hayley sniffs in exaggeration, pretending to be offended. "I can pull it off."

I'm catching my breath while I shake my head at her. "I love you, sweetie, but no, you cannot."

"Hmph."

Martha's gaze snags on mine, and we snicker some more.

There isn't a mirror so I have no idea what my two friends are turning me into. Now that the laughter has died down, they have concentrated looks on their faces, peeling off stickers and placing them on my head. I'm a little antsy and nervous about the outcome of this. I know Hayley wants to boost my confidence, but I'm afraid I'm going to look more like a circus performer than anything.

"What were these stickers originally supposed to be used for?" I ask Martha to distract myself.

"A *Rainbow Fish* craft." Her focus never leaves the spot behind my ear that she's working on.

"The book about the fish with the glittering scales who shares his sparkle with the other fish?"

"That's the one."

I keep my upper body still but reach out a hand and snatch a sheet of stickers out of the storage container. Peeling one off by feel alone, I place the ruby-red jewel on the apple of Martha's cheek, followed by another on Hayley's.

"What are you doing?" Hayley lightly touches the sticker.

"Sharing my sparkle." The words are trite. I can hear that.

But when Martha and Hayley squish me in a hug sandwich, I know they understand the depth of what I truly mean.

"There. I think that does it." Hayley places one last gem to the crown of my head, then straightens.

Martha leans her shoulder against Hayley's and inspects their collective work. "Chin up, Evangeline. You've got your glow back, and you're not going to let anyone snuff it out again, you hear?"

I sniff against the tingle of emotion threatening to fill my eyes and nod.

"Aunt Missy really likes Martinelli's Sparkling Blush but never buys it for herself because she thinks it's too fancy for some reason. Anyway, if you show up with a couple of bottles, she'll be tickled pink with you."

"I can do that."

Both Martha and Hayley look at me expectantly.

"Oh, you mean now? But my shift isn't over."

"We'll cover for you," Martha assures.

"That way if you want to go to the store a couple towns over and share your sparkle"—Hayley waves her hand toward my bedazzled head that I still haven't gotten a look at—"while not worrying about running into anyone you know, you can."

Martha nods in agreement. "Now shoo." She swats the air like she's trying to get a pesky bug to leave.

"I'm going, I'm going. Sheesh." Before I leave the closet, I carefully place my wig on my head so I don't accidentally knock any of the stickers off. "I'll see you tomorrow." I grab my purse from behind the front desk, then do as I'm told—I get.

When I turn into the parking lot of a grocery store three towns away, I take a deep breath and pull down the visor in front of the windshield. My reflection stares back at me in the tiny mirror. *This is the last time*, I promise myself. The last time I drive out of town like I'm ashamed of myself or have a deep dark secret.

"No more hiding." My fingernails graze my nonexistent hairline and hook under the webbing of my wig. I lift the headpiece and let my scalp breathe.

The afternoon sun shines through the side window, bouncing off every ridge and plane of the paste jewels stuck to my scalp, throwing light in a million directions. My breath hitches at the sight. Lyrics from a Danny Gokey song blaze through my mind: *"You were made to shine."*

I have to squint against the sun's brightness as I step around a poorly parked car. The store is busier than I would've expected, and there are quite a few people navigating the parking lot, pushing carts full of grocery bags.

"Mommy, look. It's a princess."

I can barely hear the little girl's voice over the clattering of shopping cart wheels, but my gaze scans the area, looking for said princess. Sometimes the high-school girl named that year's town royalty shows up for events in a ball gown and sash. I don't see a teen with ringlet curls, though. I do, however, see a little blond girl about four years old sitting in a racecar-designed cart staring straight at me.

"I want to be a princess like her and have a crown of jewels like that."

I press on one of the colored rhinestones as my throat thickens. The girl's mom leans toward her daughter and says something I can't hear, then she straightens, smiles at me, and nods as we pass each other, her to her minivan and me toward the automatic doors whooshing open in front of me.

The blast of arctic air-conditioning snaps me out of my momentary daze. I refocus, looking at the hanging aisle signs to find where the beverages are shelved. I turn down a row with a line of glass bottles on one side and scan their labels, looking for the nonalcoholic brand Tai's mom likes.

There. I grab two bottles and pivot toward the checkout counters. I pass a few fellow shoppers, and I'd be lying if I said I didn't notice them noticing me—or my head, more precisely.

But I keep my shoulders back and my chin up. They may pity me or come to their own wrong conclusions, but at least one person today said I was a princess and that's probably more than they can say about themselves.

In true small-town style, there isn't a self-checkout register, so I enter the short line to pay, one customer ahead of me. He only has a deli-made hoagie sandwich and a can of Coke, so it doesn't take long before I step in front of the cashier and put the two bottles of sparkling blush onto the conveyor belt.

I smile congenially at the cashier, who appears to be so ancient that she was one of the eight occupants on the ark. "Hello. How are you doing today?"

She grabs one of the bottles by the neck as she squints at me then points with a gnarled finger at my head. "Why'd you do that to yourself?"

My chin tucks as I flinch in surprise. "Excuse me?"

She jabs the air with her finger again. "Your hair. Why'd you do that to yourself?" She slowly slides the first bottle across the scanner, and the machine beeps.

I blink, shock chilling my core and causing me to shiver. I've never been called out and confronted like this. Judged silently, sure, but this? Never.

"Umm. I didn't *do* anything to my hair. I have alopecia so it fell out on its own." *Not that it's any of your business.*

She nods as she takes hold of the second bottle. "You know they make wigs, don't you?"

I grit my teeth. "Yes, I do know that."

"But you aren't wearing one."

"No, I am not."

Beep goes the machine.

Finally. I can pay and get out of here.

"Good for you."

I still, replaying what Grandma Noah just said. Surely, I heard wrong. "Excuse me?"

She slides the bottles into a paper bag. "Good. For. You, honey." She enunciates each word like I'm the one hard of hearing. "You're an inspiration, I say. You never know who you're going to encounter each day, who you're going to influence. You don't even have to say a word. You just have to be yourself."

A throat clears behind me, drawing both the elderly cashier's and my attention. A haggard-looking man in a rumpled flannel, buttons mismatched and bags under his eyes, stands with his arms at his sides and a cellphone in his left hand.

"Sorry for eavesdropping and, uhh . . ." He holds up his phone. "I guess I should also apologize for sneaking a picture of you without your permission." A photo of me in profile shows on his screen. "You see, my daughter is going through chemo right now, and it's been rough, as you can imagine. When I saw you, I thought, *I wish Abby could see her* because I knew she'd think how you celebrated your baldness was beautiful and maybe it would help her to see her own beauty, even without her hair."

"I . . ." I swipe at the tear trailing down my cheek. "I don't know what to say."

"You don't have to say anything. Except maybe . . ." He flushes, clearly embarrassed. "Yes to a better picture?" He shrugs adorably.

I laugh despite my tears and wipe my eyes again. "Yes, of course."

Grandma Noah winks at me. "See? An inspiration."

36

O kay, Kitty Purry, what do you think?"

The sparkling blush is chilling in the refrigerator. I've changed out of my work clothes and into a flowy dress that hits mid-calf, a row of cork buttons marching down the front. Teardrop leather earrings in the same shade of blue as the dress hang from my ears and frame my face. The paste jewels have come off my head, and so far, that part of me is bare.

I eye the wig draped over the bust on the counter. Kitty Purry must have the same idea because her yellow eyes go that direction as well. One of her tiny paws reaches out and bats at the synthetic tresses.

I take a deep breath as I meet my own gaze reflected in the mirror. "I think I'm going to go without it, Kitty."

There's nothing wrong with wigs or wearing them. There is, however, something injurious in the path my thoughts have traveled since losing my hair. In how I've viewed myself since then.

Tai calls me beautiful, and I'm beginning to believe it. Strangers in a grocery store say I'm an inspiration, and I want that to be true. Tai loves me. It's about time I start loving myself.

Kitty Purry stares at me, her head tilted. I know she has no idea what I'm saying so I don't take it personally when she hops off the bathroom counter and slinks around the door to somewhere more interesting.

I pick up the tube of lipstick from my makeup bag and swipe the cherry color over my lips. My gaze strays back to my bald head. It just seems so naked. Bare.

A mental picture of the woman with the henna tattoo on Tai's social media materializes. My phone is lying face-up on the counter, and it only takes a few swipes and taps before the photos are on the screen. She's gorgeous in a raw and powerful way. In an *inspiring* way.

I look between the photo and my own reflection in the mirror, a seed of an idea, of want, burrowing into my soul. But then I catch sight of the time and I scramble to collect my things. If I don't leave soon, I'm going to be late.

I grab the two bottles of sparkling blush from the refrigerator. "Wish me luck, Kitty," I say as I sling my purse over my shoulder. Predictably, she doesn't even look up from where she's grooming herself on the couch.

Tai's parents live on the other side of Little Creek, closer to the foothills and a little deeper into the woods. Their driveway is a bit on the steep side, and I'm glad I'm not attempting it in winter without the help of four-wheel-drive. The house comes into view over a rise, but I don't spend too much time noticing the homey porch or the welcoming pots of hanging plants because I'm too relieved to see Tai's Challenger parked in front of the garage door.

I park behind him and kill the engine. By the time I gather the beverages from the passenger seat, my door is being opened and Tai is standing there, grinning down at me. He offers me a hand, and even though I'm perfectly capable of exiting a vehicle under my own steam, I slip my palm into his and let him help me out of the car.

He immediately tugs me to him, and I fall against his chest as he wraps his arms around the small of my back. "I've changed my mind. Let's skip dinner and get out of here," he says against my neck right before I feel his lips press a kiss to my thrumming pulse.

"You don't want me to meet your parents?"

"I don't want to share you. Can't I keep you all to myself? Once my mom gets ahold of you—"

"Tai, stop hogging the poor girl and bring her here," a woman's voice calls.

Tai groans but pulls away, tucking me into his side. "You look amazing, by the way."

My fingers twitch with the need to self-consciously touch the base of my scalp, but I keep them by my side. Tai leads me toward the house and the petite woman standing at the top of the porch stairs. She smiles with her whole face, the same way Tai does, and the resemblance somehow calms the butterflies in my stomach.

"I'm so glad to meet you, Evangeline." She pulls me into a hug, squeezing me tight.

"Mom, you might want to let her breath." Tai's voice hums with humor.

His mom releases me and steps back. "I'm sorry. I'm just happy to meet you. My son never brings girls home. I was beginning to despair."

I look over at Tai and raise my brows at him.

He smirks back at me. "I told you I wasn't a rake."

Mrs. Davis glances between us, confusion written on her face. "Why would you be a garden tool, Tai?"

Tai folds his arms over his chest and casually leans against a porch pole. "Yeah, Angel. Why would I be a garden tool?"

My face heats, but there's no way I'm explaining to Tai's mom the historical romance definition of the word. I clear my throat and make a show of looking around the front porch. "What a lovely house you have here, Mrs. Davis."

"None of that Mrs. Davis nonsense. Call me Missy. And thank you, dear. Let me show you around." She links her arm with mine and pulls me through the front door, Tai trailing behind. "Walter's out back manning the grill. I hope you like barbecue."

"What's not to like?"

"My thoughts exactly."

Missy takes the paper bag from me and hands it to Tai with instructions to put it in the kitchen, then shows me around the house, including the timeline of photos of Tai as a child that hang in the hallway.

"He was such a cute kid," Missy says.

"That hasn't changed, has it, Angel?" Tai winks at me as he joins us again.

"I'm afraid if I answer that your head will no longer fit in this house."

Missy laughs like that's the funniest thing she's ever heard. "Oh, I like this girl."

"Me too, Mom." Tai's look is heated.

I flush, but Missy breezes past me without noticing, thank goodness.

"Let's go outside so you can meet Walter."

I step behind her to follow but am halted when Tai snakes an arm around my waist and hauls me against his front.

"Come on. We can still sneak out while she's not looking," he says low in my ear.

He's kidding, but that knowledge doesn't stop the thrill of pleasure his words send down my spine. Being wanted is extremely heady. I turn my chin and peck a kiss onto his cheek, then thread my fingers through his and tug, following his mom outside.

Tai's dad is standing in front of a steaming grill, brushing barbecue sauce onto glistening cuts of meat. He finishes, closes the grill's lid, wipes his hands on a Grill Master apron, then turns to me with a wide smile. "Well, well, well. If it isn't the librarian we've been hearing so much about."

I shake his proffered hand. "Thank you for having me."

"I'm going to head inside and grab some of the other food." Missy hooks a thumb over her shoulder and pivots on her heel toward the house.

"Go help her, son."

"Oh, I could go," I offer.

"No can do," Walter says. "I need you for something out here. Tai can go."

Tai holds up his hands as he turns to follow his mother. "I guess Tai will go, then."

I turn to Walter. "What did you need my help with?"

He waves me over to the table. "Not sure you knew we'd be eating outside. Didn't want your head to burn if you hadn't put sunscreen on already." He holds out a tube of lotion with palm trees on it with one hand and rubs his hand over his shiny pate with the other. "Take it from me. A burned head is not fun."

I wordlessly accept the offering. I have no idea if Tai told his parents about my condition beforehand or not, but at this moment, I realize there's no elephant in the room. No surreptitious curious glances. No outright questions.

"This may be the first time I've ever given this compliment— and pardon me if it's in any way untoward—but you have a beautifully shaped skull."

"I . . ." No one has ever said that to me before. As far as compliments go, I doubt it's one that has passed many lips, but it's also one that warms me more than any other. "Thank you."

The sliding glass door opens, and Missy and Tai step out,

holding platters of baked beans, coleslaw, sliced tomatoes, and corn fritters.

"Wow. This looks amazing." I take the bowl of baked beans from Missy and set it on the patio table already set for the meal.

Walter plucks barbecued chicken off the grill and heaps a serving dish full of smoky drumsticks.

After a quick blessing over the food and the passing around of dishes, Missy jumps back into conversation. "I promised Tai I wouldn't pester you with questions right away, and since you've been here at least twenty minutes, I'd say I've kept that promise."

"Mom." Tai's voice holds exasperated warning in its tone.

Missy shoos away her son's complaint. "This is your fault. I had to hear from Bella Johnson that you were even seeing someone. Imagine my surprise when she said the romantic tension from you and the new librarian would put Elizabeth Bennet and Mr. Darcy to shame." She picks up her fork, then wags the utensil at Tai. "And don't think Hayley is off the hook either. A romance happening under her nose and she didn't tell me? Tsk."

"Hayley's the reason we met, actually," Tai supplies.

"That girl is going to get an earful next time I see her. Come on. Spill the beans. What's the story?" Missy turns to me. "If Hayley is a part of the plot, I can only assume one of their little dares was involved. And then what happened?"

I look past Tai's mom and latch onto the man's gaze. He's shaking his head, but every revolution only tugs at my lips. He sees my burgeoning grin and hangs his head in mock defeat.

I look back to Missy, letting my smile break free. "And then we struck a bargain in which my end required me going out with him."

She gasps a *no* while Walter's silverware clatters onto his plate and he glares at his son with threatening malice. "You forced your attention onto a woman? Stand up. You and me need to have a conversation right now."

Tai lifts his head and pins me with a look that promises retribution. A look that has me curling my toes in my strappy sandals.

I clear my throat. "That's not necessary."

"The devil it isn't," his dad says.

Oh dear. Maybe I shouldn't have used Tai's parents to tease him. "It really isn't. Tai didn't circumvent my consent. Well, technically I guess he did, but somehow he knew my refusal came from a place of hurt and that I needed someone who wouldn't give up on me. Not that I'm saying any man shouldn't take a woman's no as the final answer, but in this case—" I scrub a hand down my face. "Wow. I'm really muddling this up."

"You aren't here against your will?" Walter is still scowling at Tai like he wants to find a willow switch and drag his son behind the woodshed.

"No, I am not." I meet Tai's gaze again, hoping he can read the apology in my eyes.

"And you're with Tai because you want to be? No other reason?" Missy sounds as if she's afraid to hear the answer.

"I'm with Tai because he's the best man I've ever met. He's shown me what unconditional love looks like at a time when I thought love had given up on me. I'm with him because there's no other person I'd rather be with. I fell in love with him, and he has my heart."

"I am so in love with you, Angel. Even your favorite romance authors wouldn't be able to put what I feel for you into adequate words." He stares at me with fire in his eyes.

"Well." Missy fans her face with her fingers. "That was . . ." She trails off, not finding a satisfactory adjective.

Tai winks at me across the table.

"So, Evangeline, where are you from originally?" Missy tries to bring the conversation back to polite get-to-know-you grounds.

"I grew up in Chattanooga."

"Such a nice city. Are your parents still there?"

I take a bite of baked beans and chew, giving myself a moment to think. I've already made the conversation awkward once. No need to do it again by mentioning my parents' accident. I swallow and take a sip of water. "My grandparents are. They're about to celebrate their fiftieth wedding anniversary."

"How lovely." Missy pauses. "There's something I've wanted to say ever since I saw you step out of the car, but I didn't want to be gauche."

My muscles tense as I prepare for whatever she plans to say next. But then I surprise myself as I hear my voice saying, "It's about this, I suppose?" I wave in the direction of my bald head. "Did Tai not tell you beforehand?" I'd been wondering. Assumed he must have since the topic hadn't come up yet.

Missy narrows her eyes at her son. "Like I said, Tai told us nothing." She looks back at me, her expression softening. "I just wanted to say how striking you are, dear. Seeing you immediately put me in mind of Nefertiti. Both of you with your long, elegant necks and regal beauty. Simply striking."

My spine hits the back of my chair as shock puts me in a temporary paralysis.

"That reminds me of that tattoo you did a bit ago, Tai," Missy continues, as if she hasn't left me utterly speechless. "The one on that woman's head."

"You looked through my online portfolio?" Tai asks her incredulously.

"Of course I keep up with your art." Missy sounds affronted. "Just because I don't want you to jab me with needles doesn't mean I'm not proud of you."

"Wow. Thanks, Mom."

"Actually." I finally get my vocal cords working again. "I was just looking at those photos earlier today myself." I take a deep breath, then put to words a desire that has taken root and bloomed inside me. "I want to be your next canvas, Tai."

37

My phone vibrates in my palm. I look down and click on the text that just came in.

"What are you grinning about?" Tai asks as he flicks his gaze toward me before promptly returning his attention to the road, adjusting his grip on the steering wheel.

I look up at him, the joy inside pulling my lips in a wide arc, my eyes crinkling with my happiness. "Oh, you know. Just the fact that your mom loves me." I dance the phone in the air between us. "I have proof."

"Do I even want to ask?"

I pull the phone back toward me. "This is the fourth article she's sent me on cortisol levels and their correlation to hair loss. Hayley told me your mom's love language is an abundance of unsolicited medical advice, so the evidence suggests your mom is head over heels for me."

Tai takes one hand off the steering wheel to squeeze my knee. "Is this where I tell you I knew my parents would love you?"

"No one likes a know-it-all."

He laughs and returns his grip to the steering wheel, changing lanes. "What about me? Do I need to be worried about your grandparents' first impression of me? Will they jump to any conclusions because of my tattoos?"

"Oh, most definitely."

Tai blanches, and it's hard to swallow the giggle bubbling up in my throat. I school my features, going for a deadpan look. "Especially since you've so obviously led me down the path of iniquity with you."

Tai glances at me again, and this time he must see something on my face that gives me away because he visibly starts to relax, the color returning to his cheeks. "Make fun all you want. I don't usually care if people judge me rashly because of what I do or my own body art, but your grandparents are different."

I pat his leg. "What was it you told me? They'll love you because I love you."

He lets one of his hands fall and squeezes my fingers that cover his thigh. We drive like that in silence for a few minutes before he speaks again. "What do you think they'll say about your tattoo?"

"Honestly? I'm not sure. They've been surprising me lately—like with Grampie's new macabre hobby—so anything is possible, I guess."

"And you? No regrets?"

There's a vulnerability in his tone. He'd spent hours designing and redesigning the piece, wanting to make it perfect for me.

And it is. Absolutely perfect.

Intricate and delicate fine lines weave in a pleasing pattern over the crown of my head, dipping down like a jeweled widow's peak across my would-be hairline. The head of a mythical, majestic phoenix perches over the top of one ear, its fiery feathers curving along the base of my skull, evaporating into a garden of flowers: peonies, daisies, and—my favorite—an exact replica of the rose that decorates the side of Tai's own neck. The same lines and rich tones that have mesmerized me since the first time I ever laid eyes on them.

I'd cried when I saw my reflection in the mirror when Tai had finished the tattoo. I'd never told him my thoughts of the phoenix, how I could relate to the symbolism of regeneration and resilience. Looking at myself with Tai's art marked into my skin, it was like I was able to see myself through his eyes for the first time. I felt stronger and more empowered than maybe I had felt in my whole life.

I felt—*feel*—loved.

"Absolutely zero regrets."

Tai's throat bobs. This whole experience has been a bit emotional for the both of us.

"That's good," he says, his voice thick.

My phone buzzes again, this time with an incoming call. Penelope's name flashes on the screen. I tap the green accept icon. "Hello, Penelope. Before you start to freak out, yes, we're almost there."

"And you remembered the backdrop with Granny and Grampie's letters displayed? And the personalized stationery we're using in lieu of a guestbook, along with the keepsake box to keep the letters in? Oh, and you didn't forget your vintage typewriter, did you? We need that as decoration for the—"

"Penelope, stop. I have everything. I had it the first time you texted a reminder. I had it the fifth time you texted a reminder. I have it now. Stop stressing."

"Right. Sorry. It's just, it's Granny and Grampie, you know? I want the party to be perfect for them."

"I know, and it will be."

She takes a deep breath. "How far out did you say you were?"

I scan out the window, noticing certain landmarks. "We should be there in about ten minutes."

"Okay, good. Ten minutes is good."

"Try not to have an aneurysm before then."

"Yeah, okay. I'll try," she says way too seriously before hanging up.

"Your sister's stressed?" Tai flicks on the blinker and merges onto the exit ramp.

"That's an understatement." We've been working on this party for months, though. Nothing is going to detract from our grandparents' big day.

A realization bolts into my mind, echoing in my ears like thunder. "Oh no!"

"What? What is it?" Tai shoots a quick look at my face, the car decelerating. My outburst must have made him lift his foot off the gas pedal.

I slump down in the passenger seat. "It's my grandparents' big day."

"And . . ."

I straighten. "And I'm showing up like this." All ten of my fingers point to the artwork covering the curves of my head. "It's like someone proposing at their friend's wedding, stealing the attention when everyone should be celebrating the newlyweds."

What was I thinking? My grandparents' anniversary party isn't the time or place to step out of the shadows. The spotlight should be on them. If I arrive without a wig, without trying my hardest to blend in and not make a statement, everyone's going to be talking about me instead of focusing on Granny and Grampie's epic love story.

But I didn't bring a wig with me. Or a scarf. I have no way to cover up. Maybe Penelope—

"Or, and hear me out here—" Tai interrupts my downward spiral. "They love you so much that the greatest gift you could give them is by being your true, authentic self."

I try and slow my stampeding thoughts long enough to consider what he's saying. It's . . . possible.

He pulls the car along the curve and puts the car into park.

Either way, we're here. There's no turning back now. Both Tai and I exit the car and round toward the trunk where the party supplies are. The slap of a storm door echoes in the background.

"Good. You're here." Penelope scurries across the street in four-inch heels. She stops beside me, her gaze running over me from head to toe with the speed of a flip-book. I'm sure she's reading me just as quickly and easily as well.

"First off, love this." She sweeps her hands through the air in front of me. "You look amazing, that tat is epic, and I am one hundred percent here for it." She reaches into the trunk and lifts out the ancient typewriter I bought at an estate sale last year. "But gushing is going to have to wait because Granny and Grampie will be here soon and we still need to finish setting up."

I grab the custom-made backdrop that's rolled protectively in a cardboard tube, then hurry after Penelope. She's almost to the front door by the time I catch her. "How'd you get them out of the house?" I ask, a little out of breath.

Her hand pauses for the briefest of moments as she's reaching for the door handle. So briefly, in fact, that I wonder if I imagine the momentary delay.

"They're with Brett and his family."

Nope, not my imagination. She'd flinched on my account.

"Brett and his fiancée got a puppy. His grandparents had offered to be the diversion to get Granny and Grampie out of the house, and I guess they figured a new puppy was a good lure."

I take in the information and wait for the familiar feelings of loss and worthlessness to grip me, but nothing happens.

There's no anchor tied to my emotions at the news, nothing pulling me down and threatening to drown me. Instead, I feel relief. I know I'm not going to be able to avoid Brett entirely, but I feel like some cosmic judge has granted me a reprieve.

Tai has caught up to us by this point, his arms full of the stationery, quills, and letterbox for guests to write notes for our grandparents. My sister directs him to the small desk and chair she's set in the corner of the backyard near the house while I find the area we'd agreed the backdrop of their love letters would go.

People have already started to arrive. Some help with last-minute details while others mill around, waiting for my grandparents to arrive and the party to officially begin. Most of the faces are familiar. I notice the pastor and his wife from my grandparents' church. Then there's Grampie's old coworker at the advertising agency he worked at for over thirty years.

"I love your new artwork, Evangeline," a familiar voice says from my right.

I finish securing the corner of the backdrop to the tall privacy fence, then turn to Nanette, Granny's scrapbooking buddy. The three of us used to pour over pictures, stickers, and fun background paper to make our memory books. Nanette moved to Memphis about five years ago when her husband's job transferred him.

I move to give her a hug, her scent of honeysuckles bringing back waves of memories. "It's good to see you again."

She squeezes me in return. "You too. And this—" She leans back to look at me. "Girl, you're on fire."

I open my mouth to demure but am interrupted by a voice behind me.

"She's right. You're making a statement, and I love what I'm hearing." A woman who looks familiar but whom I can't place steps beside Nanette. "It must have hurt a lot though, huh?"

"They're here!" Penelope whisper-shouts from the French doors leading into the house. "Everyone quiet!" She steps into the house and shuts the doors behind her, pulling the curtains closed.

Nanette and the other woman drift away. There aren't really places to hide, and Penelope and I agreed having people jump out and yell "Surprise!" at our aging grandparents may not be the best idea. We want their hearts to be touched by emotions, not a defibrillator.

An arm wraps around my waist, and Tai pulls me to his side. The yard is quiet except for the hum of a lawn mower in the far background and the faint sounds of a passing car. There's the unmistakable click of the front door shutting. A few moments later, the curtains move, then the French doors open. Granny steps out with her eyes wide, both hands raised to cover her mouth. Grampie is a step behind her. He's grinning, but there's a telltale sheen to his eyes.

"I can't believe you did this." Granny pulls Penelope into a hug.

"You should be up there too," Tai whispers into my ear.

I wipe away a tear with the pad of my thumb. "I will be," I assure him. Right now, I'm enjoying the front-row seat to their joy.

Granny looks over the backyard slowly, taking everything and everyone in. "Nanette, dear, I haven't seen you in ages. And Phyllis. Ron, can you believe this?"

Grampie wraps his arms around Granny. "We're talking about our girls, here, Carol. Of course I can believe it."

Granny leans her head on Grampie's shoulder. "Speaking of our girls, where's Evangeline?"

Every head turns my direction. I'm faintly aware of the four other people who've joined Granny and Grampie on the small patio, but my focus is trained on the two who have loved me so well my entire life. I know the moment they spot me. Their reaction to the surprise party was what Penelope and I had hoped for, but I never could have pictured the looks on their faces when they see me. Whatever trepidation I felt about how they'd react to my tattoo quickly blows away. They're looking at me exactly how Tai said they would—like I'm the best gift they could've been given.

They move in tandem down the two plank steps and rush toward me. Tai steps aside so Granny can wrap her arms around me on the left, Grampie on the right. I faintly hear Penelope issuing instructions and see movement of activity from the corner of my eye.

"Oh, my sweet girl. I have prayed for this." Granny wipes a tear away from her cheek.

"You've prayed I'd get a tattoo?" I tease her, trying to replace her tears with a smile.

She swats my shoulder.

"I think your grandmother means," Grampie says, "that we prayed you'd let that brilliant light within you shine again and not let anyone dull it. That you'd stop running away from love long enough to see that love will never stop pursuing you."

"Speaking of love . . ." I motion Tai over and introduce him to my grandparents. They inspect my tattoo closer, oohing and ahhing over the intricate details and design. Granny admits she's always been fascinated with body art, even when it had been taboo and frowned upon in society. Tai offers to give her her first. We talk of everything and nothing, and my heart has never been happier.

Granny and Grampie drift away to mingle with their guests, and I watch them go.

Tai tugs on my hand. "Come on. Let's get something to drink."

Penelope's directing the caterers with the food, but a table has already been set up with a trio of large glass beverage dispensers—ice water, lemonade, and sweet tea. I lift a clear cup from the top of the stack then hold it under the spigot to fill with tartly sweet lemonade.

"I really don't know what she was thinking."

Every muscle in my body freezes. I'd know that voice anywhere. I let go of the nozzle just as my cup is about to overflow.

"Why would she want to draw attention to the fact that she's bald?"

Tai stiffens beside me. I place a hand on his forearm, his tendons pulsing under my touch. It's sweet that he wants to defend me, but it's also not necessary. Brett no longer has the power to hurt me.

"It's such a shame, really. She used to be so pretty, but then . . ."

I don't have to see his face to envision the disgust there. The look used to haunt me. Used to eat away at my confidence like a virus.

"It really is a shame." I raise my voice, done letting his be the one that I hear.

He pivots, an expression of surprise mixed with just a hint of shame. His small audience looks everywhere but in my direction, clearly uncomfortable.

"It really is a shame," I state again. "You used to be such a kind man, but then . . ." My voice trails off like his had, letting each individual fill in the blank.

"Evangeline." He chokes on my name. "I didn't know you were there."

"No, I suppose you didn't, though that in no way excuses your behavior—now or in the past."

"I don't—"

I hold up a palm, cutting him off. "You said you didn't

know what I was thinking, well, let me enlighten you. I was thinking that I'm done letting your opinion or anyone else's define me. I was thinking that if being who I am and living my life out loud could help someone else, then the snide remarks and judgmental glances from little people like you would be worth it. I was thinking it's about time I embrace my beauty. Because I am bald and I am beautiful, so deal with it, Brett."

I turn on my heel and am greeted with the sight of Tai's adoring face. He hands me my drink without breaking eye contact. "You're so unbelievably amazing, you know that?"

We move over to give room for others to access the drink table.

"Don't look now, but it appears your grandfather is no longer happy with the guest list," Tai says over the rim of his cup.

I glance over my shoulder and watch as Grampie escorts Brett to the back door.

"Come here." Tai sets both our drinks down, then takes my elbow and guides me to the secluded spot in the backyard protected by the large rhododendron bush. As soon as we're out of view, he steps between my feet, brackets my head in his hands, and captures my mouth with his own. My fingers come up and grip his wrists, hanging on for dear life, grounding myself in this moment while his kiss attempts to send me into other dimensions of euphoria.

I lose all track of time. A minute could have passed or an hour. I don't know, and I don't care. There's no place I'd rather be than here with Tai.

He pulls back but barely, just enough to look into my eyes. "I want this to be us in fifty years, Angel."

"Making out behind a bush in my grandparents' backyard?" I reply.

His thumb strokes my cheek. "Celebrating our love. One

that has only grown stronger, dug deeper, bloomed wider with the years. What do you say?"

I smile into Tai's eyes, feeling his love written on every page of my story as Stacey's words ring in my ears. "I say yes. I love you. I didn't think it was possible, but this librarian has finally met her overdue match."

DISCUSSION QUESTIONS

1. Evangeline wasn't sure what to think of Tai when she first laid eyes on him. How do appearances play a role in first impressions?

2. Evangeline thinks everyone falls into one of three categories: hero/heroine, secondary character/side-kick, or villain. Do you agree with her assessment? What category would you fall under?

3. Evangeline doesn't see herself as a heroine even in her own story because of messages she's seen and heard around her. How have spoken and unspoken messages in our society shaped your own self-image?

4. How important is representation in fiction? In what ways do you think the industry can improve?

5. If you were to be matched with someone based off your library checkout history, what sort of person would you be set up with?

6. Tai's deal with Evangeline could be seen as opportunistic as he manipulates the situation to get what he wants—a date with Evangeline after she'd already

turned him down. What was your reaction to his proposal?

7. Romance sometimes gets a bad rap, but as Tai points out, Jesus is the lover of our souls and pursues us unceasingly. What would your response be to someone who doesn't believe Christians should indulge in romance?

8. When Evangeline shares her struggles with her friends, Hayley and Martha rally around her and give her support. Has there been a time in your life when a friend came alongside you and helped you during a difficult time?

9. Do you have any tattoos or would you get a tattoo? If so, of what?

10. As Evangeline learned, there is empowerment and the chance to be an inspiration when we are vulnerable. Was there ever a time you were inspired by another person's vulnerability or vice versa?

11. What piece of advice would you give to Tai or Evangeline?

AUTHOR'S NOTE

Dear Readers,

I've wanted to write a story with a heroine who has alopecia for a while now. If you read the dedication page of this book, then you already know the personal reason for that burning desire. But if you skipped that part, then I'll go ahead and tell you now.

One of the most beautiful women to walk this earth—my mother—has lived with alopecia in some form since she was a teenager. Different dermatologists attempted to give her explanations and treatments, but the hair would fall out in circular patches on her scalp and grow back on its own timeline. About ten years ago or so, the hair loss didn't stop at patches. It continued until she experienced the loss of most of the hair on her body. She is strong and radiant and the most beautiful bald woman I know, rocking her killer vintage feather hat head tattoo proudly. But there has been a journey to her confidence and acceptance. One that, at times, has probably felt all too lonely for her.

Fiction is powerful, uniting us in stories that are our own as well as those that are not. Broadening our perspectives and compassion through a cast of diverse characters who we may not have personally encountered off the page. Spotlighting those who feel forgotten or unseen and celebrating them in ways they deserve. In the thousands of books I have read in my many years as a book devourer, I have sadly only come across one romance novel where the heroine experienced a loss of her hair. In a world where there are an estimated 160 million people dealing with alopecia, I think it's safe to say that the condition is grossly underrepresented in fiction. We all deserve to be seen as heroes and heroines of our own stories.

Not everyone's experience is the same, and the fictional character of Evangeline Kelly and the journey that she goes through in this book may or may not be similar to others living with an alopecia diagnosis. While I consulted with and absorbed firsthand accounts from those who wrestle with hair loss, the fictional experiences illustrated in this story are not to be taken as a blanket representation and portrayal of an entire community. While some may say it's only hair, others will find those same words deeply hurtful. Please extend grace.

If you want to learn more about alopecia, you can go to the National Alopecia Areata Foundation website at naaf.org. High-quality, real hair wigs can be very costly. There are organizations that accept hair donations and provide free wigs to children and young adults with medically related hair loss like alopecia. Some of these organizations include Wigs for Kids, Locks of Love, and Hair We Share. Please visit their websites if you are interested in making a hair donation to support the creation of these wigs.

Best wishes,
Sarah Monzon

ACKNOWLEDGMENTS

The journey this book has taken to publication looks so different from my previous books. While I've never been truly alone in my writing, relying on critique partners and a talented editor, I've never really felt like I was part of a team either. That's what publishing this book has felt like—having teammates that I can depend on and who care about this story as much as I do. Each and every one is an MVP.

Many thanks to my agent, Rachel McMillan, who took a chance on me even though I completely butchered my pitch because I was so nervous. Thank you for believing that I actually can string some coherent words together even though I didn't demonstrate that skill at all during our Zoom meeting. I am more than happy to let you pitch every story idea from here on out.

To the publishing team at Bethany House, especially my amazing editors Jessica Sharpe, Jennifer Veilleux, and Bethany Lenderink. Thank you for believing in this book even in the raw stages and lending me your expertise and story insights to help make it shine. Go, team captains!

Toni Shiloh, we are like Kelce and Mahomes, Jordan and

Pippen, Ruth and Gehrig. Okay, not really, but I know you get what I'm trying to say here. You are the one person who has been on my team from the beginning, and I can't imagine writing a book without you.

A special thanks to Dianne Semones, my mother, who has been a huge source of encouragement to my creativity since I began writing stories in kindergarten. Thank you for always believing in me. And thank you for being open and vulnerable and helping me with this book in particular.

Thank you to the women and men in the social media alopecia support groups who took the time to share your experiences and insights. The community you have cultivated is beautiful and inspiring.

I couldn't write without the support of my husband who works so hard to provide for our family. Thank you, José, for your dedication to our own little battalion.

And most importantly, thank you to my God, the lover of my soul, pursuer of my heart. Help me to love like You.

Read on
for a *sneak peek* at
the next book in the

CHECKING OUT LOVE

series.

Available November 2025

1

HAYLEY

Y'all cannot be serious," I say as I take in the heap of junk littering the corner of the library's parking lot. The monstrosity looks like it needs a tow truck to take it to its eternal resting place in the junkyard, not at all like a vehicle primed and ready for its reincarnated life as Little Creek's new bookmobile.

"Deadly serious." Evangeline breathes the words out, also staring at what has become my newest worst nightmare, dethroning my recurring irrational fear of getting stuck inside the *It's a Small World* ride at Disney World.

"Maybe we shouldn't use the word *deadly*." Martha winces.

I'm sandwiched between our small town's other two librarians, the three of us in a disbelieving stupor, still trying to make sense of the . . . *thing* . . . parked cattywampus and taking up multiple parking spaces. When Marge from the town council had dropped by yesterday to say there would be a surprise waiting for us in the morning, not in a million years would our imaginations have come up with something like this.

And our imaginations are Olympic-level, let me tell you. We're librarians, after all. We practically marinate in the creative realms, and yet we've still been blindsided.

"Yeah, new rule. *Deadly* and all of its synonyms are no longer a part of our vocabulary when referring to—" I wave my hand in front of me, gesturing to the heap of metal.

Someone has an even better imagination than we do to think this relic could ever function in a literary capacity. The paint is chipping and peeling, the seams are flaking iron oxide at an alarming rate, and I can't imagine the mechanicals under the hood are in any better condition.

Bookmobiles are to bibliophiles what ice cream trucks are to children. This thing is more like a horror movie waiting to happen.

It still needs a name, though.

I swipe my hand in its general direction again. "Cletus."

Martha whips her head toward me, her wide, caramel-colored eyes disbelieving. "Cletus? Really?"

Evangeline lets out a soft laugh. "Hadn't you noticed Hayley's little quirk of naming everything?"

Martha shakes her head, her curly hair growing bigger by the second due to the humidity in the air. She says she hates the wild volume because it makes her look like Medusa and scares the kids during story time, but I think it's because she finds it harder to go unnoticed when her hair is practically screaming for attention like a beauty pageant contestant armed with Aqua Net.

"Okay, fine. But Cletus?" she huffs.

I shrug, not seeing why she's so put out with my choice. "It looks like a Cletus to me."

She turns so her whole body is facing me. "The name Cletus is of Greek origin. It means 'illustrious.'" Now it's her turn to wave her hand at the unwanted automotive hand-me-down. "Does that thing look illustrious to you?"

I purse my lips and pretend to inspect the newly acquired bookmobile, hiding another wince by tapping my mouth with my finger. "It does have a certain *je ne sais quoi* about it."

"If *je ne sais quoi* means 'tetanus shot,'" Evangeline mumbles more to herself but loud enough that we can hear.

"The definition is actually a quality that cannot be described," Martha supplies helpfully, which is no help at all. "And *that*, ladies"—she punctuates by pointing a finger at Cletus— "can be described with a litany of negative adjectives."

"We're in the foothills of southeastern Tennessee, not the cliffs of Santorini, so of course I meant the hillbilly version of Cletus and not the Greek rendition."

I'm sorry, but when I think of Greek names, Zeus and Poseidon and Hercules pop into my head. Not Cletus. Cletus is the hunched man who used to live on the edge of town in a run-down old hunting cabin people only talked about in whispers. He never showered, never shaved, never laundered his clothes, and had an illegal moonshine still he'd built himself out of a Dutch oven, along with a few bungee cords, a lunchbox-type cooler he stole from a construction site, and a rusty refrigerator coil, also suspected of being stolen from a trash heap. You have to admit, if people were vehicles, the nightmare in front of us would remind anyone of that type of Cletus.

"Maybe we shouldn't look a gift horse in the mouth." Evangeline's voice holds a note of forced optimism.

Optimism I'm just not seeing at the moment.

Martha's eyes brighten at the word *horse*. "Did you know that the first bookmobiles precede anything with an engine? Library deliveries to the remote regions of the Appalachian Mountains were made with horses as the means of transportation. It was called the Pack Horse Library Project. I know I have at least one book about it in the children's section, so I wouldn't doubt there's something in both nonfiction and fiction on the adult shelves. We should check it out."

I cock my hip. "I'm pretty sure this is the perfect time to look a gift horse in the mouth. Because if this was the 1930s, then that gift horse would be a lame swayback nag. The kind that would probably keel over on the first strenuous incline to a hollow where we—so sorry, *I*—would've been left stranded to fend off wildlife and the elements or perish."

"Someone is being a bit dramatic." Martha attempts but fails to quell her grin.

"Also, *perish* could arguably be a synonym of *deadly*, which we said was no longer in our vocabulary in reference to . . . Cletus." Evangeline isn't in the habit of calling nonliving things by human monikers and stumbles over the syllables in her mouth.

I sigh as I let my chin fall to my chest. We've gotten off topic. "Explain to me one more time how we inherited Cletus."

"Mayor Breckenbridge made acquiring a bookmobile for the library one of his reelection campaign promises. He failed to inform the good citizens of Little Creek, however, that when he said *bookmobile*, what he really meant was turning the beat-up rust bucket on his front lawn into the mobile library." Evangeline tsks.

"And how did the responsibility of mobile librarian fall on my shoulders again?"

"I can't drive a manual transmission," Martha answers simply.

I spin on my heel and clamp desperate fingers to Evangeline's shoulders, pinning her in place. "You can. My cousin taught you. I've seen you driving Tai's Challenger around town."

Maybe I'm overreacting. It's just driving, right? Not something on par with letting a tarantula walk on your face. But I can't shake this queasy feeling in my stomach every time I picture myself behind the wheel. Like there should be ominous music playing in the background. If my life were being written by some cosmic author, this is when they'd be cackling with ill-conceived glee at laying down breadcrumbs of foreshadowing for some major event filed under the words *conflict* and *raising the stakes*.

Evangeline eases out of my grip, a small, fake-innocent smile playing at her lips. "Ah yes, but you see, it's your turn." She says that last bit in a singsong voice.

My jaw slackens. I've never hated my words being thrown back in my face more.

She rubs her chin dramatically. "I seem to recall a time when I asked you to help me out with the certain matter of a critter stuck in the book return receptacle. Do you remember what you told me?"

"That it was your turn," I grind out, then throw my hands up in frustration. "But this is different!"

Her tattooed-on eyebrows rise ever so slowly. "You might possibly need a tetanus shot. I could've possibly needed a rabies shot. I think we're even."

I seal my lips against the mild curse pushing to be released. Not curse as in a bad word. Curse as in curse. Like hex. No, not like voodoo doll stuff. I'm not into any of that. We live in the South, but New Orleans is another brand of South all together.

No, I just sometimes wish for a tepid inconvenience to be brought down upon another person's head. Nothing nefarious. Still this side of innocent. Like, *may you never have matching Tupperware containers and lids.* I don't want real harm to befall anyone I'm mildly annoyed with, but the idea that they could be somewhat inconvenienced makes me feel better and cools my negative feelings toward them in the moment.

I do not, however, wish these curses on my friends. Ever. And Evangeline is one of my best friends.

Mayor Breckenbridge, though . . . Oh yeah, he definitely deserves a curse.

My nose wrinkles as I think of a particularly bothersome disruption to wish upon him. The Tupperware lid thing isn't quite annoying enough if I really have to climb behind Cletus's deathtrap wheel and drive it on our windy, rural back roads.

My lips turn up at the sides. *Mayor Breckenbridge, may you only ever find one square of toilet paper left on the roll for the rest of your life.*

"Why does she look like she's hatching an evil plan?" Martha stage-whispers out of the side of her mouth.

Evangeline lifts a hand to shield her eyes from the sun, squinting. "Is it revenge evil or overthrow-the-government evil?"

"Um." Martha frowns. "Both?"

Evangeline lowers her hand and flicks me lightly on the forehead. "I love ya, Hayley, but I don't have money to bail you out of jail, so just don't, okay?"

I snort and plant a palm on my hip. "One, I'm as sweet as peach pie so I don't know what y'all are even talking about, and, two, like Sheriff Jacobs would ever arrest me. I babysit his kids on every single date night he takes with his wife. If he puts me in a cell, he's going to have to be the warden of his own brood of inmates, and we all know that's unlikely to happen."

"It is kind of ironic how unruly the sheriff's own children are," Martha agrees.

"Anyway, I wasn't scheming anything nefarious, thank you very much. It's nice to see what y'all truly think of me."

"I truly think you're a force to be reckoned with." Evangeline loops her arm through mine.

"Peach-pie sweet but with a hefty splash of spicy bourbon added to the recipe." Martha links her arm with mine on the other side.

I take in a deep, bracing lungful of air and let it out slowly.

"I guess Cletus and I should get better acquainted. Maybe we can come to some kind of agreement for our working relationship." I force cheerfulness into my voice. "He won't break down on the side of the road and leave me stranded, and I won't accidentally forget to put the parking brake on and hope he rolls off the side of a mountain."

"That's the spirit?" Martha's voice pitches high at the end. "Okay, ladies, I'm off to get ready for preschool story time." She unhooks her arm and gracefully glides toward the library's entrance like some kind of literary book fairy. It's no wonder all the kids who come in love her.

Evangeline moves to stand in front of me. Her eyes have lost their teasing glint, and she's looking at me seriously. The early morning sun is hanging in the sky just behind her head, casting her in a slightly shadowed silhouette. "Tell me the truth. Are you really scared to drive that thing? Because if you are, you don't have to do it. I mean, you were right. I know how to drive a stick shift now too. Driving that thing isn't exactly on my bucket list, but you shouldn't be afraid of coming to work just because of Mayor Breckenbridge's, uh, generosity."

I snort at her liberal use of the word. Mayor Breckenbridge wasn't thinking of anyone but himself if he'd planned all along to bestow this hunk of junk on us. But it's not fair to ask Evangeline to shoulder the responsibility either. I may be more than a little nervous at the idea of driving Cletus farther than ten feet, but Evangeline has faced enough fears and been brave beyond measure this year alone. She's earned herself a nice long reprieve.

I let my gaze roam over the beautifully artistic tattoo inking her bald scalp. The lacework lines, colorful bouquet of flowers, and the striking image of a rising phoenix. A few months ago, she'd been hiding the fact that she has alopecia, afraid her friends and the townspeople would view and treat her differently simply because she'd lost her hair to the autoimmune disease. She'd nearly given up on the idea that anyone would ever love her or find her beautiful just the way she is. Now she more often than not forgoes wearing any of her wigs, proudly displaying her new tattoo that Tai created for her and making us all gag with the very public displays of affection she and my cousin can't seem to stop putting on.

I might have thought an extra second before setting them up if I'd known I'd have to endure so much PDA.

Oh, who am I kidding? I'd do it all over again in a heartbeat. At least the back corner of the reference section is finally getting some foot traffic, if you know what I mean.

Anyway, there's no way I'm going to ask her to do this instead of doing it myself. Like she said, driving Cletus isn't high on her bucket list. But it is on mine.

I mean, the words *Drive Cletus* obviously aren't written down physically on a piece of paper anywhere, but I can remedy that real quick since I add to my bucket list (if that's what we're going to call it) every day anyway. Literally.

Every day starts with a blank page in the little notebook I carry around with me, looking for something to jot down and check off. All under the same heading: *Make It Count.*

I can never pay back my debt, but I'm really hoping I can pay it forward.

A Carol Award finalist and Selah Award winner, **Sarah Monzon** is a stay-at-home mom who makes up imaginary friends to have adult conversations with (otherwise known as writing novels). As a navy chaplain's wife, she resides wherever the military happens to station her family and enjoys exploring the beauty of the world around her. You can follow her at SarahMonzonWrites.com.

Sign Up for Sarah's Newsletter

Keep up to date with Sarah's latest news on book releases and events by signing up for her email list at the website below.

SarahMonzonWrites.com

FOLLOW SARAH ON SOCIAL MEDIA

Sarah Monzon, Author   @SarahMonzonWrites   @MonzonWrites

More from Sarah Monzon

Mackenzie Graham's work crush, Jeremy Fletcher, has barely noticed her—until they compete for the same much-needed promotion. But winning has less to do with work performance and everything to do with showing the most Christmas spirit. As their yuletide duel progresses, it might be more than a job they risk losing.

All's Fair in Love and Christmas